D1085703

MY FRIENDS
WOULDN'T LET ME

A Story of Courage, Determination . . . and Love

John A. Broadwell

Copyright © 2019 John A. Broadwell.

All rights reserved. No part of this book may be used or reproduced by
any means, graphic, electronic, or mechanical, including photocopying,
recording, taping or by any information storage retrieval system
without the written permission of the author except in the case of
brief quotations embodied in critical articles and reviews.

LifeRich Publishing is a registered trademark of
The Reader's Digest Association, Inc.

LifeRich Publishing books may be ordered through booksellers or by contacting:

LifeRich Publishing
1663 Liberty Drive
Bloomington, IN 47403
www.liferichpublishing.com
1 (888) 238-8637

Because of the dynamic nature of the Internet, any web addresses or
links contained in this book may have changed since publication and
may no longer be valid. The views expressed in this work are solely those
of the author and do not necessarily reflect the views of the publisher,
and the publisher hereby disclaims any responsibility for them.

Any people depicted in stock imagery provided by Getty Images are
models, and such images are being used for illustrative purposes only.
Certain stock imagery © Getty Images.

ISBN: 978-1-4897-2371-0 (sc)
ISBN: 978-1-4897-2372-7 (e)

Library of Congress Control Number: 2019909001

Print information available on the last page.

LifeRich Publishing rev. date: 07/29/2019

ONE

Bobby Murphy turned seventeen almost a year ago. An excellent student, he was also a huge sports fan. He liked all sports, but his first love was baseball. Before the accident, Bobby was a star player on the Brookside Rangers baseball team. He also played football and basketball, but his fantasies usually had him pitching or playing third base at Wrigley Field or Fenway Park. This was to be the year Brookside won the state 5A baseball championship in Oklahoma.

He woke to a bright, sunny morning and reflected on how he used to love the promise of days like this. Now, he was in no hurry to get up. Why bother?

He remembered how he and his friends, Rog and Andy, had been to a local college football game and were coming home. The silver Ford F-150 Rog was driving hit a spot of black ice and spun out, colliding with an oncoming semi. Bobby, lying by the side of the road, realized he had a head injury, not a difficult diagnosis since blood was all over his clothing, but what really frightened him was he could not move his legs. He couldn't feel any pain below his waist, but he couldn't get up either.

The truck driver was uninjured and called for an ambulance. Rog, Andy and Bobby were loaded up and taken, siren screaming, to the Hospital of the Plains in town. Bobby went in and out of consciousness for the next twenty-four hours.

The head injury was not as serious as it first appeared. But, the major lasting effect was somewhere in his back. His legs and feet had no feeling, no movement. He remained in the intensive care unit for a week and then was moved to a private room. Altogether he was in the hospital for three weeks before being referred to the regional neurological center in Tulsa.

Fearing the potential psychological impact on Bobby, no one had told him the status of Rog or Andy. After he was relocated to the private room, his Mom gave him the sad news. While Andy had suffered fairly serious trauma to his legs and back, his prognosis was for a complete recovery in time. However, Rog had died in the ambulance on the way to the hospital. The news was devastating to Bobby.

After a month at the neurological center, the doctors sent him home. "We're referring you to a physical therapist, but, truthfully, we don't think you will ever walk again," the lead doctor said. "You need to have the physical therapy so the rest of your body, your upper torso, shoulders and arms will regain their strength. If you work hard at your therapy, you'll be able to lead a pretty normal life."

And so, Bobby was driven home by his solemn parents. He knew his Mom and Dad loved him, and they thanked God he had survived, but now . . . They tried to be upbeat and encouraging, but all three of them were scared to death.

Bobby sank into a funk. Before the accident, he was tall, trim and athletic, approaching six feet. His sandy brown hair, trimmed to just above collar length, and his blue eyes that always seemed to be smiling, had given him a look the girls found handsome. Now when he looked in the mirror, he saw only a shadow of what he had been.

Between Rog's death and his own situation, Bobby's depression deepened. He couldn't help but feel he was somehow to blame for Rog's death. *Why did Rog die and not me?* It just wasn't fair.

Bobby did his physical therapy half-heartedly. He missed school.

He missed playing sports. And he missed his friends. Andy, who had suffered serious injuries in the accident, dropped by every couple weeks, but his visits felt awkward. His closest friends, Eddie Smith and Riley McGee, came by every so often, but he missed the daily camaraderie. He felt sorry for himself and found it difficult to do anything. He even entertained thoughts of ending it. *I'm no good to anyone; just a burden on Mom and Dad.* His Mom had taken a leave of absence from her job at the library to take care of him.

They had hired a home health care attendant to help him get out of bed in the morning, get dressed and prepare for the day. *I hate this. I should be doing it for myself.* The fact that he couldn't depressed him further. After getting help dressing in the mornings, he had to be carried to the bathroom and then out of his bedroom to his wheel chair; the doorway wasn't wide enough for the chair to roll through. Then he was able to wheel himself down the hall and into the kitchen for breakfast. *Thank goodness we have a one story house.* The physical therapist came and was gone by noon, leaving him to his thoughts for the rest of the day until it was finally bedtime.

As depressed as he was, he had to admit his attendant, Carl, and his physical therapist, Karen, were good company. Despite hating the fact he needed them, they gave him someone besides his Mom and Dad to interact with.

Bobby particularly enjoyed his time with Carl. Carl had graduated from Brookside five years earlier and had started a home health care business after attending the local tech school. He had played both football and baseball at Brookside and loved telling stories about "the old days." Like the time he and some of the others on the team got into Coach Brawley's Red Man chewing tobacco one night at a game and all got sick as dogs. Carl stood about six feet tall and still had his athletic physique. With his mid-length light brown hair, he was ruggedly handsome. *Just like an athlete should look*, Bobby thought.

Trim and pretty, with short blond hair, Karen had also graduated from Brookside. Her dream had been to become a doctor, but

3

studying physical therapy at Oklahoma State, she found her niche. Her family really didn't have the money to send her to medical school, and after she married, she didn't want more student debt. She tried to encourage Bobby with stories of people in as bad, or worse, shape than he was, and how they got better with time and hard work. Bobby thought she was a little slim to be very athletic, but he had to admit she knew her stuff.

Bobby tried, but it was a struggle. Carl and Karen helped a lot, and his Mom was going by Brookside High to bring home assignments so he'd be able to keep up with his classes. His teachers were all sympathetic and promised to help. Miss Winn, his guidance counselor, was particularly helpful and had come to see him a couple times. The burden of getting his old self back, in the face of no legs and a dead friend, seemed too much.

Then one sparkling, cool late winter day, the doorbell rang. Mrs. Murphy opened the door and found a crowd of Bobby's baseball teammates on the porch. Bennie Brown, the team's co-captain with Bobby before the accident, spoke for the group. At six feet, three, with short dark hair and a chiseled face, Bennie was a natural leader. He wore his baseball tee shirt tucked into his jeans and seemed to take over any room he entered. "Mrs. M, we're here to see Bobby. He hasn't returned any of our calls and we're not gonna let him lie around and feel sorry for himself."

"Well," Mrs. Murphy said, "he's taking a nap. But, he takes a lot of naps. Maybe you can cheer him up."

So in they went, crowding into Bobby's bedroom. Sure enough, Bobby was dozing. "Bobby, wake up. We're not here to watch you sleep," Bennie said.

"Yeah," skinny Charlie Levin, the shortstop, said, his long brown hair bouncing up and down, "wake your sorry ass up. Oops, sorry Mrs. M."

Bobby came out of his slumber and looked around. "What are you guys doing here?"

"Well," Bennie said, "we're here to see how you're doin'. We've been worried about you."

"Yeah," Tommy Jones, the catcher, said. "We're here to cheer you up and get you back into circulation. You can't just lie around and feel sorry for yourself." Tommy was an old friend who had played baseball with Bobby since they were eight years old. Tommy had grown, not quite chubby but solid, a stereotypical build for a catcher. He had a round face that looked perpetually tan, but it was his dimples the girls all noticed.

Long, lean Brick Nelson, the center fielder, declared, "We're not gonna allow it. And, we want you back. The team needs you." Brick's demeanor gave him a relaxed, confident appearance. With his shoulder length hair, he almost looked like a young Ringo Starr. Bobby had always envied that look.

Bobby perked up a little. "What's going on with the team?" he asked. "How's the pitching look this year?"

Bennie, who played first base, said, "It looks pretty sorry. Miserable group of rag arms, I'd say." With that, he gave a little poke with his elbow to Al Tarkinton, the lone pitcher in the group.

"Hold it right there," Al said. "It's tough to be a good pitcher when the infielders are wearing boxing gloves trying to field the ball. Kind of like a bunch of monkeys playing with a football." Al, who was almost as tall as Bennie, but several pounds heavier, pretended to be offended and shook a meaty fist at the captain.

"Seriously," Bennie said, "our home opener against Millville's comin' up. It'd be great if you could be there."

After about an hour of the banter teenage friends have normally, poking back and forth at each other, the guys all left, with the promise to be back.

Bobby found himself feeling a little more upbeat. But, then, not long after everyone was gone, he thought: *That was really nice of them to come, but they probably won't be back. They'll get bored with me pretty quick.* And he drifted off to sleep.

The next morning, when Bobby woke up, he thought about

his friends' visit while Carl helped him get cleaned up and dressed. *Those guys really are good friends. I hope they'll be back when they can. And it was a lot of fun kidding back and forth.* The thought made him feel a little better despite himself, and he felt more motivated doing his physical therapy.

Karen noticed his improved humor. "Bobby, you're tearing these exercises up this morning," she told him. "Keep this up and you'll be a new man in no time."

After lunch, he even took marginally more interest in his classroom assignments.

As she helped him with his geometry and history, his Mom observed the change. "Bobby, it's so good to see you smile," she said. "Even over geometry." He thought smiling over geometry was a stretch, but he had to admit to himself he felt a smile over something.

TWO

The upbeat feeling Bobby got when his teammates came calling faded overnight. *Sure, it was nice of them to come, but they probably won't be back. I'm still helpless. I still can't use my legs. I hate being this way. I hate having to depend on other people for me to do anything at all. I even have to have someone help me get in and out of my bedroom. I can't even get in bed without help.*

Two days after the visit from his baseball friends, he got another surprise. The doorbell rang and in marched three of his friends from school, two guys and one girl. *Oh my God, it's Laura Sue Medlin.* Bobby had a crush on Laura Sue since the fifth grade, but he never got up the courage to ask her out. Laura Sue, at five feet, two inches, with eyes of blue, a great figure, short blond hair fixed in a ponytail, and the cutest smile ever, was the perfect girl. She wasn't stuck-up either, like some of the others.

"Hey man, we've missed you," Riley McGee announced. Riley was a big guy, over six feet. With his brown hair, fair complexion and toothy smile, he made people think of Opie from "The Andy Griffith Show." The others chimed in with their own greetings.

Eddie Smith, one of his closest friends, and the one he had seen most since the accident, said "Bobby, you need to get out. I've cleared it with your Mom for you to go to the baseball game tomorrow afternoon. Me and Riley'll be by after school. I've got my Mom's Explorer, so we can load you in the car and put your chariot in the back. How 'bout it?" Eddie and Riley both played on the football team with Bobby and were easily strong enough to lift Bobby and his chair. Eddie was about the same size as Riley, but had bright red hair, and the fair complexion to go with it. He had an infectious smile that naturally drew people to him. Both Eddie and Riley were wearing their letterman jackets.

Bobby had only been out a couple times since coming home from the hospital, and that was with his parents. The thought terrified him. He was just about to tell Eddie he couldn't go when Laura Sue spoke up. "Hey Eddie, don't leave me out. I'm going too." She gave Bobby a little smile.

When he saw her smile, he almost forgot about the wheelchair. "Got to tell you Eddie, it's really scary to be going out for the first time, but I've gotta do it sometime." He gave Laura Sue a big smile back, then turned red as a beet. *Real smooth, Captain Cool.*

"Oh, and one more thing I almost forgot," Eddie said. "While we're at the ball game, Mr. Dowling is coming over tomorrow with a crew to widen your bedroom door and the door into your bathroom. We've cleared it with your Mom and Dad." Mr. Dowling was the shop teacher at Brookside. When Bobby had taken his class in the tenth grade, they had hit it off. He used Bobby as an assistant in the eleventh grade.

Bobby was stunned. He couldn't think of a thing to say, so he looked over at his Mom, who was standing at the edge of the room trying to hide her tears.

After another half hour or so of catching up on things at school, Eddie said "Well, we gotta go now. See you tomorrow." Laura Sue hadn't said much, but directed several smiles his way and even some eye contact. Or, was that just wishful thinking? *Don't get your hopes up Bobby. She's too pretty, too popular at school, to see anything in . . .this . . .* He thought of his useless legs.

Each of the guys gave Bobby a pat on his back on their way out. Was it his imagination, or did Laura Sue sort of linger a moment and touch his hand as she said goodbye? For sure she did say, "See you tomorrow Bobby."

When the door shut, Bobby's Mom had tears running down her cheeks. "You sure do have some good friends, Bobby. "I was floored when Mr. Dowling offered to widen the doors. That will help you so much." All Bobby could do was nod his head.

A little while later, he heard his Dad's car pull up in the driveway. As soon as his Dad walked into the room, Bobby told him about the afternoon. When he told his Dad about the doors, his Dad said "That's great, Bobby. And when that's done, we'll mount some bars on the wall in the bathroom, so you can pull yourself up, and we'll need to design some sort of pulling bars for you to get yourself in and out of bed."

"Maybe Karen or Carl will have some ideas. I'll ask them tomorrow," Bobby said.

Bobby's Mom and Dad exchanged glances. Both were trying not to let Bobby see how emotional they were. This was the first real sign of any enthusiasm from Bobby in a long time. They had an upbeat family dinner that night. Bobby talked on and on about the doors, going to the game tomorrow and even accidentally mentioned Laura Sue and that he had especially enjoyed seeing her again. And, he turned bright red.

THREE

When Carl arrived the next morning to help Bobby get ready for the day, he found a different Bobby. "C'mon Carl, we've got work to do," he said with excitement. He told Carl about his friends' visit, all but the Laura Sue part. When he got to the part about Mr. Dowling and the doors, Carl interrupted him.

"Bobby, I've been waiting for you to get to this point. I've got some ideas that'll help you. One thing my company does, besides what I've been doing for you, is design and install the kind of bars you're talking about, not just in the bathroom, but also in the bedroom so you'll be able to get in and out of bed by yourself. Let's let Mr. Dowling get the doors widened. Then we'll get on that job--if you're Mom and Dad want me to do it, that is."

Listening from the doorway, Mom said, "You bet we do, Carl. Why don't you work up a design and an estimate, and I'll run it by my husband? I'm sure he'll agree. I want to get Karen's input, too. Maybe you two could work together. If he can combine some of his basic needs with the physical therapy, it'd be even better."

"I'd be glad to do that, Mrs. Murphy," Carl responded. "Karen and I have worked together on projects like this before."

When Bobby told him about going to the game that afternoon, Carl said "I'll be there. I haven't missed a Brookside home opener in baseball, basketball or football in all the years since I graduated.

You may not know it, but I helped us win the state championship in baseball my senior year. Had major league scouts looking at me, even."

Bobby already knew the story about the scouts. Carl had been sent to warm up their star pitcher, who the scouts were there to see, and had been positioned between the scouts and Fred. They couldn't miss him. But, Bobby wasn't about to embarrass him by saying that he knew that.

When Karen came, she felt the same sensation Carl had—Bobby was upbeat and really got into his exercises. His upper body was becoming stronger and his flexibility increasing. "You're getting there, Bobby." Bobby beamed.

FOUR

The rest of the day passed slowly for Bobby. All he could think about—besides Laura Sue Medlin--was getting out with his friends for the baseball game. Bobby's Mom had a hard time getting him to focus on his school work. In the months since the accident, she had tried a lot of ways to motivate him. But, he just didn't care very much. But, today's problem was different.

Finally, his Mom said, "Bobby, I know you're excited about going to the ball game with your friends this afternoon, but your studies are really important. Look at it this way: Your friends are seniors and they'll be graduating. If you don't keep up while you're not in school, they'll graduate and you'll be left behind. Think about when you were playing ball. You still had your studies to keep up, and you did. Your grades have always been good. How cool will it be for you to make the honor roll while you're studying at home?"

"Mom, I know I need to do it. It's just that I'm so fired up about this afternoon. And, to be honest, I'm a little scared, too."

"Bobby, you're going to face a whole lot of new challenges. Even if you weren't in a wheel chair, you'd have some scary times. Everyone does. Remember last summer when we watched the Paralympics on TV; how some of those competitors didn't even have arms or legs, but still did their best? And, their best a lot of times was pretty darned good. Many of them had to overcome a lot more than you're dealing with, but they didn't give up, or let down.

And, I bet a lot of them didn't have the support of all the friends that you have." She let that sink in. "Now, let's do some chemistry."

Bobby knew his Mom was right. Strange thing, the chemistry was starting to make a little sense. *What's with this?*

Finally, it was time for school to let out. Carl had laid out a new pair of jeans and a Brookside Rangers sweatshirt, navy blue, trimmed in gold, and helped him get dressed. The jeans were a little roomy, but Bobby hardly noticed. When his friends arrived, Bobby was in the living room waiting. "Man, I thought you guys would never get here," he said, as Eddie and Riley came into the room.

Trying to sound casual, like it was no big deal, Bobby asked "Where's Laura Sue? I thought she said she was coming."

His buddies exchanged glances, trying not to laugh. "She's clearing out the back seat. Don't worry, lover boy, she wouldn't miss this for the world."

Bobby turned bright red.

"Oh, yeah," Eddie said. "We brought you a new baseball cap. Coach Brawley said 'If our co-captain's here, be needs to have on the right headgear." With that, Eddie produced the blue cap with a script style "B" in gold. Across the back were the gold letters "Co-captain." *Coach really said that? Wow. He's including me as part of the team.* Mrs. Murphy showed the boys how to fold and unfold the wheelchair and Eddie and Riley made a little seat for Bobby by locking their arms. Both Eddie and Riley were big guys, over six feet tall and on the plus side of two hundred pounds. They had no problem lifting Bobby and helped him into the rear seat, where Laura Sue was waiting.

"Hi, Bobby," Laura Sue said, with that cute smile that made him miss a heartbeat.

"Oh, hi, Laura Sue," Bobby said, trying to sound casual. "I was afraid you wouldn't be able to make it."

"Now, Bobby, why on earth would you think that?"

"Um, uh, I dunno." *Captain Cool again. I've really got to work on my small talk.*

The trip to the baseball field was only a couple miles. Bobby could see the team doing their pre-game infield practice, while Coach "Booger" was hitting fungos to the outfielders. Bobby chuckled to himself as he recalled the day Coach Booger earned his nickname. Coach Brawley was absent that day and Coach Albright was leading practice. As he addressed the team at the end of the practice, Bennie had blurted out "Hey Coach, you got a booger hanging out of your nose." Good thing Coach Albright had a sense of humor.

Eddie parked the Explorer in the lot, leaving a wide space between it and the black Toyota Camry on his right. He and Riley got the wheelchair out, unfolded it and carefully lifted Bobby out of the backseat and into his "chariot."

"All right, King Tut, we're here," Eddie said, and he pushed Bobby out of the parking lot toward the grandstand behind the Brookside bench. As they got closer, the infield practice ended and the team came off the field. Bennie Brown and Charlie Levin both spotted Bobby at the same time and broke into a run.

"Hey, Bobby, you made it. We told Coach Brawley you'd be here. He wants you at the end of the bench, with the team," Bennie said.

The rest of the team came over, gathering around Bobby's chair, patting him on the back, and telling him how much they needed him there for encouragement. Bobby hardly knew what to say. Then Coach Brawley and Coach Albright came over. Coach Brawley was a large man, six, two and weighing at least two hundred and thirty pounds—no fat, just muscle. His shaved head and black handlebar moustache gave him a fierce look, which matched his gruff personality. While they remained slightly intimidated by the Coach, the team knew the gruffness was mostly a front. At least they thought it was.

"Murphy," the Coach growled, "get your butt over there. You're at the outfield end of the bench. I expect some input from you. I can't coach this team by myself, and Booger here ain't much help sometimes."

Coach Albright just grinned and gave Bobby's shoulder a squeeze. "Hey," he said, "what's all this muscle? You been working out?"

"Sure have Coach," Bobby said with a grin.

The players headed back to the bench. All of a sudden, it dawned on Bobby, *what about Laura Sue? She went to all this trouble to come to the game with me, and I won't even be sitting with her.*

Seeming to sense Bobby's discomfort, Laura Sue stepped in front of Bobby's chair. "Bobby, you need to be with your team. I'll be back in the stands. Anyway, I have to leave early. My Mom's picking me up. But," she added, with that smile that drove Bobby crazy, "I'll see you tomorrow."

"Brown, Murphy get over here," Coach Brawley said. "First game of the season and I want my captains to go out with me for the pre-game meet and greet. Can you manage that thing, or does Bennie need to push you?"

"I got it Coach," Bobby said, pleased that the Coach wanted him included.

While the warm-ups were taking place, a good size crowd, mostly students, had filled the stands. As they noticed Bobby, the buzz from the stands increased, and by the time he, Bennie and Coach Brawley reached home plate, people were standing and cheering.

"What's everyone so excited about?" Bobby asked Bennie. "I've never heard the crowd making so much noise over a pre-game meeting."

"You idiot," Bennie said. "They're cheering for you."

"Why would they cheer for me? I'm not playing."

Rolling his eyes, Bennie said, "Beats me."

After the coaches and umpires reviewed the local ground rules, Coach Brawley introduced his captains. The Millville coach, a big, muscular guy, with a buzz cut, said "I remember reading about you last winter Murphy. Glad to see you out."

"Thanks Coach. It's good to be here."

To raucous applause and cheering, the three Rangers made their way back to the bench, where the team was gathered. Coach Brawley stepped in. "Okay. Murphy's here, so now that you've said 'hello', let's get to a baseball game. You all know what to do—at least we've practiced enough that you should. So, let's go out and win a ball game."

The team ran onto the field. Al Tarkinton took his warm-up tosses. The first Millville hitter stepped in and drilled the season-opening pitch solidly into center field for a lead-off single. The second batter bunted him over to second. The third Millville batter launched a long fly ball to center field, which Brick Nelson tracked down for out number two. But, the Millville runner tagged up and took third. Clearly rattled, Al threw the first pitch to the clean-up hitter in the dirt past the catcher and the runner scored from third. One-nothing Millville. Calling time out, Tommy Jones went out to try to calm down his pitcher. After giving Al a few soothing words and a pat on the butt, Tommy resumed his spot behind the plate. The batter nailed the next pitch, hitting it right on the button, but, fortunately for Al and the Rangers, right at shortstop Charlie Levin.

Al walked slowly off the mound and took a seat next to Bobby at the end of the bench. One by one, the Brookside players all stopped by to offer Al some words of encouragement. "Hang in there Al. They got lucky on a couple pitches." "Don't worry buddy, we'll get it back." And so on.

Al looked over at Bobby. "I don't think I've got it today. Those were good pitches they drilled. Maybe I ought to tell Coach to take me out."

Bobby thought a moment. "Al, over the last several months, I can't tell you how much I felt sorry for myself and just wanted to give up. In fact, when you guys showed up at the house last week, I was about to. Don't you dare give me that BS about not having it, and telling Coach to take you out. You can't quit on your teammates that easy. You're a good pitcher and they got lucky, like Charlie said. They haven't given up on you, so don't give up on yourself. You've worked too hard to get to this point to quit after one inning."

"I know Bobby, but it's hard."

Bobby looked away, then back. "Hard? Al, you're my good friend, but don't tell *me* it's hard."

Al didn't respond, and Bobby didn't know if he had gotten through to him or not. *Was I talking to myself or Al?* Meanwhile, the first three Brookside hitters were out on ground balls to the infield. As Al got up to head back to the mound, he looked at Bobby and said "Thanks buddy."

While Al was taking his warm-ups, Coach Brawley came down and stooped in front of Bobby. "You talk to him?" the Coach asked.

"Yeah, Coach, but I don't know. . ."

"We'll see," the Coach said and moved away.

Al proceeded to set Millville down one-two-three, striking out the first two batters. He returned to the spot on the bench beside Bobby. "Nothing to it," he said, smiling at Bobby.

"Don't let up," Bobby said.

The game progressed quickly, neither team scoring until Brookside finally broke through in the bottom of the eighth. Tommy led off with a solid single to left and Brick's single to right moved him to third. With two outs and runners on first and third, Charlie Levin went "yard" on the first pitch, a long fly ball over the leftfield wall. Brookside led three to one.

Justin Moore, a senior, came in in the ninth to shut down Millville and seal the win. While the team took the field to celebrate, Coach Brawley came over to Bobby. "Good job Murphy. You earned your keep today. See you here on Friday"—sort of a question, sort of a command. Bobby thought to himself, *I really didn't do anything. I hope I can make it on Friday.*

As Bobby began wheeling himself across the grass, Eddie and

Riley intercepted him. "Let's go, Jocko," Eddie said. "Good start to the season."

Bobby, feeling a slight glow over the game and just being there, suddenly realized someone was missing. "Where's Laura Sue?" he asked, forgetting she told him she would need to leave early. It also occurred to him that he had completely forgotten about her during the game.

"She had to leave about the fifth inning," Eddie said. "Her Mom came over to pick her up. Something at home. She said to tell you she'd come by tomorrow after school."

FIVE

On the ride home, the three friends talked about the ball game and filled in Bobby on what was going on at school. Andrew Schmuck's cat had gotten trapped in the washer and scratched up his Mom pretty good when she went to get Tabby out. Bubby Short was suspended; somehow Mr. Doud, the assistant principal, found out he was the one who put the cherry bomb in the commode. Annie Jones got caught with a little weed, and was also suspended. Marylou Reed had been accepted into Texas A&M, not that anyone was surprised; the class generally conceded that Marylou would probably be the first astronaut from Brookside. Oh, and Mr. Payne, the assistant principal, had been arrested, but no one knew why. And so on.

As Eddie and Riley deposited Bobby and his wheelchair at the front door, Riley said "I'm not gonna be able to get by tomorrow. My Mom's taking me, get this—to shop for socks after school. Then we're gonna meet Dad for dinner. But, I'll be by on Friday to pick you up for the ball game."

"Great," Bobby said. He couldn't think of the words to tell them how much the afternoon meant to him. "Thanks."

"Our plan's to make sure you get to all the games this spring, at least the home ones. Believe it or not, Coach Brawley assigned us to it. He said if we ever couldn't do it, to let him know."

"You're kidding."

"Nope," Eddie said. "For some reason we can't figure out, he wants you there. Prob'ly in case someone really useful gets hurt; he can haul them off in your wheel chair."

"I know you're lying, but thanks."

When Bobby rolled into the house, he saw Mr. Dowling talking to his Mom. Even though Mr. Dowling and Bobby had gotten along well when Bobby was in his class, he was still a little intimidated by Mr. Dowling's sober demeanor. Tall and slim, he had a thick gray moustache that gave him a look Bobby thought was distinguished.

"Hi Mr. Dowling. How's it going?" Bobby asked.

"Well, Bobby, we got the doorways widened so you can get in and out of the bathroom and your bedroom with your chair. Still have the cosmetics to finish—the paint and hardware for the new doors. A couple of the young guys from shop class came over to help me. Buddy Medlin and Jay Schmidt."

Bobby was surprised at the mention of Laura Sue's younger brother. "Really nice of them to help out," Bobby said.

"We still need to install some grab bars in the bathroom and your bedroom. Carl called and told me he and your physical therapist designed a system for you. When it comes in, me and the boys will be back to put them in. We'll do the painting and stuff while you're gone to the ball game on Friday."

How did he know I'm going to the ballgame?

Mr. Dowling said, "I've been talking to Coach Brawley. He wants you to be at all the games. After all, you're the co-captain. He figures you being there will be good for the team."

What good can I do? I can't even move by myself, much less play. But, he kept the thought to himself. Instead, he said "Mr. Dowling, I really appreciate what you and your class are doing for me. I don't know how to thank you."

"We'll figure out a way," the shop teacher said, leaving Bobby to wonder what he meant. "Now I've got to get home for dinner. Mrs. Dowling gets anxious when I'm late."

After Mr. Dowling left, Bobby rolled down the hall and

through the newly widened door. He looked across the room to the bathroom door, which also had been widened. Without the bars, he still couldn't get in and out of the wheelchair to use the bathroom or get into bed by himself, but he was encouraged by the promise of more personal freedom.

Bobby's Mom came into the room while he was admiring the doors. "Looking good," she said. "How was the game?"

"Great game for an opener," Bobby said. "Al really pitched well once he got his groove. And, Charlie hit a homer. Coach Brawley said he wants me to be at all the games. I'm not sure I understand why, but I told him I'd try. He seems grouchy on the outside, but I don't think he's all that gruff."

"No, I don't either. I know he wants you there when you can get there. But, keep in mind, just like if you were playing, you've got to keep your grades up."

How did Mom know Coach Brawley wants me at the games? She must have been talking to him. "I know I need to keep my grades up, Mom," he said. "You don't need to nag me about it."

Just then the front door shut and his Dad hollered, "Where is everybody? No one out here to welcome home the hard working warrior?"

"We're back here," Mrs. Murphy called, "admiring the job Mr. Dowling and his crew did this afternoon."

Mr. Murphy came down the hallway and stopped short. "Wow, they got all this done just today?"

"They worked hard and fast," Mrs. Murphy said. "You haven't even seen it all. Come on in here and see the bathroom doorway. They're coming back Friday afternoon to put on the finishing touches—paint the new wood and hang the doors."

"I just can't believe all this," his Dad said. "Lot of work for someone without even being asked.

"And they're coming back when the grab bars come in to do the mounting. Now, dinner's waiting, so let's move to the dining room."

Bobby rolled his chair down the hall, easily maneuvering through the newly widened door. Fortunately, their house had an open style and the rooms in the front part of the house were easily accessible to him. He'd been assigned the place at the end of the table so he could roll right up to it without having to make any tight turns.

Over the meal, Bobby told his Dad about the ball game. He even told his Dad about Mr. Payne getting arrested and Andrew Schmuck's cat. Mom and Dad let Bobby chatter away. It had been a long time since he was so upbeat, and they enjoyed seeing their son acting more like the old Bobby.

SIX

Thursday morning, Carl arrived to help Bobby get up and meet the world. Bobby was still happy from his successes the day before He told Carl about the ball game, and asked him if he knew why Mr. Payne got arrested. Carl deflected the question, which made Bobby think he knew. Carl instead said, "You're not going to believe what happened to Andrew Schmuck's cat. It climbed into the washing machine when Mrs. Schmuck was putting in the clothes, and she somehow didn't see it. Well, when she started the washer, the cat set up a scream out of a horror movie. When she opened the washer to get it out, this soaking wet ball of fur came flying out like a rocket, almost knocking her on her butt. The cat ran around the utility room for a few minutes and took off down the hall. They haven't seen it since."

After they finished laughing at the image of a three pound furry, wet projectile coming out of the washing machine, Carl said, "Looks like Mr. Dowling and his boys did a nice job on the doors. That's gonna help you a lot. I expect the grab bars should be here over the weekend. When they come in, I'll get with him to set up a time when we can install them. You'll be a lot more independent when we get them up."

They continued to chat while Carl helped Bobby get cleaned up and dressed. "One thing I'm really looking forward to," Bobby said, "is being able to shower and use the bathroom by myself."

"Well, it's gonna take a little practice, and patience, but you'll get it," Carl said. "Okay, buddy, I'm out of here. I'll see you tomorrow. Want me to roll you out to the breakfast table?"

"Thanks, but I can do it." He followed Carl to the front door.

"We need to put a ramp out here," Carl said as he looked at the front steps. "One thing at a time, I guess." And he was gone.

As Bobby finished his breakfast, Karen arrived for his physical therapy. After admiring the work Mr. Dowling and his crew had done on the doors, she got down to work. The workout Bobby did each day was designed to build his upper body strength, but she always spent a little time moving his legs, flexing his ankles and knees, even though he had no feeling from about mid-thigh down. He asked her about it. "Why work with my legs? I can't use them anyway."

"We need to maintain some muscle tone and flexibility down there. Also, by moving your legs around, it'll help keep your circulation going and prevent blood clots."

"I get the circulation and blood clot thing," Bobby said, "but worrying about muscle tone and flexibility seems like a waste of time."

"Maybe so, but, humor me. If a miracle occurs, I want you to be ready."

This was the first time anyone had held out even a faint glimmer of hope that he might someday regain the use of his legs.

Sensing what Bobby was thinking, Karen said "Look Bobby. I don't want you to get your hopes up. Like the docs said, your ever walking again is such a long shot that it's just not going to happen. But, we do need to keep your circulation going and be sure no clots build up. And, you'll just feel better. I want you to be prepared to live your life independently. I want you to be able to do everything you can without the use of your legs. Believe me, you can do a lot. If you're willing to work at it, you can have a normal life, do most everything your friends do, and go almost anywhere."

"Even Coach Booger, oops, Coach Albright, noticed my upper

body strength getting better yesterday at the ball game. So, I guess you must be right." Bobby smiled. "And, when I get those grab bars installed, I want to be able to get myself in and out of this chair."

"I'll do my best to have you ready," Karen said. "Matter of fact, you're ready now, but we've still got more to do."

Karen finished the therapy session and, after a brief discussion with Mrs. Murphy, left. "I'll see you tomorrow, Bobby" she said, as she walked out the door.

"Time to study, Bobby," his Mom said. He eagerly plunged into his school work; maybe a little less eagerly with chemistry. He found geometry came easy to him and he enjoyed studying about the opening of the Oklahoma territory in 1889. He was struggling a little more with the chemistry. The stories about the land run and the '89ers, and where the term "Sooners" originated made good reading; he had no trouble retaining that. But, chemistry was more challenging. He struggled to make sense out of the idea of atoms and such floating around somewhere, invisible, and then magically coming together to make something.

After a break for lunch, Mom said "Okay, Bobby, time for English. By the time three-thirty came, Bobby was finished studying for the day. His Mom made a good, patient teacher and seemed to enjoy some of the subject matter, too.

Normally, when he was finished with his school work for the day, Bobby took a short nap. But, today he was too keyed up. He knew he shouldn't let himself create an expectation that his school chums would come by after school every day, but he couldn't help himself. He wanted to show Eddie and Riley his newly widened doorways and tell them about the grab bars. He was anxious to learn what had gone on in school. And, he found himself hoping Laura Sue might come.

About 4:30, he heard the doorbell ring. He was reading, and put down his copy of Ted Williams by Leigh Montville. Bobby thought Ted Williams was the greatest player ever to don a uniform and had already read three other books about him. He thought this one was the best of all. He was at the point in the book where Ted's son, John Henry, was forcing the elderly, infirmed Williams to sign all kinds of memorabilia to sell, and keeping Ted's old teammates and friends from visiting. John Henry, he decided, was a jerk and ought to be hung with a new rope.

Bobby wheeled himself down the hall and into the living room as his Mom answered the door.

"Hi, Mrs. Murphy. Is Bobby seeing visitors?" he heard Laura Sue ask.

Mrs. Murphy said, "I suspect he'll make time from his busy schedule to see you. Come on in."

"Captain Cool" kicked in as Laura Sue walked through the front door and Bobby wheeled his chair into the side of the sofa. "Oops," was all he could think of to say.

"Bobby, why don't you and Laura Sue go into the den? I'm just getting ready to take a fresh batch of chocolate chip cookies out of the oven. Laura Sue, I know Bobby wants some cocoa with his cookies. What can I get you to drink?"

"Cocoa would be really good, Mrs. Murphy. It's a little nippy outside and that sounds just right."

The den had already been set up for Bobby to easily access. It was a welcoming and comfortable room with book shelves lining one wall, family pictures, mostly of Bobby growing up, on the other two walls. It was painted a soothing shade of beige, offset with oak stained crown and floor molding. A slow moving ceiling fan kept the air moving. There were two stuffed chairs, a tan leather Lazy Boy recliner and a couch. Although not on at the moment, Mr. Murphy had installed a large screen TV.

Laura Sue sat down in the Lazy Boy, allowing Bobby enough room to park his chair nearby for easy conversation, not that he could think of any sophisticated things to say. Fortunately, Laura Sue had no such inhibitions.

"You've already heard about Andrew Schmuck's cat haven't you?"

Bobby nodded that he had.

"Well, the latest is that it came back and they think it's pregnant. Must have been something in the water, everyone thinks. And, you also know about Mr. Payne getting arrested. The rumor is that he approached some young kid in a public bathroom at the mall. At least that's what's going around."

"I hope that's not true," Bobby said. "Mr. Payne was always a pretty decent guy and a good class sponsor. Whenever he came to any of our events with his wife, I thought she looked like she was sucking a lemon. She never looked like she wanted to be there. I always wondered if she just didn't like us. Looks like they had other problems."

"Yeah, it does," Laura Sue said. "Oh, and we think we've figured out how they caught Bubby for blowing up the toilet. The moron had been trying to get a date with Emily Parsons. I guess he was trying to impress her with his – I don't know what – and told her what he'd done. He didn't take into account that she's vice president of the Pep club, and she turned him in. At least that's what we think happened."

"Bubby's always had more mouth than sense," Bobby said.

"You'd never do something like that, would you?"

"What? Blow up a toilet, or admit it to someone?"

"Either one," Laura Sue said.

Sensing that she was asking a serious question, Bobby said "No, I wouldn't do something that stupid."

Before he could say any more, Mrs. Murphy walked in with a plate of warm chocolate chip cookies and two steaming mugs of hot cocoa. "Dig in," she told them. "And there's more in the kitchen, if you eat all these. Just let me know."

"Thanks, Mom."

Yes, thank you very much Mrs. Murphy," Laura Sue said. "They look delicious."

Bobby chewed his cookie and took a sip of cocoa. *Laura Sue always seems to know the right thing to say. I, on the other hand, can't ever seem to say the right thing, especially around her.*

"You know, Bobby," Laura Sue said, "I knew you wouldn't do something like that. You always seem to know just what to say or do in most any situation. I was talking to Al Tarkinton today at school and he told me how you had exactly the right words for him when he was struggling at the ball game yesterday. I would never have known what to say to him."

While Bobby was contemplating the compliment, Laura Sue went on, "Speaking of the game, I'm sorry I had to leave early. My Mom was picking me up and we were going out for dinner. Buddy couldn't make it. I think he was actually over here with Mr. Dowling working on your doors."

"No problem," Bobby said, remembering he was so wrapped up in the game that he hadn't even noticed she left. "I really appreciate the work Buddy and Mr. Dowling did. It's gonna help me be a lot more independent. It's really been frustrating having to depend on someone else just to get in and out of this chair."

They continued to talk about school, what their friends were doing and the baseball team until Laura Sue looked at her watch. "Wow," she said. "Time has really flown. I need to get home so I won't be late for dinner. I won't be able to make it to the baseball game tomorrow. I agreed to baby sit for the Randalls. They have tickets to a play in Tulsa and won't be back until well after midnight. Lucky for me their kids are well-behaved."

"Heck, Laura Sue, I sure hope you have a good evening with the Randall's brats." *Oops, not too bad until that last part, but maybe not what Laura Sue expected.* "I didn't mean the Randall's kids are bad brats, or even good brats, or even brats." At this point, he recalled Will Rogers' advice: "When you find yourself in a hole, stop digging." So, he shut up.

Laura Sue laughed and said, "I know what you mean, and thanks. I'll try and get by to see you sometime over the weekend."

They went to the door together. As she turned to leave, she

looked back and gave Bobby a little peck on the cheek as she said "Bye."

Bobby, feeling himself turn into a mass of cherry jello, tried to get out a farewell, but his tongue got stuck on the roof of his mouth and he said "Bllllrh." *Sheesh. How Smooth.*

SEVEN

Bobby woke up early Friday morning. He couldn't get out of bed until Carl arrived to help him. He felt himself growing more and more agitated. *Why can't I move like other people? It's not fair. Life's not fair.* He lay there a few more minutes, his mind whirling. *Get control of yourself Bobby. Sure, life has dealt you a lousy hand, but you have a lot of help dealing with it. Everybody doesn't have this much help.*

That sorry excuse for a pep talk didn't help. I want to get up and I can't. He heard his Mom clanking dishes together as she took them out of the dishwasher and put them away. "Mom," he called. "Can you come here?" He instantly regretted calling his Mom. *She's busy with her housework and doesn't need to be coming in here every time I start feeling sorry for myself.* His frustration continued to build. By the time his Mom got back to his room, he was in a full scale bad mood.

"Mom, I hate my life. Look at me. I can't even get out of bed by myself. And now I'm interrupting you from doing things you need to do. I know my friends have been coming by, but I'm even a burden to them. They have their own lives and don't need to be planning everything around helping me do things I should do for myself." He felt a tear roll down his cheek as he let out his frustration.

Mrs. Murphy was taken aback. Bobby had not been this upset in quite a while. Usually, he wakened more upbeat. His mood swings were mild and generally later in the day. She said "Bobby, I'll help you get into your chair, but you need to get out of this funk. You've got too many good things going for you right now." With that she moved the chair over by the bed and held out a steady arm for support. Using his Mom's arm and the wheel chair, he was able to swing himself out of the bed and into the chair.

He turned his chair around and, without waiting for his Mom, wheeled himself to the kitchen. When his Mom arrived, he was sitting there looking up at the cabinet where his cereal resided. He looked up at the box of Honey Nut Cheerios and felt the frustration rising again. "Look at this. Here I am, three feet from my cereal and I can't reach it for myself." He swung his chair around angrily, almost colliding with his Mom, and stormed back to his bedroom. When he got there, he had tears of frustration rolling down his cheeks. *I'm useless.*

He was still sitting beside his bed in his pajamas, fuming, when Carl arrived. He felt his rage continue to grow inside.

"Hey, buddy," Carl said, as he walked through the door. "Your Mom said you aren't doing very well today. What's wrong?"

"What's wrong?" Bobby said. "What do you think is wrong? Here I sit. I can't do anything for myself, and you ask what's wrong." Although he had had a few bouts with feeling sorry for himself while Carl was there, this was worse than any of them. Carl had always continued his assistance with a cheerful demeanor, and Bobby gradually worked his way out of his bad mood.

But, not today. Carl stepped back and looked Bobby in the eye. "You need to cut this crap out. I work with a lot of people. And a lot of them are in worse shape than you. A few of them can't get out of their bed at all. One guy is paralyzed from his neck down. He'll never be able to take care of himself, or do much of anything. He can't wheel himself around the house. He doesn't have friends dropping by to see him, doesn't even have anyone to talk to most of the time except me and a couple other caregivers.

"You, on the other hand, are mobile. You can get around the

house, entertain friends and even go the baseball games, all with just a little help. You've got a whole team helping you. Karen and I've designed a grab bar system for your bedroom and bathroom. We've started planning some other places in the house to help you be more independent, like in the kitchen. Mr. Dowling and his shop class are doing the installations—not for the money. They aren't getting paid a penny. Your friends and your teammates come by pretty regularly. Do you think they're doing that because they feel guilty, or somebody's making them? Hell, no. All these people are in your corner because they care about you and want to help.

"So get over yourself. Sure you got a bum deal, but you can choose to be a plus, a minus, or just a blob. You've got a great set of friends and caregivers, like me and Karen. But, let me tell you: you can drive all of us away. We've been upbeat with you because we care. But, if you don't care about yourself, or just want to sit around and whine, you're liable to find yourself whining by yourself. Is that what you want for a future?"

Carl had never said this much to Bobby, and he was obviously passionate about his subject. He took several deep breaths while Bobby sat there in shock. *What the hell is wrong with Carl? Why is he so angry at me? Well, screw it. I'm the one who can't move, not him. I'm the one in the wheelchair, not him.*

While he helped Bobby get cleaned up, dressed and finished in the bathroom, Carl had little more to say. Bobby accepted Carl's ministrations, but said little himself. Finally, Carl finished. As he went out the door, he turned back to Bobby and said "Bobby, remember what I said. The choice is yours. I hope you get your act together, but I can't make you. Neither can anyone else. So, what kind of a life do you want?"

As Bobby sat there, he heard Carl's footsteps fading down the hallway. Bobby was still in shock over Carl's tirade. *I thought he was my friend.*

Before leaving, Carl stopped into the kitchen where Mrs. Murphy was loading the dishwasher. "I hope I wasn't too hard on him. It seemed to me it was time for some 'tough love.' Please let me know how he is through the day. I care too much about Bobby to let him wallow in self-pity."

"Carl, you were great," she answered. "I was listening from the hall and thinking how much Bobby needed to hear all that from someone other than me. He's a bright kid, and he has a wonderful support structure in place. He'll get to thinking about it, and work his way around to know what you said to him is all true. Thanks. It's much more effective coming from you than from me."

Carl left and, after a few more minutes sitting there and sulking, Bobby rolled out into the kitchen. His Mom had his cereal, toast and orange juice on the table. He ate his breakfast in silence, looking up to scowl now and then. She didn't press the issue. When Karen came for his physical therapy, she also noted that Bobby was more withdrawn than normal.

After his exercise program, with much less talk between them than usual, Karen stopped by the kitchen. "What's going on with Bobby?" she asked.

Mrs. Murphy said, "He got up this morning in a really foul mood. He's feeling sorry for himself. Carl lit into him and I think it stunned him. He's used to everyone rolling over and catering to him when he gets depressed and we didn't do that this morning. Carl gave him a lot to think about. I just hope it sinks in. Bobby needs a little time to absorb what Carl said, and I think he will."

"Let me know what I can do to help," Karen said. "He's special and, whether he realizes it now or not, he has a bright future."

"Thanks, Karen. I really, really appreciate everything you and the others are doing for him. I think it'll sink in, and I know deep down he appreciates your help, too."

"See you Monday," Karen said as she went out the door.

After Karen left, Bobby sat in his chair, thinking about everything Carl had said. *Carl's right. I know that. I understand it. I do have a lot of people helping me. And I know they aren't doing it for any reason except they care about me. But, I hate being this way. Even if everyone in the world likes me and cares about me and wants to help me, I'm still the same. Now, Carl, Mom and probably Karen are mad at me. I can't have that. I don't know how, but I've just got to suck it up and, even if I don't feel like being cheerful, at least don't take it out on the people trying to help me.*

Bobby wheeled himself out to the living room, where he found his Mom sitting on the couch. Mrs. Murphy was wearing her bright red Oklahoma Sooner sweatshirt and black jeans. Despite his funk, Bobby couldn't help but think, *Mom really looks sharp. She's putting up with me and my bad mood, and she still looks cheerful.* What Bobby failed to see, since his Mom was facing away from him, were the tears in her blue eyes. Hearing Bobby and his chair roll into the room, she quickly dabbed her eyes with the Kleenex and turned to Bobby with a smile.

"Feeling better?"

"I guess so. Mom, I know I acted like a jerk, but sometimes I can't help myself. You weren't in there, but Carl really let me have it this morning. And, I wasn't very nice to Karen, either. Never mind how I treated you. Please forgive me and try to understand."

Mrs. Murphy had a catch in her throat and didn't immediately reply. When she regained her composure, she said "I understand, probably better than you know. You've got enough on your plate that you're going to have some setbacks from time to time. I'm not giving up on you, and neither is Carl. As long as you keep your eye on the big picture, the end goal, you'll be okay.

"You know when your Dad and I met, I was a fighter pilot in the Navy. I flew F-18's on and off carriers. In the 'heads up' display on the windshield of the plane coming in for a landing is a ball display. Keeping your eye on the ball and keeping it centered on the cross hairs is critical. Lots of things can go wrong—wind shears, speed changes, the deck bouncing up and down—but keeping your eye on the ball is how you get past all that and keep from crashing. Bobby, keep your eye on the ball and don't let the daily ups and downs keep you from your focus. Now, let's get after some chemistry."

Stewing in his own problems, Bobby had forgotten about his Mom being a pilot. She had even been to Top Gun school. *She must have been, must be, one tough lady. And what a wimp I'm being. Shape up Bobby.*

They spent an hour on his chemistry. "Well, I think you're coming along pretty well with chemistry," she said.

"Yeah, I think I just saw a molecule, or an atom, or something go by."

"How about a bite of lunch before we tackle your math and history?" she asked. "I have some homemade vegetable soup, and I can fix you a ham sandwich. How does that sound?"

"Maybe with a little cheese?" Bobby replied with a grin.

"You got it," Mom said.

EIGHT

The afternoon passed quickly. Before Bobby realized it, he had covered an extra chapter in his history lesson and missed his nap. It was almost time for the gang to pick him up for the ball game. He and his Mom went back to his room and she helped him get his clothes changed. *Got to look sharp for the crowd.* He put on a clean pair of jeans and a special new navy blue sweatshirt with "Brookside Rangers" embroidered on the front in gold letters. The ensemble was completed with his Rangers' baseball cap.

Just as he finished dressing, the doorbell rang. "Hey, Mrs. M," Eddie said, as he strode through the door, Riley trailing in his wake. "Just me and McGee today. We've gotta get going. Coach Brawley cornered me after last period today and made it clear we need to get you there ASAP. So, let's get moving."

Under the watchful eye of former Lieutenant Murphy, the boys smoothly loaded Bobby, then his chair, into the Explorer.

"So long, Mrs. M," Eddie and Riley hollered.

"Bye Mom," Bobby chimed in.

They pulled up to the gate at the stadium. Eddie and Riley got Bobby out of the Explorer and into his chair.

"I've got it from here," Bobby said. "Go ahead and park the car."

As Bobby made his way to the field, the Rangers were just starting infield practice. He started to settle in at his spot beside the end of the bench when a voice like a jackhammer almost caused him to turn over his chair.

"Murphy, get your butt out to second base. Freeman's not got his footwork down and he's throwing the ball all over the place. Get out there and work with him while we're doing our infield." Coach Brawley was, by this time, standing right beside him.

"Got it, coach. On my way."

Wheeling himself out to second base as fast as he could, he saw the second baseman, "Red" Freeman looking pale and shaken. Red was a sophomore and, Bobby recognized immediately, still intimidated by Coach Brawley's tough façade. Bobby also knew that Red had a lot of talent and would be a big contributor to the team.

"Hey, Red, what's happening?" he said.

"Bobby, what are you doing here?" Red replied.

"Coach sent me out here to see if I could help you with your throwing. What's going on? You've never had problems like this before."

"To tell you the truth, I'm so nervous about screwing up, I screw up all the more. I really want to play, but I'm not good enough to start on this team yet."

"Number one," Bobby said, "we don't have time for this BS right now. We only have a few minutes for infield and then the game starts. Whether you think you're good enough or not, you're starting. And, you're starting because you're a good player. Coach knows what he's doing and he knows you're a real asset for the team."

"He's only starting me because he doesn't have anyone else."

"More BS. He told me you have more potential than almost anyone else on the team." A little exaggeration, but Red seemed to be listening.

"When you get this ground ball he's fixing to hit you, I want you to pick it up, pause for a second while you plant your feet, and step through the throw with your right leg. End up facing the first baseman. And, if your throw is a little off, no sweat. Big Bennie over there will bail you out. Important thing is, don't think about it, other than your step. Just do it like you do every day in practice?"

Bobby rolled his chair back toward right field so he wouldn't be in the way. Red fielded the ball, paused, planted his feet, and let it go—right over Bennie's head. "One more coach," Bobby called. He turned to Red, "Okay, pick it up and throw it; don't aim it and don't think about it."

This time, the ball was not straight at Red. He had to quickly move to his right to get it. As he did, in one motion he picked it up, planted his feet and threw a strike to Bennie at first. No wasted motion.

"You've got it," Bobby told him. "Key is to have the great mechanics, but just do it. If you think about it, you have a better chance of throwing it away. You should have seen me when I first started playing ball. I was a wild man. But, Coach Booger spent some time with me when I was in junior high and, you know what? It helped. You have all the talent in the world. Just use it and don't think about it too much."

"Thanks Bobby. I really appreciate it. Spending time with me… that's special." Red picked up his last grounder, threw a strike to the catcher and ran off the field.

Bobby made his way back to the bench and looked around. *Decent crowd for an afternoon game.* It was good just being back on the field, surrounded by his teammates. Spring had definitely arrived. The grass was the shade of green only found in the early spring, before the hot summer sun arrived to leave the grass with a bleached-out look. There was something about the contrast between the manicured grass and the carefully raked and smoothed brown infield dirt that just made a ballplayer come alive. And, Bobby still thought of himself as a ballplayer.

Coach Brawley came over. "Murphy is Freeman going to be okay with his throws?" he growled.

"I think so Coach. I think he was overthinking them instead

of just doing what he knows how to do. His last two tosses were on the money."

"Keep your eye on him during the game," the Coach said. "Also, I told Roberts to come sit on your end of the bench between innings. He likes to get down on himself if any little thing goes wrong. When he does, he just clams up and lets it eat at him. Keep him loose and as upbeat as you can. Plus, you know how moody those southpaws can be." With a "hrrumph," a sound falling somewhere between a grizzly bear waking in a grouchy mood and rocks grinding in a landslide, Coach Brawley started to move away. Turning back to Bobby, he added "I want you out here to exchange the line-ups. Their coach is sending their captain, so I'm sending you and Brown."

About that time, Bennie Brown, the team's co-captain, along with Bobby, arrived. "You want me to push you out there, buddy?" he asked. "Guess not," he said when Bobby gave him a look that would melt a stone statue.

Bobby wheeled himself out beside Bennie. The Branford captains hustled out when they saw the two Rangers and the umpires waiting. After introductions and handshakes, Bennie and Bobby went back to the bench area. The team surrounded the coaches and the two captains. "All right guys," Coach Brawley said, sounding a little less guttural than earlier. "We won our opener, but this team is a good bit better than Millville was. Branford was runner-up for the state title last year, in case you forgot. Every one of you knows what to do. And, you that aren't in the line-up today stay ready. You never know when you might be needed."

With a loud "Go Rangers," the huddle broke up and the starters took the field. Ray Roberts strode to the mound to begin his warm-up. *He doesn't look nervous. In fact, he looks a little too cocky. That's good if it all works out, but, if he gives up a couple hits, he's liable to go too much the other way.*

Branford's lead-off hitter took the first pitch, a fast ball for strike one. Then, on the next pitch, he dropped a perfect bunt down the first base line, catching the Brookside infield by surprise. Roberts looked over at him on first base and went into his stretch. The runner took his lead. The first pitch to the second batter was a little inside, just enough that Bobby felt sure Roberts was sending him a message. As he prepared to throw the second pitch, the base runner took just a little longer lead. *He's gonna try to steal second,* thought Bobby. *I hope Ray notices that.*

Ray did notice, and, with an excellent move to first, picked the runner off. With no more base runner, Roberts went into his wind-up and three pitches later, the batter had struck out, frozen in place by a wicked curve ball for strike three. The next batter hit a ground ball to Charlie Levin at short, and the inning was over. No runs, one hit, and no errors—a good start for the game.

Ray came over to his assigned seat on the end of the bench and sat down beside Bobby. The catcher, Tommy Jones, sat on the other side.

"Good start," Bobby said. He didn't know Ray well. Ray, lean and fit, with a look that reminded Bobby of a young Alan Alda, had transferred to Brookside last fall when his family had moved down from Wichita. It could be hard to change schools at the beginning of your senior year, Bobby knew, but, Ray seemed to have made a good adjustment. And, the team was excited to have a pitcher of his quality.

"Thanks," Ray replied. "What's the deal here? How come Brawley wants me sitting down here with you?"

As Bobby looked over at Ray, weighing how to answer the question, he noticed Tommy Jones looking at him, also waiting for the answer. Bobby had played on the same teams with Tommy off and on since they were in Little League, and Tommy had often asked Bobby's opinion. Tommy was a thoughtful player, as many catchers are, and valued other people's input. His Dad had played five years in the Cardinals' farm system and passed on a lot of knowledge to Tommy.

"Coach asked me to sit with you and let you know if I pick up anything that might be helpful," Bobby answered. "Last game, he had Al sit here, and we just talked about stuff between innings. I'd noticed a couple things that he hadn't and it seemed to help him."

Tommy said, "Last year Bobby was our team leader. We were counting on him to lead us to State this year."

At Tommy's words, Bobby caught a sharp breath. *Bad enough I can't play, but here's my old bud Tommy telling me how much I've let them down.*

But, Tommy didn't stop there. "Now, he can't help us with his play, but he's our inspiration. He knows more about baseball than any of us and, just the fact he's here for our games, is really big. He's helping us get to State, like we planned, just in a different way. Look how Coach talks to him before games. Bobby's still our leader."

Wow. Can I live up to those expectations? Gotta try!

Ray said, "Well, did you notice anything last inning?" Bobby wondered if he heard a little sarcasm in the question.

Not rising to the bait, Bobby replied, "As a matter of fact, I did. I noticed a few things. First, I noticed that, after that guy bunted, you threw inside on the next pitch. I assumed you were sending a message. Then, I noticed the base runner extending his lead ever so slightly after the first pitch and I figured he was getting ready to steal on the pitch. I saw that you noticed it too, and picked his butt off. Good job, by the way."

"Yeah, I did notice that," Ray said, impressed that Bobby had picked up on all that. "Thanks for the observation."

Brookside went down one-two-three in the bottom of the first, and Ray headed back for the mound. As he got up to go out to catch, Tommy looked over at Bobby. "Way to go. Ray's a little cocky, but he's a good guy, and a really good pitcher. Speaking for myself, I'll appreciate any help you can give either one of us."

"Go get 'em," Bobby replied.

The game settled into a rhythm. By the end of the sixth inning, the only hit was the leadoff bunt. Bobby didn't have a lot to offer, but the way Ray was pitching, he didn't need much. They chatted back and forth about little things related to the game, and Bobby cautioned him to expect another bunt, since the Branford batters couldn't seem to hit what Ray was throwing.

As the team took the field for the top of the seventh, Coach Brawley ambled over to the end of the bench. "What do you think, Murphy?"

"Couple things, Coach. First, Ray's really pitching well. He's good. Second, Branford's got some good hitters and they can't hit him. I think they'll start bunting to try to take Ray out of his rhythm, and also get us to make some mistakes."

"Good observation Murphy. I've been thinking the same thing myself. They're just starting through their batting order the third time and we need to be ready."

Branford's first batter squared around to bunt on the second pitch. Luckily, he bunted it straight back to the pitcher and Roberts threw him out easily. Coach Brawley signaled the first and third basemen to play a little shallower, just on the edge of the infield grass. The next batter delayed showing bunt, but, at the last second, dropped one down the first base line and beat it out by a hair.

The third batter set up to bunt as soon as Ray started into his stretch. Sure enough, Ray threw a hard one inside and brushed him back on the first pitch. On the second pitch, the batter was still showing bunt, but when Ray cut loose with the pitch, he came out of his bunt stance and struck it sharply past the hard charging third baseman. The ball went into left field and, by the time the left fielder got it back into the infield, the runners were on second and third.

Bobby watched Ray closely. He was obviously rattled. How would he deal with this? Coach Brawley pulled the infield in on the grass, wanting to keep the run from scoring. Would they bunt again? *I would,* Bobby thought. He looked down the bench and saw Coach Brawley motioning to the first and third basemen. As Ray threw the pitch, both of the infield corners came charging hard. Sure enough, the batter laid down a squeeze bunt. But, Bennie, coming in from first, picked it up and flipped it to the catcher, who applied the tag. Still runners on first and third, but now there were two outs. Branford's next batter hit a sharp ground ball to Red Freeman, who threw him out with a perfect throw to end the threat.

Ray came to the bench. "Coach is pulling me. He had me on a pitch count and I got there, so I'm out of the game. Any thoughts?"

"Yeah, Ray, a couple. First off, you pitched great. If you keep pitching this well, you'll be drafted, or get a scholarship when you graduate. I'm not a pitcher, so take what I say with a grain of salt. The only thing I noticed is you seem to let the base runners distract you a little. I'd suggest you pay attention to them and keep them close, but not quite so intently. You also wear your feelings on your sleeve. I think it would help you if you could at least not show your distress when something doesn't go right. Neither of these things is a big deal."

"I hear you," Ray said. "I know I let baserunners get to me, and I also know I need to keep more calm out there. I'm trying, but it's hard."

"One other thing I'd suggest," Bobby said. "Stay close with your catcher. He's right on top of everything that's going on with you, and you've got a good one. Tommy's been playing a long time and his Dad played in the minors. He can be a lot of help."

"I'll do that, and thanks. You were a lot of help; just knowin' you were watching me and all."

They turned their attention back to the game just as Bennie Brown cracked his first home run of the season, a three run blast, clearing the left field wall with ease. Rangers led 3-0. Justin Moore, Brookside's closer, took the mound in the top of the eighth and pitched two shutdown innings.

Red Freeman approached Bobby after the game. "What you said about me belonging in the line-up—you still believe it? I did okay in the field, but I didn't get any hits."

"Red, Chipper Jones didn't get a hit in every game. Mickey

Mantle even went hitless sometimes and struck out over a hundred times one season. Your time will come at the plate. I watched how you approach it, and I like the way you get set. Just be patient and don't get too tense. The hits will come."

"Thanks, Bobby," Red replied, not sounding fully convinced, but a little more confident.

As Red moved away, Bobby sensed a presence, confirmed by a gruff "hrmph" behind him. "Murphy," Coach Brawley started in without preamble, "you did a good job working with Roberts. He's a bit of a 'head case' sometimes. And, I heard what you told Freeman. Good stuff. Hope we can get him turned around at the plate."

"I have a suggestion, Coach. He just needs to make some solid contact with the ball. Maybe if you had him bunt a few times, it would build his confidence. He's fast and might even beat some of them out."

"I'll think about that," the coach said. "Any chance you could get out for a few practices between games?"

Bobby was moved. Coach Brawley wanted his help. *Wow!* "I'll do my best Coach. I have to depend on someone to pick me up and take me home, but maybe my Mom will help. I can't promise to be here every day, though."

"If you can get here, we'll take care of getting you home. You've got a way of talking to these kids that they'll listen. Sometimes, they don't seem to be listening to me."

"You'd be surprised, Coach. Every one of the guys would die trying to please you. And, to get a compliment—that would make their day. You're our hero."

Coach looked a little uncomfortable and, with another "hrmph," walked away.

Eddie and Riley were excited about the win. On the ride home, they talked about the game and what was going on at school. As they helped Bobby into his chair when they reached his house,

Eddie said "Next game is Tuesday. Away. At Pawhuska, I think. Gonna be tight to get there on time."

"I'll see if my Mom can get me there on Tuesday," Bobby said. "Could you bring me home?"

"You betcha," Eddie and Riley said in unison. "I gotta get home now," Eddie said, "so we won't be able to come in. I'll come by over the weekend, probably Saturday afternoon."

"Thanks, guys," Bobby said, and he rolled through the door.

NINE

The first thing Bobby noticed was the aroma coming from the kitchen. He looked at his watch *Seven-thirty. No wonder I'm so hungry. It smells like Mom's making lasagna.*

He made his way to the kitchen, where his Mom was indeed busy creating one of her specialties—baked lasagna. He started to tell her all about the game when he noticed an addition on the wall beside the counter. "Is that a grab bar?" he asked.

"That's exactly what it is. Go take your jacket back to your room. Your Dad is back there and you can tell him dinner's almost ready."

Bobby wheeled himself back to his bedroom. First, he noticed a grab bar on the wall beside his bed. Then, he noticed new grab bars in the bathroom, one by the toilet, one by the sink and two in his shower beside the small seat.

"Wow, Dad. When did all this get done?"

"While you were at the game, Mr. Dowling and a couple of his students came by and did the work. Carl was here to show them where they go. And he said he'd show you how to use all this when he comes tomorrow."

Bobby thought back to the way he had acted with Carl that morning. *I'm embarrassed. I owe Carl a big apology.* Then, he thought about how he had reacted when Karen told him she wanted to maintain some of his muscle tone in his legs. As he pondered that, he looked across the bedroom and saw a free standing set of parallel bars about six feet long. "What are they for?"

"Carl said Karen would show you when she comes on Monday," Mr. Murphy replied. "Now let's get back out to the dining room before our dinner gets cold."

Bobby was unusually quiet at the dinner table, but in a thoughtful way. "How was the game?" his Dad asked.

"We won. A new guy on the team, Ray Roberts, pitched really well. Coach had me working with another new guy before the game, a sophomore named Red Freeman. He was having trouble controlling his throws to first and I helped him some. Then, he had Ray sitting next to me during the game and we talked about what was going on and some stuff I noticed. It seemed to help him, too."

"You may be looking at a whole new career in baseball—as a coach," his Dad said with a grin.

"It is kind of fun to be able to help someone correct a problem, or build their confidence," Bobby said. "In fact, Coach asked me if I could come to as many practices after school as possible. I told him I wasn't sure. By the time some of my buddies got over here after school to get me, practice would be mostly over. He said, if I could get there, he'd make sure I got home."

Exchanging a knowing look with her husband, his Mom said, "I guess this is the time to tell you. Coach Brawley called me and asked if I could help with that part. He said you have a natural knack of recognizing things on the ball field, not just with correcting players' problems, but also with strategy in the games. He wants you to be a student assistant coach and seemed to really think you might make the difference in the run to the state championship."

Bobby was stunned. He knew Coach had asked him to talk to a couple of the guys, and he remembered a short discussion of strategy, but he never imagined Coach was doing anything more than trying, in his own grouchy-sounding way, to make him feel like he belonged. *A student assistant coach! Wow.*

"What did you tell him, Mom?"

"I said 'No way'. I don't want to make that ten minute trip to the school every day."

Bobby was crushed. He knew it was a lot to ask of his Mom, who was already spending a good part of each day home schooling him so he'd be able to graduate on time in June. But, this was also important to him—a chance to have a real part on the baseball team and do something worthwhile.

Then, he looked up at his Mom. She had a grin on her face. "Okay, Bobby, I'll do it. We'll get started Monday. How could I tell Coach Brawley no?"

"Mom, you're the best, just in case I never told you that before."

TEN

Spring moved quickly for Bobby and his family. He took his role as student assistant coach seriously and missed very few practices. Most of his teammates genuinely appreciated his contributions and the younger players began to look up to him, practically on the same level as the coaches.

Bobby also put additional efforts into his studies. When the class at school had tests, his teachers sent them along to his Mom, who oversaw Bobby completing the tests just as if he had been in the classroom. At mid-term, he was making almost all "A's", falling to a high "B" only in chemistry. He was on track to graduate with honors with his class in June. He missed being at school, though. He thought his Mom was doing a great job, and made learning fun, but he missed the interaction with his friends. He did get to see his baseball teammates at practices and games, and his other friends came by regularly. Laura Sue was especially good about visiting.

Bobby was also thinking about some of the school-related activities he was missing while being at home. The senior class had a few get-togethers that he'd missed. And, the prom was coming up. The thought of it troubled him. He wanted badly to go, and to take Laura Sue. But, how could he? He couldn't dance, he couldn't even get in and out of a car by himself. He couldn't do much of anything without someone to help him, someone to load his chair into a car, someone to drive him places. He just couldn't do that to

Laura Sue. She deserved to have a fun time at her prom, and to not be saddled with his disabled self.

Carl's job had become markedly easier as Bobby learned to use the grab bars. He had mastered getting in and out of bed, into his chair, getting himself bathed and dressed, even using the bathroom. After his outburst at Carl, he had apologized so many times to him that Carl finally told him to shut up about it. They became closer and Bobby felt he could talk to Carl about "stuff", the kind of guy stuff he couldn't talk to his Mom and Dad about. When Bobby told Carl about not asking Laura Sue to the prom, Carl told him "Just wait and see. You never know what might happen. Life takes some strange twists."

While Carl's work with Bobby became easier, Karen was pushing him hard with his physical therapy. He not only worked on his various grab bars every day, he also spent a good deal of time using the parallel bars. His upper body strength was increasing dramatically. He had little trouble navigating from one end to the other on the parallel bars. Karen continued to massage his legs, and one day he noticed he was actually using his legs for support—not much, but more than he would have imagined a month earlier.

Bobby's birthday was coming up on April 15, the ides of April, he had learned. During the weeks approaching, he noticed his Dad seemed a little more pre-occupied than normal. When he asked his Mom if anything was wrong, she just brushed off his question. Was she brushing him off with a secretive smile? He couldn't tell and she wouldn't tell him any more.

His birthday had always been a fun time for him. Mom and Dad had thrown him small parties over the years, but he had no great hopes for this year. The day arrived with no fanfare. It was a Friday, so he had his normal routine beginning with Carl and Karen, followed by his studies with Mom. It got to be four o'clock and not even Mom had mentioned his birthday. *Oh well, not really much to celebrate this year anyway.* It was raining outside, so he didn't even have baseball practice. *What a bummer of a day!*

The doorbell rang. "Bobby, would you get the door please?" his Mom shouted from the kitchen.

"Okay." He hoped it might be some of his buddies coming by for a visit. He opened the door, and there was a crowd of his friends led by Laura Sue Medlin front and center. His mouth fell open and he didn't know what to say.

"Bobby, aren't you going to invite us in?" Laura Sue said, with that smile on her face that gave him fits.

"Sure, come on in everybody."

"It's about time," Eddie said. "We were fixin' to get wet." Riley traipsed in with Eddie, followed by six of his baseball teammates.

"No practice today," Bennie Brown said, "so we had nothing else to do. Thought we'd come by."

Funny all of them arrived together. A real coincidence. I smell something coming from the kitchen.

At that moment, Bobby's Mom entered the room carrying a chocolate sheet cake with eighteen flaming candles. The whole crowd began singing "Happy Birthday to you. . ." Bobby was speechless.

Finally, he got his composure back. Looking first at Laura Sue, *boy is she ever cute,* he said, "Thank you all so much. I really thought no one even remembered it was my birthday."

"Okay, okay," Charlie Levin said. "Let's get after that cake."

Laughing, Mrs. Murphy began cutting and serving the cake.

"Good thing you made a big one, Mrs. M. This is great," Eddie said. Everyone chimed in with thanks and compliments on the cake.

After cake, Bennie got up and said "Everyone shut up. I've got something to say. First, Coach Brawley and Coach Booger couldn't be here, but they said to tell you 'happy birthday'. Justin Moore and Al Tarkinton wanted to be here, but they said you didn't like pitchers, so they were afraid to come."

Bobby started to protest, but Bennie cut him short. "Just

kidding Bobby. They both had doctors' appointments. But, they'll be there on Saturday."

"Way to go, Bennie," Eddie said. "Let the cat right out of the bag. Laura Sue, why don't you tell Bobby about tomorrow?"

"Bobby, you need to be at shelter 'C' at Bud Wilkinson Park on Saturday at one o'clock," Laura Sue announced. "Don't eat lunch before you come. And don't be late."

"Wow," Bobby said. "I can't believe all this is happening just for my birthday."

"Don't get a swelled head, Murphy," Tommy Jones said. "We just needed an excuse for a party."

"No we didn't." Laura Sue flashed Tommy a look. "No we didn't. You're our friend, and we want to do something nice for you."

"Yeah, Jones. You listen to Laura Sue," Bobby said. And then he blushed a bright shade of red, to everyone's amusement.

The group spent the next half hour kidding each other, prodding Bobby with affectionate insults, and generally having a good time. Finally, it was time for everyone to leave. Bobby stationed himself by the door so he could tell each one how much he appreciated them coming. Laura Sue was the last one to depart and she leaned over and gave Bobby a little kiss on the cheek. Then, she turned and fled out the door.

Mrs. Murphy, watching them leave, hid a little smile. "You've really got a lot of good friends, Bobby," she said. "And, I sure do like Laura Sue. She seems to like you, too."

"Aw, Mom, she's just being nice."

"Uh, huh."

ELEVEN

After his friends left, Bobby rolled himself back to his room, lifted himself with his grab bars and dropped onto his bed. He wasn't sleepy, but just needed to think. *What a great group of friends, remembering my birthday and all. And, to throw me a party at the park tomorrow—really cool. But, they're gonna get tired of hauling me around one day. I've just got to get more mobile.*

About the time Bobby was just on the verge of thinking himself out of his good mood and becoming depressed, his Dad came through the door. "Happy Birthday, son," his Dad said. "Time for dinner. You need some help getting out to the table?"

"Not me. Just watch." And with that, he reached over to the bar on the wall nearest the bed and did a neat pirouette into his chair. "I've been working at this. The more I can do for myself, the more independent I'll be."

"Well done," his Dad said. "I have an idea that you'll like to help you another step toward that goal. We'll take a little ride tomorrow morning and see what we can find," he added cryptically.

"What are you talking about?"

"You'll see."

At dinner, they had a lively conversation. Bobby told his Dad about the surprise visit from his friends, and the party at the park on Saturday.

"Yeah," his Dad said. "I know all about that. Your Mom and I are invited, too, you know."

"No, I didn't know that," a surprised Bobby said. *Something's going on I don't know about. Maybe I can get it out of my Dad, or Mom, if I can't get him to spill his guts.*

But, try as he might, Bobby couldn't get any more out of his Dad. He finally asked him directly what was going on.

"Are you ready for some birthday cake?" was his entire answer. "Mom?"

"I'll get the cake," Mom said, and headed for the kitchen.

In a few minutes, she returned with the cake. It was Bobby's favorite, one of his Mom's homemade carrot cakes, festooned with lettering saying "HAPPY BIRTHDAY BOBBY—18". She disappeared into the kitchen again and returned with a carton of Blue Bell vanilla ice cream.

"I've died and gone to heaven," Bobby exclaimed. "It can't get better than your special carrot cake. But, that chocolate cake we had this afternoon was good, too. Can't remember when you've made two cakes in one day."

"Just wait until morning," his Dad said. Bobby looked at him, wanting more information. His Dad looked back and smiled.

After dinner, they all pitched in to clear the table and help with the dishes. Then, in the living room, his Dad turned on the TV and turned the volume down.

"Bobby," his Dad said, "have you given any thought to college next year? Or, if not college, what you might do?"

"As a matter of fact, I have. Sometimes I think I want to be a lawyer, like you Dad. Then, I think maybe I'd rather be a teacher. But, I realize I probably won't be quite ready to navigate OU or OSU next year. I think I'll start at the community college, take some basic courses and get them out of the way, while I work on getting around. I talked with Miss Winn, the counselor at school, last week. She said she'd help me with the application. She didn't think I'd have any trouble getting admitted."

"Sounds like you're on top of it. We should probably have had this conversation before now. But, I think you'll be okay. Have you considered how you'll get there and back?"

"I'm trying to take it one step at a time, Dad, but I'm hoping I can get into a carpool, or that Mom can help me out with that."

"Well, like you said, 'one step at a time.' Let's see if the Braves are on TV." His Dad had played two seasons in the Atlanta Braves' farm system until tearing his ACL in the off-season.

Sure enough, the Braves and Cardinals were on; the Braves had a 2-0 lead in the second. The three lapsed into a comfortable silence watching the game. Bobby watched intently, enjoying the time with his Mom and Dad. Every now and then, his Dad would offer a comment on the game, generally acknowledging a good play, or noting a mental error by one of the teams. Bobby was struck by how much about baseball he had learned from just spending time with his Dad. *I wonder if I could be a real coach one day?*

After the game, which the Braves lost 4-3 in ten innings, Bobby said his good nights, and headed for bed. He no longer needed help to change into his sleeping clothes, or to use the bathroom, thanks to the bars. As he climbed into bed, his mind was racing. So many things. His friends all coming by. The small birthday dinner with his Mom and Dad. *Hmm, they usually give me some presents. Maybe, since I turned eighteen, they think I'm too old for what Dad's being so mysterious about?*

Then his mind turned toward the next day, and the events his friends had planned. He fell asleep thinking about Laura Sue.

TWELVE

S aturday morning, Bobby woke up early. No Carl or Karen on Saturday, but he was able to get himself up, bathed and dressed. He rolled himself out to the kitchen. His Mom had moved his cereal and other breakfast supplies to a lower cabinet, one he could reach from his chair. He got out his Honey Nut Cheerios and a bowl. Moving to the refrigerator, he opened the door and took out the milk for his Cheerios. It was a little tricky getting all this to the kitchen table, but a small removable folding shelf his Dad had installed on his chair helped a lot.

Bobby was at the table eating his second bowl of cereal when his Mom appeared in the doorway. "Bobby," she said. "You've come a long way in such a short time. Two months ago, if someone told me you'd be getting yourself up and dressed, and making your own breakfast without any help, I wouldn't have believed it." She walked over to him and gave him a big hug.

At that moment, his Dad came into the kitchen. "Right, Bobby, you've come a long way. Now, go mow the lawn."

Realizing his Dad was kidding, Bobby said "Look outside Dad. I did it before you got up."

Without thinking, his Dad took a quick look out the window.

"Gotcha," Bobby said, and they all laughed.

"Do you remember my friend, Al Nelson?" his Dad asked.

"Yes, he's Brick's Dad. You know Brick's our left fielder, don't you?"

"I do, but Al's a car salesman down at Sooner Ford. I've been thinking about getting a new car. He's expecting me at ten and I thought you might want to go with me."

"Sure I would," Bobby said, "but don't forget we're supposed to be at the park at one."

"No problem. We'll be back in plenty of time."

Bobby had to have a little help getting into the Explorer. His Dad stowed the wheelchair in the rear and they drove away. Bobby thought it was a little strange that his Dad wanted him to go with him to look at new cars. Besides, the Explorer was only a year old and his Dad always kept his cars several years. *Maybe he's buying a new one for Mom.*

The Ford dealership was only a mile from their home, so they were there before Bobby could ask questions. They pulled into a parking space by the door and his Dad helped him out of the front seat and into his chair.

"Hi Bobby. Hi Jack," the salesman said, as he met them at the door. "Bobby, it's nice to see you. You look good."

"Thanks, Mr. Nelson. I feel pretty good, too."

"Al, we don't have a lot of extra time this morning. Why don't you take us out to the vehicle you and I discussed," Mr. Murphy said.

Mr. Nelson led them across the paved lot, past rows of new Explorers and Expeditions. They reached the used car lot and now Bobby was really confused. *Why would Dad be looking at a used car?* He grew even more confused when Mr. Nelson pointed them to a white Dodge mini-van that appeared to be at least two or three years old.

Mr. Nelson pointed the remote key fob toward the car and Bobby heard the click of the doors unlocking. Then, a strange thing happened. The right rear sliding door began to open. When it was fully open, a small ramp dropped slowly from the inside, creating a ramp wide enough for a wheelchair to board the vehicle. Bobby was still puzzled.

"Come over here Bobby and roll yourself into the van, so you can see the interior."

The first thing Bobby noticed was the lack of center row seats. The floor was smooth. He rolled himself in and looked around. There was no driver's seat. There was some hardware on the floor in front of the steering wheel, but Bobby didn't make the connection.

From behind, he felt Mr. Nelson take hold of his chair. "Let's try something, Bobby." He maneuvered the chair into place, reached beside Bobby and snapped the bracket on the floor onto Bobby's chair so it wouldn't move. As he did this, Bobby noticed the hand controls in front of him. He began to shake. His Dad got into the front passenger seat. "Do you think you could learn how to drive this using your hands?"

Bobby just sat there and nodded his head up and down, speechless.

"I'll take that as a 'yes.'" He and Mr. Nelson had big grins on their faces when Bobby finally spoke.

"Dad, I can't believe this."

"I think you're ready," his Dad responded. "Al took this in on a trade last week. He called me and asked if I thought you might be interested. I said I thought you might, but we'd have to let you see it first. This will be your birthday present and graduation gift, a little early."

"Bobby," Mr. Nelson said. "We've known this vehicle was coming in on a trade for a couple months. A fellow from Owasso wanted a new van with this same special equipment on it, so we worked out a trade and special ordered it for him. I talked to Bob McGee, our general manager, and we cut your Dad a special deal on it."

"That's Riley's Dad?"

"Yes, it is," Mr. Nelson said. "He felt the community should be doing more to help you and this opportunity just came along at the right time."

"But, how will I learn to drive it?"

"Here's the neat part. The guy that bought the new van offered to come over next week and give you a lesson. He's a really nice guy and wanted to help. He was in the same spot you're in just three years ago. He said a few minutes, a little practice and 'Bob's your uncle.' Can you come by here on Monday about three?"

"I'll be here if I have to walk. I can hardly wait."

THIRTEEN

Riding back home with his Dad, Bobby grew even more excited. "Dad, I still can't believe this. Having my own wheels will open up so much for me. I'll be able to get to practices, and other places, without having to depend on Mom or my friends. And . . .". He almost said "And take Laura Sue to the prom." But, he decided to keep that idea to himself for now.

They pulled into the driveway. Bobby's Dad helped him out of the Explorer and into his chair. He rolled in as fast as he could. "Guess what, Mom?" he shouted, as he burst through the front door.

"Well, let me see," she said. "Dad got you a hamburger for lunch."

"No, no Mom." Then he realized his Mom was kidding him again. Of course she already knew about the van. She grinned back at him.

"Now you can ask Laura Sue to the prom," his Mom said. Bobby's face turned bright red. *Can she read my mind?*

"I want to. But, what if she doesn't want to go with me, or already has another date?"

"Only one way to find out." She didn't tell him Laura Sue had already confided in her that she hoped Bobby would ask her. "Right now, you better get ready to head for the park, or we'll be late. And, you're the guest of honor."

"I just need to put on a clean shirt," Bobby said.

It was only a ten minute drive to the park, so they arrived in plenty of time. Bud Wilkinson Park was a city-owned facility, named after the famed Oklahoma University football coach. The park had a lot of shade trees, a small lake and three shelters at intervals along the edge of the lake. When they pulled into the parking lot nearest the largest shelter, several of Bobby's friends came out to meet them.

Eddie Smith led off. "Bout time you got here Murphy." Eddie led the procession back to the shelter. Others came up to greet Bobby.

Riley McGee said, "Is what I heard this morning true? About the van?"

"Yes," Bobby said, "but keep it to yourself for now. I still have to learn to drive it."

"You won't have any problem with that," Riley replied.

Carl came up from behind Bobby. "No, you won't. I'll be there on Monday to help you. We'll get the basics from the guy who's trading the van in, and then we can work together until you get it down."

So much for the word not getting out.

As he pondered the extent of the knowledge about his van, his baseball teammates began approaching him, with long, lean Bennie Brown leading the way. "Hey, Murphy, how's it going?"

Almost the whole team was there. He had pretty much expected to see the guys he had played with for years—Charlie Levin, the shortstop; Tommy Jones, the catcher; Bennie, Al Tarkington, the pitcher; Brick Nelson, the left fielder. But, he was a little surprised to see some of the new guys. Red Freeman, the sophomore second baseman came over to shake his hand. He really had not been sure that he and Ray Roberts had hit it off all that well, but there was Ray with a big smile.

Just as he was thinking it couldn't get any better, he saw Laura Sue drive into the parking lot with her brother, Buddy. As she got out of the car and began walking to the shelter, Bobby noticed she was wearing a nicely fitting pair of jeans, her blond ponytail falling over the collar of her western shirt. *She's so cute.*

Eddie said, loud enough for several of his friends to hear, "Okay guys, we'll have a tough time gettin' Bobby's attention now." As they all laughed, Bobby tried to hide his embarrassment, but his crimson face gave him away, which caused them to laugh even more.

"Hi, Bobby. What's everybody laughing about?" Laura Sue asked, as she walked up.

"Nothing much," Bobby said, still in full blush mode. "Hey, Buddy, thanks for coming. And, thanks for all the stuff you did at the house."

"No problem," Buddy said. "Least I could do for Laura Sue's boyfriend."

Bobby's embarrassment grew and now he was joined by Laura Sue. "Buddy, you've got a big mouth," she said. The crowd around Bobby was thoroughly enjoying their discomfort.

"You go, Buddy," Eddie said.

"Gee, Bobby, we'd never have guessed," Bennie chimed in.

To Bobby and Laura Sue's great relief, at that moment Coach Brawley and Coach Albright arrived. "Murphy, we're here to wish you a happy birthday. From the sound of it, sounds like we're almost too late," the Coach growled.

"Happy birthday, Bobby," Coach Albright said. "You're looking good."

"Thanks Coach and Coach, I really appreciate your coming," Bobby said.

Mr. Dowling and Miss Winn arrived and greeted Bobby. "Hi, Bobby," Miss Winn said. "Happy eighteenth. Can you come by the school one day next week, so we can talk about a few things?"

"Sure," Bobby said. "I'll give you a call on Monday to set a time."

"Happy Birthday, Bobby," Mr. Dowling said. "How's the new layout at home working?"

"Mr. Dowling, I can't tell you how much everything you and your class did for me means. I'm trying to learn to be as self-sufficient as possible, and the changes make that a lot easier."

"Glad we were able to help."

The last arrival at the party was Karen. She came over to greet Bobby. "This looks like quite a party," she said. "You're lucky to have so many friends."

When Karen walked away to say hello to Bobby's parents, Laura Sue leaned over and whispered in Bobby's ear. "Your physical therapist is really pretty."

Bobby didn't know what to say, so he said, "Yeah, she is." *Did she sound jealous? Naw.*

Bobby called for Carl and Karen to come back up to the front and, in a voice loud enough to get everyone's attention, said "Most of you know each other, but I want you all to meet the best support anyone could hope for. Carl's been coming by almost every day for months to help me get up and dressed in the mornings. He's taught me so much to help me function on my own. And, to be honest, when I've gotten down and started to feel sorry for myself, he's kicked my butt.

"And, this is Karen, my physical therapist. She's been making sure I keep up my upper body strength and muscle tone. Without her help, I'd be a puddle of soup. Between Karen and Carl, I'm gonna to be able to make it on my own one day."

"Let's hear it for Carl and Karen," Bennie shouted, and everyone cheered.

Eddie came forward next. "I just want to say, Bobby Murphy is my best friend in the world, and I'm so proud of how tough he is. Lot of people would have given up, felt sorry for themselves; crawled into a shell. Not Bobby. I wish I had just half his courage. Happy birthday, Bobby, and many more. Now, let's have some hot dogs." He pointed at the large charcoal grill where Riley and

Bobby's Dad were busy cooking. Actually, Riley was manning a spatula, threatening the blue jay that was eyeing the hotdog buns, waiting for its chance.

While the crowd made its way to the grill, Laura Sue said, "Bobby, I'm sorry Buddy had to open his mouth, especially in front of everybody."

Wow. The only part she's sorry about is him saying it in front of everyone? Does that mean. . .?

She started to say something more, but before she could get it out, Eddie and Bennie arrived. The four of them made their way over to the grill, where Riley, having sufficiently terrorized the blue jay, had transitioned into serving the plates of food.

"When you get all the hotdogs you want, we have ice cream and cake for dessert," Riley announced. He pointed to a table next to the cooking spot and Bobby saw a large sheet cake. His Mom was serving chocolate cake with what appeared to be a cream cheese icing, and butter pecan ice cream in copious quantities.

"This is my fourth hotdog," Charlie Levin said. "Whose birthday is it, anyway?"

Laura Sue looked at him with a grin. "Charlie, are you sure that's just your fourth hotdog? I hear you can eat more than the average hog at the feed lot when you're not paying for it."

"Right on, Laura Sue," Brick Nelson chimed in. "This guy can out eat everybody I know. Wonder how he stays so scrawny? But, whose birthday is it?" They all laughed at Brick's lame attempt at humor and got up to go get ice cream and cake.

"Bobby, can I bring you yours?" Laura Sue asked.

"That would really be nice," Bobby said.

The rest of the afternoon passed too quickly. Coach Brawley made a short speech announcing he was naming Bobby an official volunteer student coach for the baseball team. And, Bobby's Mom closed the festivities by thanking everyone for coming and for all the support they had given Bobby.

As the people came by for a final birthday wish, Laura Sue sat by Bobby's chair. "I'm so glad all your friends came today Bobby. You deserved a great party. I was hoping to come by to see you tomorrow. Your Mom invited me over for Sunday dinner. But, I have to go with my Mom up to Pawhuska to see my aunt. I'll definitely see you on Monday after baseball practice." She gave him a little kiss on the cheek. "Happy Birthday, Bobby," she said as she and Buddy headed for their car.

FOURTEEN

The rest of the weekend was a blur for Bobby. All he could think about was the new van, and his coming increase in mobility. Monday morning finally arrived. Carl came to help him get ready and found Bobby already dressed and in the kitchen eating breakfast.

"Looks like you're getting to where you won't need my help much longer. But, today I'm meeting you and your Dad at the Ford dealer at three. You're gonna drive that van home." As Carl left, he said, "See you then."

Karen arrived about nine for his physical therapy session. Bobby was still excited and dived into his exercises with more energy than usual. As she massaged his legs, she told Bobby, "A lot of these exercises are ones you can do on your own without me. I think maybe we'll cut back on my visits a little. Maybe two or three times a week for a massage and we can see how you're doing with the exercises. I also think it may be about time for you to begin going back to school. I think that would help you a lot."

"You heard about my van, didn't you?" When Karen nodded that she had, Bobby went on. "I'll be able to get myself there and back without Mom having to disrupt her day. And Miss Winn asked me to come by to see her one day this week. I'll talk to her about it."

Karen left at ten thirty and Bobby rolled himself out to the kitchen where his Mom was making banana nut bread. She looked a little sharper than usual.

"Mom, you're all dressed up. Are you going somewhere?"

"Yes," she replied. "In fact, we are going somewhere. Miss Winn called while you were doing your therapy with Karen and asked if we could come by about noon. So, as soon as I get this banana bread out of the oven, we'll go."

"Do you know what she wants to see me about?"

"I don't think it's anything to worry about. I suspect she wants to see if you're ready to come back to school. I think you are. You've been doing very well keeping up with your classwork and, with your own transportation, it should be doable for you. It'll be an adjustment, but you're used to making adjustments, and this will be just one more."

"Mom, I think you're right about school, but I'm still nervous about one other thing. I want to ask Laura Sue to the prom. But, she may already have a date, or maybe she won't want to be saddled with these useless legs at the dance."

Since Mrs. Murphy already knew Laura Sue was waiting for Bobby to ask her, she answered: "Only way to find out is to ask her. Wouldn't it be a shame if she does want to go with you and you're too shy to ask?" She also felt a warm glow. Most teenage boys would not feel comfortable talking to their Mom about this sort of thing.

The buzzer on the oven sounded and Mrs. Murphy took out the banana bread. She turned the baking pans on their side and said, "Are you ready to go?"

Bobby and his Mom drove in her white Honda the short distance to school. At the front entrance, she pulled up into the passenger unloading area and came around to help Bobby out and into his chair. Before she could get the door open, Bennie Brown and Tommy Jones came rushing out of the school.

"We'll get him out, Mrs. M.," Bennie said. "We saw you drive up from the cafeteria."

"Thanks boys," she said. "I really appreciate it. This guy is a handful to lift around."

"If you could please quit talking about me like a sack of potatoes, and get the job done, this 'lump' would like to get inside," Bobby said, as they all laughed.

When he was seated in his chair, Bobby led his Mom into the school and down the hall to Miss Winn's office. Miss Winn was wearing a red blouse and a navy skirt, much like the one Mrs. Murphy was wearing. "You guys must have gotten the same memo about what to wear today," Bobby said.

"Bobby, it's so good to see you. I really enjoyed the party at the park on Saturday. It was nice of y'all to invite me."

"Well, Miss Winn, you've really helped me, not just this year, but the whole time I've been in high school. And not just me. A couple of my friends wouldn't be going to college next year if you hadn't given them some direction. And, I wouldn't be where I am today without you." Realizing what he had just said, Bobby stammered "Not exactly where I am, in this chair, but you know what I mean."

"I do, Bobby, and it's nice of you to say that. The reason I wanted you and your Mom to come by today is to talk a little about where you go next. Graduation is only a little over a month away, and I think it would be good for you to come back to your classes for the rest of the year. Not only will it be good for you psychologically, but it'll help you prepare for what you'll face when you start college next year; you know, the logistics of managing yourself and your disability. I also think you're ready to step right back in academically. Your Mom's done a great job helping you keep up in all your classes. I've talked to all your teachers, and they're ready for you. If you need a little help here and there to get back on track, they'll help you. What do you think?"

Bobby looked at his Mom. "Do you really think I'm ready, Mom?"

"I don't have any doubt," she said. "We may need to help you a little here or there, but I see no reason for you not to come back to school."

He took a breath. "Then, I'll do it. I was going to be coming over every day for baseball practice anyway. Coach Brawley wants me to help with the team. And, the playoffs start soon. We're gonna win the state championship this year, you know. Can I start returning to classes on Wednesday?"

"That sounds perfect," Miss Winn said. "I'll have everything ready for you. I know you're getting a vehicle, so you can park in the handicap space in the front of the lot. Why don't you come see me on Wednesday morning, and we'll make sure everything is ready for you, and answer any questions you may have."

"I will, and thank you so much, Miss Winn. See you Wednesday."

After stopping through the Burger King drive-in window for lunch, Bobby and his mother drove home. With all the excitement of meeting with Miss Winn, Bobby hadn't thought about picking up his van. But, as he and his Mom ate their burgers and fries, he began to get antsy.

"You're so fidgety," his Mom said. "Let's catch up on your school work so you can have it out of the way when your Dad gets home."

FIFTEEN

Bobby spent the next hour studying chemistry and Oklahoma history. Finally, about two thirty, his Dad walked through the front door. "You ready to go, Bobby?" he asked, realizing that was probably a dumb question.

"Ready? I've never been so ready. Let's go."

When they reached the Ford dealer, they found Carl already talking to Mr. Nelson and another man, who was in a wheelchair like Bobby's. Bobby's Dad helped him out of the car and into his chair. Bobby rolled over to where the three were waiting.

"Hey, Bobby," Carl said. "I've been talkin' to Mr. Angelli here about operating this bus. You're gonna have no trouble learning how to do it."

"Bobby Murphy, Jack Murphy, meet Roger Angelli," Mr. Nelson said. "He's ready to help you get started."

"Bobby, it's a real pleasure to meet you. Please call me Roger. Let's get started. First thing you need to know is how to get in." He pulled the remote control out of his pocket and pointed it at the sleek, freshly washed and waxed white van. When he pushed the 'open' button, the right side door slid back and a small ramp dropped one end to the pavement. Roger rolled in, motioning Bobby to follow him. He proceeded to the driver's position, where the seat had been removed, and rolled into a bracket on the floor, with a handle control up to the height of the wheelchair. Pushing the handle forward, he locked his chair into place in front of the steering wheel.

"You can move the bracket forward or back, but just eyeballing it, I think it's adjusted about right for you. Come up here as close as you can, so you can watch me."

Carl had moved into the passenger seat and Mr. Murphy sat in the rear seat. The center row of seats and the console between the driver and front passenger seat had been removed. Bobby locked the wheels on his chair. He and Carl watched closely as Roger started the van with the push button control on the dash. He shifted the vehicle into Drive and slowly moved one of the two lever controls on the right side of the steering wheel forward. As he did, the van accelerated gently. Then, taking his hand off the right hand lever, he slid it over to the lever on the left and pulled back. The van slowed and stopped.

"In a nutshell," Roger said, "that's all there is to it. You need to get a feel for the right pressures for the accelerator and the brake, and be sure you know which is which is by feel. You'll have to really concentrate until you get used to it, but it'll come quickly and become instinctive, just like using the accelerator and brake in a normal car with your feet. When you need to back up, you have your mirrors and a back-up camera. There's also a warning sound if you're in reverse and a car's coming from one side or the other, like if you're backing out of a parking space and can't see past the cars beside you. Obviously, when you're accelerating or braking, you need to steer with your left hand and I suggest you always keep your left hand on the wheel so, if you have to brake quickly, you can stay in control.

"Finally, always plan ahead. Use your turn signals just like you would in any car. Plan ahead where to park. Remember, you'll need room for the ramp to come down on the right, and for you to get out with your chair. Most handicap spaces have extra room on the right side that'll work for you. But, not all, so be sure you park where you can't get trapped either in or out. Other drivers are mostly considerate, but they may pull up and park, not realizing your need for space. So, you come back and need to get in, but don't have room.

"If you're ready to try it out, I'll ride around the lot next door with you a few times while you get the hang of it." Next door to the Ford dealership was a large parking lot for a plant that had been closed.

"I'm ready," Bobby said.

"Let me drive us over there, and you can take over," Roger said. "First, see that bracket on the left? You need to lock your chair into that, and put on your seat belt."

When they reached the empty lot, Roger stopped the van, turned off the engine and opened the door. "It's a little awkward, but we both have to get out so we can change places." They got out and Bobby rolled in first. It took him a couple tries to line up his chair with the bracket, but he soon had it locked in place. After putting on his seat belt, he waited for Roger to secure his chair behind him. Carl watched Bobby from the passenger seat.

Bobby pushed the start button and the engine came to life. Remembering what he had seen Roger do, he shifted the transmission into Drive. The brake lever automatically stayed locked in place until he manually released it. Then, he moved his hand to the other lever and pushed forward slowly. The van crept ahead. As he increased his pressure on the accelerator lever, the van sped up. He made a couple turns around the large lot before he returned to the brake. He pulled back on the brake lever and the van slid to a stop, a little abruptly. "I need to work on that," Bobby said. "Anything else I need to know?"

"The only thing I noticed that you didn't do was adjust your mirrors before you set out. Other than that, I think you'll be fine. Why don't you drive me back to my car and I'll be on my way?"

Oh boy. This means I have to go out onto the street with other cars. But, I've got to do it sometime.

"I'll be glad to, Roger. Thanks for taking your time to help me."

"If you have any questions after you've practiced for a while, give me a call. Here's a card with my number. I'll give your Dad one also."

Bobby drove to the exit of the parking lot, stopped, waited for a car to pass and pulled onto the street. The Ford dealer's parking lot entrance was just down the street and Bobby, coordinating his accelerator and brake levers smoothly, if a little slowly, pulled into the lot and drove up to the new navy blue Ford Transit van. Roger deftly opened the new vehicle's door, dropped a ramp similar to the one in Bobby's van and looked over to the door. "Bobby, you need to let me out of here," he said with a smile. "And, one more thing: you didn't use your turn signals when you left the parking lot or when you turned in here. It's important so other drivers know what you are getting ready to do, especially while you're getting used to driving again."

Bobby opened the door for Roger to get out and waited until he had gotten into the Transit. Roger waved and left. Bobby looked over at Carl, and at his Dad. Carl said, "Let's go back over to the parking lot for a little bit and practice some more. We can also work on your backing up. Is that okay with you, Mr. M?"

Bobby's Dad said it was fine with him, so Bobby shifted into Drive. Carl cleared his throat ominously. "Oops," Bobby said, as he shifted back into Park and adjusted his mirrors. He drove carefully back to the parking lot, this time using his turn signals. They drove around the lot a few times and practiced backing up. After some initial struggles, Bobby could back into one of the marked parking spots on the first try.

"I think you've pretty much got it, Bobby. As you drive more, you'll get better at it," Carl said. "I really didn't think you'd get it this quick."

"Your Mom and I will go out with you for a while so you can get comfortable driving it before you go out alone," his Dad said. "Now we need to get you over to the school for baseball practice.

Coach Brawley's expecting you. Carl, would you mind riding home with Bobby in the van? I'll bring you back to get your car."

"No problem, Mr. M," Carl said. "But, why don't Bobby and I go straight to baseball practice? I want to watch it anyway, and then when we get back to your house, you can bring me back to get my car."

"Good plan," Mr. Murphy said. "Let's drop me back at the Ford dealer so I can pick up mine."

Bobby and Carl arrived at the baseball field as the team was beginning to take infield. "Where have you been, Murphy?" Coach Brawley said in his gruff way. "You're late. Get out there at second and work with Freeman. He's starting to screw up his throwing again."

Bobby rolled out to the second base area. "Hey, Red. Let's work on those tosses to first." He spent the rest of the infield drills with Red, helping him with his mechanics. Then, as the team took batting practice, he watched the hitters carefully, making a few observations and suggestions as Coach Albright did the pitching. After practice ended, Bobby called Red over.

Nicknamed because of his full head of red hair and ruddy complexion, Red was about five feet, eight inches tall, small for a ball player, but Bobby could see a lot of potential. "Red, your throwing's getting better. All you need to do is focus hard on your mechanics, and then just let the ball go. Once it gets automatic, you won't even think when you get ready to throw it. But, here's something else. I'd like to see you pay a little more attention to how you look."

Red looked puzzled. Bobby continued: "If you look like a ball player, you have a better chance of performing like one. Tuck your uniform shirt in, for example. Even if you're only at practice. Don't wear your cap backward. It makes you look like a smurf, not a ball player. Plus, you have a lot of potential. You're really good. Make yourself a leader. I know you're just a sophomore, but now's the time to start. You are the only soph in the starting line-up and the other young guys look up to you. Set an example for them, and you'll be better for it."

"Gee, Bobby, I never thought of it like that. That's great advice." Red tucked in his shirt, straightened his cap and headed for the locker room. Bobby turned to join Carl, who was walking back to the van. Out of the corner of his eye, he saw the two coaches looking his way.

"Good job, Murphy," Coach Brawley called. "Don't let that guy with you teach you any bad habits."

As they drove home, Carl said, "Bobby, you're a natural as a coach. Nobody else would have thought to give Freeman that kind of advice. He'll be a much better player if he listens to what you told him. No wonder Coach Brawley's so interested in having you stay part of the team."

SIXTEEN

The rest of the week passed like a runaway freight train. On Tuesday, after his physical therapy and studies with his Mom, she and Bobby went out in the van and Bobby drove around town. She made sure he experienced a variety of events that he might have to deal with by himself. They went to the grocery store, where he had to find a parking spot that would allow him to exit and enter the van. They drove slowly on city streets and ventured out onto the highway, where he had to drive faster. They parked in a crowded lot at the mall. Bobby had to back out of a parking space, into a flow of cars all trying to find their own spaces. They even went by Brookside, where he practiced parking in a handicap space. When they finally got home, he was exhausted. "I never realized how tiring driving can be," he said.

That evening, his Mom helped him pick out clothes to wear to school, a new pair of jeans and a navy blue polo shirt. Over dinner, she surprised him. He was telling his Dad about his day, driving around with his Mom, and baseball practice, when she said "I think Bobby's ready to drive the van on his own. He does just fine with me with him, but he needs to do it by himself."

To his further amazement, his Dad agreed. "The only restriction I want to put on you is that, at least for the first few weeks of driving by yourself, you not have any passengers. Get whatever bugs you may need to work through without having anyone else there to distract you. Do I have your promise on that?"

"Sure, Dad. It even makes sense."

Wednesday morning came. Bobby had mastered most of his tasks to get himself up and dressed, but had not yet come up with a way to get his shoes and socks on without help. Carl came by to be sure he was, as Carl described "all put together." They had rigged a basket on the chair for books and anything else he had to carry. Carl had also designed what he referred to as a "saddle bag" that hung on the left side of his chair. In a sectioned off pouch in the front, Carl loaded it with a can of pepper spray and a billy club. The club was hardwood, about 16 inches long and an inch in diameter. The rest of the bag had room for miscellaneous things Bobby might want.

"What's with the spray and the club?" Bobby asked.

"Never know when you might have to use them. In case you haven't noticed, you're not exactly gonna get up with your fancy footwork and engage someone who might want to hurt you."

"I'm never gonna need this stuff," Bobby said. "I feel silly carrying it."

"Do me a favor and keep it. Tell yourself you're just humoring old Carl."

"OK, but I still don't see any need for it."

Carl and Mrs. Murphy walked out to the van with Bobby. She gave Bobby a motherly kiss, wished him well and they waved goodbye. He saw her in the rear view mirror, still waving as he turned the corner at the end of the street.

When Bobby reached the school, he found a group of his buddies standing around the handicap space. He parked and got out of the van, to cheers and general hoop-la. Bennie Brown, ever the leader, called out, "Welcome back, Murphy. It's about time you came here to suffer with the rest of us." Everyone laughed and gathered around Bobby's chair to clap him on the back, tell him how much they had missed him, and express other "feel good" sentiments.

There were a few girls that he knew in the group, but the one he was looking for, wasn't there. *I wonder why she's not here.* Then he didn't have any more time to wonder as the merry group made its way to Miss Winn's office.

"Look who we found in the parking lot, Miss Winn," Eddie said.

"Yeah, he looked lost, so we decided to dump him on your doorstep," Riley added.

"Come on in, Bobby. This motley crew needs to get themselves to class before somebody dumps them," Miss Winn said.

After a few minutes of asking how Bobby felt, was he ready for a full day of school, and so forth, Miss Winn led him down the hall to his first class—geometry. When he rolled through the door, the class spontaneously began clapping, interrupting the teacher, Mr. Akins, in mid-sentence. Mr. Akins was very tall, about six feet, five, and slim. He was almost completely bald and was the second oldest teacher at Brookside, behind Miss Kern, the English and speech teacher. He was the only male teacher who wore a suit to school, and had a formal, serious demeanor. None of the students would have thought to try to kid, or have a light conversation with Mr. Akins.

"Mr. Murphy, if the class will control itself, I have reserved a spot in the front for you. Please make your way to the front so we can continue this morning's lesson without further interruption. We are on page 125 of our text book."

Miss Winn whispered "Go get 'em Bobby," and left the room while Bobby made his way to the assigned space.

The rest of Bobby's teachers were a little more welcoming and they all seemed genuinely pleased to have him back in their class. Lunchtime was a bit of a challenge as Bobby had to navigate the serving line in the cafeteria. The basket that Carl had fashioned for his chair included a top that acted as a shelf, and Bobby's tray fit it just right. Eddie and Riley had reserved a place for him at the end of their table. As he ate his lunch, and the friends joked and kidded with each other, Bobby realized just how much he had missed being at school, and with his friends.

He was still wondering about Laura Sue. Her lunch period was the one after Bobby's, so that explained why he didn't see her at lunch. And, she was not in any of his classes. *Have I done something, or doesn't she like me anymore?*

When his last class ended, Bobby rolled out to the baseball locker room. The school was new enough that all of its facilities were handicap accessible, so he rolled in and chatted with Bennie and Tommy while they got dressed for practice. He also stopped by the coach's office.

"Come in, Murphy. We were just looking over our practice plan. You know we only have three more games before the playoffs. I want you out there during infield spending some time with Freeman. But, I also want you to watch Charlie Levin at short and Buster Talbot at third. Levin's ok, but I'm thinking we might have to bench Talbot. He's not hitting, and his fielding's falling off. I haven't been able to get through to him, and his attitude seems to be affecting the whole team. See what you think. Now, let's hit the field." Coach Brawley got up and led them out the door.

Bobby spent infield practice moving around among the three positions. Red Freeman was glad to see him. Bobby noticed Red was spruced up. He was wearing his cap straight, had his shirt tucked in and his shoes even looked like they had been shined. Red also put a little extra into his hustle, making crisp, accurate throws and turning double play opportunities like Bobby pictured Ozzie Smith of the Cardinals doing.

Charlie was also happy to have him. They were good friends, and played together for a lot of years while they were growing up. Charlie knew, if Bobby did offer a suggestion or criticism, he would do well to listen.

When he moved over by third, where Buster Talbot was playing, his reception was less congenial. The first thing he noticed was that Coach Brawley had sent out Marty Ross, a promising junior and the back-up third baseman, to alternate taking ground balls with Buster. Buster seemed more than a little resentful. "What are you doing here Murphy?" he asked with a sneer. "You think you're gonna take my position? Ross, here, thinks he is, but it ain't gonna happen. So just stay out of my way."

Buster Talbot was a stocky fireplug, with a square jaw and a surly attitude. He was a big guy, and some said he was a bully. Bobby had not actually witnessed him bullying anyone, but had heard rumors. He was not a very good student, and, to Bobby's knowledge, didn't seem to have many, if any, friends. He certainly wasn't popular with his teammates.

"Talbot, if you don't want any advice, no problem for me. But, if you want to stay in the line-up, you better take all the help you can get."

"Talbot, you're up. Get two," shouted Coach Albright, who was hitting ground balls to the infielders. He hit a hard ground ball to Talbot, who fielded it cleanly and cut loose a throw that sailed two feet over the second baseman's head.

"C'mon Freeman. You should have had it," Talbot yelled. Then he looked over at Bobby with a scowl. Bobby shrugged and looked away.

"OK, Ross, let's see if you can make a play," Coach Albright hollered. The ground ball was hit sharply, and to Marty's right, causing him to make a quick stab across his body to catch it. He smoothly turned, planted his feet and made a perfect throw to Freeman, who made a perfect throw to Bennie at first.

"Good job, Ross," Coach Albright said, causing Buster Talbot to scowl even more.

After infield practice, the team closed with batting practice. "Stay here behind the backstop, Murphy, and watch these guys hit. Let 'em know if you see anything in their swings that might help them," Coach Brawley said, as he headed for the mound to pitch.

As the players went through their swings, Bobby offered only a few comments, mostly to the younger players. But, when

Buster Talbot came to the plate, he watched intently, remembering Coach's earlier comment about Talbot not hitting. On the first pitch Coach Brawley threw him, Talbot swung and hit it over the left centerfield wall. He turned around and glared at Bobby. "Any comments, Murphy?" he said.

Bobby didn't reply. The coach had not put much into the pitch. But, on subsequent pitches, Coach Brawley threw with a little more zip. Talbot managed to pop up three and hit three weak ground balls to the left side of the infield. After he fouled off two bunt attempts, he stalked over to the bench. Bobby met him there. "Look, Buster, I know you don't like me very much, but I'm gonna tell you what I noticed anyway. You're too valuable to the team to be benched, and I want this team to win state. So, here's what I saw."

Talbot looked even angrier than he had earlier. But, he didn't say anything and he didn't move away. Bobby continued, "It looks to me like you're trying to hit a home run on every swing. You'll make better contact if you level your swing instead of swinging up each time. Imagine you're trying to hit a line drive back at the pitcher, instead of a long fly ball."

"Murphy, you're a jerk, and I don't think you know what you're talking about," Talbot said. But I know you're talking to the coach, so just to shut you up, I'll try it."

When the batter currently up had completed his seven swings and two bunts, Bobby called out to Coach Brawley, "Coach, could you let Talbot take a few more swings?"

Coach Brawley had seen Bobby and Talbot talking. "OK, Talbot, let's see what you got."

Talbot walked to the plate, paused a moment and took his stance. Coach Brawley was through throwing "puff" balls and brought it with a little more zip. Talbot swung hard and, to Bobby's eye, level. The ball left his bat like a rocket, almost taking Coach's head off. The next pitch was a line drive that bounced off the left field wall. Three more pitches, and three more hard liners.

"Enough, Talbot," the Coach said. "I don't know what's in the water you drank, but it worked."

Practice ended, and as Bobby was rolling himself back to his van, with Bennie, Charlie and Brick alongside, Buster Talbot walked past. "Lucky guess, Murphy. I had already figured that out. And," he muttered, as he stalked away, "I'm gonna to take Laura Sue Medlin to the prom."

"What did he just say?" Bobby asked Bennie. "I must not have heard him right."

"You heard him right," Bennie said. "But, that doesn't mean she'll go with him. Haven't you asked her yet?"

"Not yet," Bobby replied. "It sounds like he's already asked her, and she's accepted."

"Probably not," Bennie said. "He's such a jerk, I doubt she'd go with him."

When they reached the van, Bobby showed his friends how it all worked. "I want a ride," Charlie said.

"In a couple weeks. I promised my Dad I wouldn't have any passengers until I get driving it down pat."

As he drove out of the school's parking lot, Bobby thought, *I better get my courage up quick, or I'm gonna lose out on taking Laura Sue to the prom.*

SEVENTEEN

When Bobby reached home, dinner was waiting. As they ate, Bobby told them all about his first day back at school, and about his encounter with Buster Talbot, leaving out the part about Laura Sue.

His Dad said, "It sounds like this Buster Talbot fellow isn't one of the good guys. You better take it easy around him. If he wants to be left alone, leave him be."

"That's the strange thing, Dad. I know he's about to be benched because of his hitting. I think he must sense it, too. And, when I made a suggestion about his swing, he made the adjustment, even if he didn't give me any credit. If he can get back on track, it'll help the team a lot. I think he really does want some help, but he's too stubborn to admit it."

Bobby began to roll away from the table, and then stopped. "I'd like to show Laura Sue my new van. Do you mind if I take it over to her house? I won't be gone long."

"Fine Bobby," his Mom answered. "Have you called her to be sure it's ok?"

"No. I think I'd like to surprise her."

To his own surprise, his Mom smiled and said "I think she'd like that."

What?

Bobby drove the ten minutes to Laura Sue's house and parked

at the curb. He rolled up the walkway and the ramp Buddy insisted on building. Before he could ring the bell, the door opened and Mrs. Medlin exclaimed, "Bobby Murphy. I haven't seen you in a coon's age. Did your Mom or Dad bring you over? Come on in." Anyone would recognize Mrs. Medlin as Laura Sue's mother, or maybe even her older sister. In her jeans and blue Brookside High tee shirt, she was a dead-ringer.

"Hi, Mrs. Medlin. It's been awhile. No, I drove myself over. I was hoping Laura Sue might be home so I could show her my new van. Well, it's new to me anyway."

"We just finished dinner and she went back to her room." Turning toward the back of the ranch style house, she called "Laura Sue, come on out here. Some one's here to see you."

"I'll be there in a minute." Hearing Laura Sue's voice, Bobby felt a tingle.

"I hope I'm not interrupting anything."

"Not at all. She'll be excited to see you, I'm sure."

Bobby felt himself turning red. *I sure do seem to blush a lot when Laura Sue is involved.*

When Laura Sue came around the corner, she saw Bobby and stopped. "Oh, hi Bobby."

Maybe this wasn't a great idea. She doesn't seem very glad to see me. What did I do wrong?

"I want to show you what I got yesterday." Forging ahead despite his discomfort, he said, "Would you come out front with me?"

Just then, the front door burst open and Laura Sue's brother, Buddy, came running in. "Who's here?" he asked. "There's a white van parked out front. Hi Bobby."

"That's mine, Buddy. Want to come see it?" Bobby said.

The three of them, Laura Sue, Buddy and Bobby, headed outside, followed by Mrs. Medlin. "I want to see this, too," she said.

Bobby demonstrated how the door opened and how he could roll into the driver's position at the steering wheel. Laura Sue watched carefully, but said nothing. Finally, Buddy and Mrs. Medlin went back into the house, leaving Bobby and Laura Sue alone.

Not knowing where or how to begin, Bobby decided to just say what was on his mind. "Laura Sue, you don't seem very glad to see me. Have I done something wrong?"

She didn't say anything for a long minute. Then, she blurted out, "Bobby, you haven't seen or called me since the picnic on Saturday. I know I was gone with my folks on Sunday, but you never even called me on Monday or Tuesday. Today at school, you ignored me—didn't even look my way."

The part about ignoring her at school threw Bobby for a loop. He thought she had been ignoring him, which he told her, and which didn't seem to help. "I'm sorry I didn't call you on Monday or Tuesday," he said. "They were both really crazy days for me." He told her about picking up his van on Monday and how exhausted he was by the time he got home, and he told her about his Tuesday. "By the time I got a chance to call you, I was afraid it was too late. And, I really was looking forward to seeing you in school today, but every time I spotted you, you were gone before I could get there."

He sounded so sincere; her stern expression appeared to soften a little. So, he went on. *Nothing to lose at this point.* "I heard today you already have a date for the prom."

"What?" she exclaimed, her mouth falling open, obviously surprised. "Where did you hear that? And who am I supposed to have a date with?"

"Buster Talbot told me at baseball practice that he's taking you to the prom."

"Buster Talbot's a cretin and a liar, if he said that. He said something about the prom one day, but I didn't take him seriously. That makes me madder than a hornet. But," she added, "no one else has asked me, so maybe I'll have to go with him."

Bobby took a deep breath. *Here I go. Please Lord, don't let me screw this up.* "Laura Sue, would you consider going with me? You don't have to tell me now, just think about it. At least you wouldn't have to go with Buster Talbot." *Shut up, Bobby. Don't keep babbling like an idiot. Here comes the blush again.*

"Bobby Murphy! You're the densest boy I've ever met. I've been waiting and waiting for you to ask me. I was about to decide you didn't like me as much as I like you." Then, befuddling Bobby even more, she gave him the smile that always turned him to jelly, leaned over and kissed him right on the lips.

She turned and ran into her house, leaving Bobby on the sidewalk thinking, *I can't wait to get older so I'll understand girls.*

Somehow, he managed to drive home. When he came into the house, his Mom looked at him. "You finally asked her, didn't you?"

EIGHTEEN

Baseball's regular season was over. Brookside easily won their district championship, qualifying the team for the regional playoffs. Four teams qualified for the double elimination tournament in Tulsa. Coach Brawley gathered his team around him after they finished practice on Wednesday.

"All right, guys" he said. "We won our district. Big deal! The only thing we get out of that is a ticket to go play in the Regional. Certainly, that's better than not getting it. But, the Regional is when things begin to get serious. If we don't win that, you can forget the state championship. We've got as much talent as any team I've ever coached, and I know we have what it takes to win it. But, all we've earned so far is a shot at it. We don't deserve anything. We have to go out and take it. Booger, you got anything to add?"

"Yeah, Coach, I do. Over this season, I've seen several of you guys doubting yourself on occasion, and going through some rough patches. Freeman, you didn't think you really belonged, and for a while, it showed in your play. All of the pitchers had their moments. Talbot, you've had a terrible hitting slump. I don't know what you did, but you seem to be back on track. My point is whenever you doubted yourselves, or when things went wrong, you fought back and corrected your problem. This team has the guts and the ability to overcome anything that hits us. Now, we've got a big challenge.

McAlester, Miami and Muskogee all think they're good enough to win it, just like us. Can we prove them wrong?"

"You bet we can Coach," Bennie Brown answered. "Right guys?"

All the players joined in: "We can do it."

"Brookside Rangers: State Champs," Bennie said. Coach Brawley came as close to a smile as the team had seen, and Coach Albright looked pleased.

"All right boys, we leave at eight o'clock Friday morning for Tulsa. Our first game is with Miami at two that afternoon. They think they're hot stuff. Still trying to claim Mickey Mantle even though he was really from Commerce. If we beat them, we play the winner of the McAlester – Muskogee game on Saturday. If we win that one, we play for the state championship in Oklahoma City the following weekend."

"Excuse me Coach," Bennie said, standing up. "You have that wrong."

"Wrong? What are you talking about, Brown?"

"You said 'if' not 'when.'"

"Good catch, Brown," the Coach said. "I like that, but don't get too cocky. These guys are just as sure they can beat us as we're sure we'll beat them. Make arrangements with your teachers about your class work for Friday and the weekend. It's too close to the end of the year to let your grades slip, and some of you need to graduate." Coach Brawley looked around. "OK, that's it. No practice tomorrow. I want you rested and fresh on Friday. Murphy, stick around a minute."

Bobby wondered what, if any, role he would have with the team when they travelled for the playoffs.

"Murphy, are you able to make it? I don't see any way we can take you on the bus with your wheel chair. But, you're my assistant coach and, if possible, I want you there. You've really helped some of these guys. I still don't know what you did to get Talbot out of his slump, but he seems to have turned it around."

"I'll have to make sure it's all right with my parents for me to drive my van down. Maybe some of the guys would be able to ride with me."

"No," the coach said. "Our insurance rules say the players all have to be on the school's bus. They aren't even allowed to drive themselves or go with their parents. But, since you're not a player, it should be okay for you to drive. Maybe Coach Albright could ride with you. And, you'll be able to stay at the motel with the team. Talk to your parents and let me know tomorrow."

Bobby drove home. He was not quite ready to have anyone else in the van with him, but he hoped his folks would agree, since it would be Coach Booger. He also thought about Laura Sue. *I haven't even seen her, other than at school, since she'd agreed to be my date for the prom. I'll call her after dinner.*

When Bobby came in the front door, his Mom was just putting the final touches on dinner. The aroma from the kitchen made him realize how hungry he was. His Dad was setting the table and said "Bobby, go wash up. Dinner's ready to eat and I'm hungry as a horse." Bobby had always wondered just how hungry horses were, or how anyone knew. But, he decided he would pursue that area of knowledge another time and headed for the bathroom to wash his hands.

Over dinner, when his mouth was not full, Bobby told them about his conversation with Coach Brawley. "Coach Albright will be riding with me, so I won't be alone," he said. "And, I feel good about driving. It's become almost as natural to me as when I had legs."

"Bobby, it's a big step," his Dad replied. "Driving a longer distance, and at highway speeds is a lot different than driving around town. But, if you'll promise to be careful and not have any other passengers, I guess you have to have a first time sometime. What do you think, Myrna?"

"Well, Bobby's been an important part of the team, and it would be a shame for him not to be there for the playoffs. I can't help but worry, but, like you said, he has to do it sometime."

"Thanks, Mom and Dad," Bobby said, with relief. He didn't think they would say no, but you never knew. "Will you be able to come to any of the games?"

"I can't make it Friday," his Dad said. "But, we'll drive down for the weekend game."

They finished their supper with Bobby giving them a position by position analysis of the team and his view of their prospects for winning Naturally, his prediction was a Brookside sweep. After dessert, Bobby went back to call Laura Sue on the extension in his bedroom.

"Hi, Laura Sue," he said. "Sorry I haven't called before, but it has really been hectic." *Lame excuse. She'll probably tell me I should have called anyway.*

"No problem, Bobby. It's been busy here, too, but I'm glad you called now. Are you going with the team to Tulsa for the playoffs?"

"Yes. I'm driving my van down. Coach Albright's gonna ride with me. I'm really excited. When I was a sophomore on the team, all of us made it a goal to win State by our senior year. We came close last year, but not quite. I just wish I were playing, but helping coach is the next best thing, I guess."

"Whether you win State or not, I'm still proud of you," Laura Sue said. "You're an assistant coach. And, from what I hear at school, you've been a big asset. Will you call me after the games and let me know how they went?"

"I promise. I have to go now, but I'll see you tomorrow at school."

"Bye, Bobby. Thanks for calling." Bobby felt a little flutter in his chest as he hung up.

NINETEEN

Thursday passed slowly for the team. They felt like Friday would never arrive. Bobby got his assignments from his teachers. They had all prepared written lesson plans to give the players. Even sober and serious Mr. Akin wished the team luck and all the teachers said they were looking forward to them bringing a state championship back to Brookside. After school ended for the day, Bobby asked Laura Sue if she would meet him at Baskin-Robbins for an ice cream.

"That sounds great, Bobby." Laura Sue was wearing a blue and green plaid skirt with a cream colored blouse. Bobby thought she looked great.

"I wish I could take you with me in the van, but I promised Mom and Dad I wouldn't have any passengers until they said it was okay."

"No problem," she said. "I'll get to ride with you soon enough. I rode to school with Anna today and I'll just ask her to drop me off. Baskin-Robbins is just around the corner from my house, so I can walk home."

"One other thing," Bobby said. "I need to go see Coach Brawley for just a minute to let him know I'm going. I'd hate to get there and not have a room."

Bobby headed for the coach's office. When he got there, he found Coach Brawley just getting ready to leave. "Murphy, I hear

John A. Broadwell

you are going with us to Tulsa," said the coach in his normally gruff voice. "I needed to know whether to reserve a room for you this morning, so I called your Mom. We're staying in a Hampton Inn, and everyone will have a roommate. I got you a handicapped room and you'll be sharing it with Coach Albright. That ok?"

"That'll be good Coach. Actually it will solve a problem I hadn't figured out a solution for. It sounds like a small thing, but about the only thing I can't do for myself is get my shoes and socks on. Maybe Coach Booger, I mean Coach Albright, can help me with that."

"I'm sure he'll be happy to help you. When we get to the field, I want you to pay attention to Freeman and Roberts. Freeman is young and may be a little uptight with all the pressure. And, Roberts considers you his mentor."

The coach's comment about Roberts took Bobby by surprise. He didn't feel like he had actually developed that close a relationship with Ray. Since transferring into Brookside last fall, Roberts was still a "new guy." He didn't seem to have bonded with many of the other players, most of who had played together for years. But, as the season progressed, he had become the 'ace' of the pitching staff. Bobby had made a point to have a few words of encouragement before games that Ray pitched, and had made a few, what Bobby considered minor, suggestions during and after games. And, Ray had come to his birthday party. He felt good to hear that Ray appreciated him.

"I will. I also want to work a little with Al Tarkinton and Justin Moore. We'll need Al on Saturday, and Justin can be a little flaky, which I guess goes with being a closer. Different mindset than normal pitchers."

"Good idea, Murphy," the Coach growled. "Be here at eight am sharp."

Bobby left to go meet Laura Sue at the ice cream parlor. When he rolled in the front door, Laura Sue already had a table for them. "I want a banana nut Sunday with chocolate sauce and whipped cream. Oh, and a cherry on top," she said by way of a greeting.

92

"That's what I'll have, too," Bobby said. "I'll be right back."

After he placed their order, he came back to the table. "Sorry to keep you waiting. Coach Brawley was a little more talkative than I expected. He kind of surprised me. He wants me to work some with Ray Roberts. I've been talking with Ray all season, especially before he pitches, but he never seemed all that impressed with what I had to say."

"Oh, Bobby, I don't think you realize just how much you influence a lot of the guys. Ray's in a couple of my classes and, since the baseball season started, he's been talking a lot about the team, and how everyone's accepted him. I overheard him telling Barbara Johansson how much you've helped him, not only be accepted, but also be a better pitcher."

Laura Sue was in a chatty mode. Bobby could hardly get in a word, which gave him some relief. He didn't have to worry about saying something dumb if he wasn't talking. So he was happy to let Laura Sue carry most of the conversation.

When Laura Sue seemed to wind down for a moment, Bobby asked "Did Buster Talbot ever ask you to the prom?" He wasn't sure why he asked her that, or if he even wanted to know.

"No," she answered. "I made sure he heard me telling my girlfriends that I was going with you. Anyway, I think he just told you that to make you mad. I'm sort of glad he did tell you, because it was right after that you finally asked me."

Bobby wasn't sure what to make of that, so he decided to keep his mouth shut. Changing the subject, she said "I learned why Mr. Payne was arrested. Turns out he was a closet sleaze. He was charged with spousal abuse. He'd been beating his wife for a long time, but no one knew it. She finally had enough and went to the police."

"Too bad about him. I always thought he was a pretty nice guy and his wife was a little strange. Guess it was the other way around."

Laura Sue looked him in the eye. "You'd never do that to your wife, would you?"

If Bobby had been a cow, he'd have swallowed his cud. *Why did she ask me that, I wonder?* "No, I wouldn't," he replied.

They finished their sundaes and Laura Sue said she needed to get home before her Mom sent out a search party. Bobby really didn't want their time together to end, but agreed he needed to go, too. After all, he had finished this huge dish of ice cream and it was almost time for dinner. They went out together and, as they reached Bobby's van, Laura Sue leaned over and gave him a little peck on the cheek. "Don't forget to call me," she said, and headed home.

TWENTY

Friday morning, Bobby got to school at 7:45. Several of his teammates were already there, as well as the two coaches. Bennie came over. "Big weekend coming up. You ready?"

"You bet I am," Bobby said. "Two wins and we're playing for State."

Coach Albright walked over to Bobby and Bennie. "I'm putting my bag in your van, Bobby. Coach Brawley asked me if we could haul the clean uniforms for Saturday. I told him we would. That okay?" Bobby shook his head in agreement.

"Well then, let's get loaded up and head out. We can get there ahead of the rest of the team and get the motel lined up."

"See you in Tulsa," Bobby called out the window to the team as he pulled away. The drive was only a little over two hours to the Hampton Inn, in south Tulsa, just a mile from Oral Roberts University, where the games would be played. On the drive they chatted.

"You know Coach Brawley really depends on you," Coach Albright said. "He told me he thinks you played a big part in Roberts pitching so well. And, he's not sure what you did to help snap Talbot out of his slump, but he gives you the credit. Coach comes over as a grouch sometimes, but he'll always have your back. He loves this team and all the guys, well almost all of them, but you'd never know it."

95

"Yeah, I've sort of picked up on that," Bobby said. "You can't imagine how much it means to me to be included with the team."

As they pulled up to the motel entrance, Coach Albright looked over and said, "Bobby, don't sell yourself short. You're a natural leader and what you've accomplished has been an example for all of us."

Coach Albright got out of the van and Bobby went to park. By the time he rolled in the front door, Coach Albright had made arrangements with the clerk for the team's check-in. All he had to do was give out the room keys to match the room assignments. The two of them moved their luggage into the room they were sharing on the first floor-- a suite, with a living area and a separate bedroom with twin queen size beds.

"Nice digs," Bobby said.

When they went back out to the lobby, the team bus was pulling up in front. Coach Brawley, followed by the players, got off. "Brown, take Levin and Jones over to Murphy's van and get the uniforms. We'll pass them out here in the lobby."

"Don't worry about anything," Coach said to the desk clerk. "I've put the fear of God into them. They'll behave and not make too much noise."

As Coach Albright handed out the room keys, Coach Brawley said to the team "Go to your rooms, get your uniforms on and be back here in twenty minutes. It's now," he looked at his watch, "ten o'clock. We play at two, so we'll have some pizza at the ballpark, and do our warm-ups."

"What kind of pizza, Coach?" someone called out.

"Whatever Mazzio's brings us," the Coach answered. "The manager used to play for me when I coached at Pawhuska and he's donating it. So, you'll either like it or go hungry." Without further comment, he turned, picked up his suitcase and left for his room.

Twenty-five minutes later, the team bus pulled out of the hotel parking lot, followed by Bobby and Coach Albright in the van. The coach had issued Bobby a navy blue Brookside Rangers pull-over shirt and Bobby wore it, with his Ranger's baseball cap, proudly. When they reached the parking lot at ORU, Bobby found a handicap space and rolled out, accompanied by Coach Albright. Coach Brawley led them all into the players' facility, which included a comfortable lounge and tables for them to eat their pizza.

Charlie Levin, the team's skinny shortstop and biggest eater, said, "This pizza is the best I've ever had." Several of the others signified their agreement.

Brick Nelson responded, "Every pizza you have is the best you've ever had."

"Don't stuff yourselves too much," Coach Brawley warned. "We've got a game to play, remember. After the game, we're going to a nice steak house for dinner, so save room."

"No problem, Coach," Charlie said, as he reached for his fifth slice.

When everyone had finished eating, they all sat around and relaxed for about fifteen minutes before Coach Albright announced it was time for pre-game batting practice. They went down the tunnel into their dugout and, as they went out onto the field, they got their first glimpse of the Miami team leaving the field after their own batting practice.

"These guys don't look so big," Brick said. Bennie agreed.

"Maybe not to you two," Charlie said. "But, you're up there in the clouds. They look big to us normal sized people."

During batting practice, Bobby hung around the cage, just watching the hitters swing. He occasionally offered an observation, which they seemed to appreciate. When Buster Talbot took his turn, Bobby noticed he had reverted to swinging up instead of the level swing Bobby suggested earlier. Against Coach Albright's batting practice pitching velocity, Buster had no problem putting several balls over the left field fence. Bobby made a mental note to watch Buster in the game, but said nothing.

When Brookside finished batting practice, the team moved out to right field for stretching exercises, led by Bennie. Bennie, as the first baseman, had some extra stretching to do. With Coach Albright's help, he stretched out his hamstrings, quads and groin muscles. Bennie had missed almost a full season two years earlier when he hadn't stretched enough and pulled a muscle in his leg.

While the Brookside team was stretching, the Miami team took their infield and outfield practice. Then, it was Brookside's turn. Coach Brawley had asked Bobby to stay in the vicinity of second base, just in case Red Freeman showed any pre-game jitters. Red seemed as poised as he ever was, and his throws were all right on the mark.

When infield practice was over, Bobby rolled himself back toward the Brookside dugout, which was on the first base side. He passed a pair of Miami players and nodded a greeting. "What's Brookside doing with a cripple?" one of them said with a sneer.

"He's probably their ace reliever," the other one said and they both laughed. Bobby ignored them, but inside it hurt. *Is that how other people see me?*

Finally it was game time. Coach Brawley went to the plate for the pre-game meeting with the Miami coach and the umpires. While this was going on, the players looked into the stands, where a small crowd had assembled. The mostly navy blue clad fans behind their dugout looked a little sparse, but Bobby saw Carl in the group. Carl waved and gave him a thumbs up.

As the designated home team, Brookside took the field first, with the green and gray clad Miami team at bat. Ray Roberts strode in from the bullpen, where he had been warming up under Coach Albright's tutelage. He looked confident as he threw his warm-up pitches from the mound. Bobby assumed his usual place at the end of the bench, where he'd be joined by the game's pitcher and by catcher Tommy Jones.

After all the build-up, the teams were both nervous. Bobby had very few suggestions to offer. Roberts had a perfect game going into the fifth inning, when Miami managed its first hit, a bloop single into left field. Meanwhile, Brookside got a run in the first inning when Tommy Jones hit a sharp line drive double down the third base line, scoring Charlie Levin from second. In the third inning, with the bases loaded, Brick Nelson hit a towering home run that just cleared the left field wall for a grand slam. They added another run in the seventh on a solo homer by Bennie Brown. Miami had its second hit of the game with two out in the eighth inning and Justin Moore, the closer, came in to finish the game. Everything seemed to be working well. All that is but Buster Talbot's bat. Buster was hitless. Nevertheless, Brookside won 6-0. Bobby made a mental note to figure out a way to address Buster's hitting.

The team returned to the hotel. Before the Coach dismissed them, he gathered them all by the indoor pool, the only room in the hotel where they could all fit. "Boys," he said in his gruff way, "we got a good win today. Miami didn't really have a very good season, but they won their district tournament, somehow, which got them here. Tomorrow will be a much tougher test. Don't get ahead of this. Whoever wins the McAlester-Muskogee game will give us all we can handle. They both have good pitching and both of them can hit the ball.

"Tarkinton, you're on the mound. Now, everyone go get a shower and put on your decent clothes. Be back here in the lobby at six sharp. Our dinner reservation is for six-thirty."

Before he left to go to his room, Al Tarkinton came over to Bobby. "I'm gonna need you tomorrow, pal."

Coach Brawley called to Bobby. "Murphy, you're screwed for a steak dinner. I want you to go with Booger back to the ballpark and scout McAlester and Muskogee. Anything we can get. We may need it. Watch for individual tendencies, and what they do in strategic situations. Booger's got the money to buy you a hamburger or something at the park. And put on 'civilian' clothes so you guys don't stand out and look like a couple of spies."

"Sure thing, Coach," Bobby said. *Man, I was looking forward to having dinner with the guys.* But then he thought about the responsibility Coach Brawley was giving him and felt kind of good.

Bobby and Coach Albright changed clothes and drove back to the stadium for the McAlester-Muskogee game. Coach Albright commented "I could get used to being chauffeured around."

"My pleasure Coach. It feels good to me not having to be totally dependent on other people to get anywhere. And, I enjoy the company."

They found seats directly behind home plate and got out their notebooks. Bobby wasn't exactly sure what he was looking for, so he decided he would try to tell what pitches the pitchers were throwing and how the individual hitters handled them. The first three McAlester batters struck out, all on fastballs. Bobby noted that the Muskogee pitcher didn't seem to throw as hard, or with as much movement as Al Tarkinton.

In the bottom of the first, the first two Muskogee batters made outs—a ground ball to second and an infield pop-up. The McAlester pitcher skillfully mixed his fastball with an off-speed breaking ball and kept them off-balance. The third batter lined the first pitch, a fastball, to center. Muskogee's clean-up hitter, Urf Bratkowski, had been named Oklahoma high school player of the year. He hit .342, with nine home runs during the regular season. No one had been able to get him out with any consistency.

The McAlester pitcher started him off with a fastball, low and on the outside corner. Bratkowski reached out and fouled it off down the first base line. The pitcher came back with an off-speed curve ball and Bratkowski swung and missed. The next two pitches missed and it was 2-2. Bobby found himself thinking: *Don't groove a fastball.* But, the McAlester pitcher decided he could throw it past him. No such luck. Bratkowski took a mighty swing, and they all watched the ball fly out of sight over the left field wall. Muskogee led 2-0.

Each team scored two runs in the sixth inning, as both starting pitchers showed signs of fatigue. Going into the ninth, it was 4-2 Muskogee. Muskogee brought in their ace closer, Mark Shadduck. Shadduck was a long, lean six foot, three inches tall, second team all-state, and had already signed a letter of intent to go to Oklahoma State on a baseball scholarship. He was also potentially a high professional draft choice.

Shadduck quickly got the first two McAlester hitters, on fastballs, Bobby noted. Then, the third batter, McAlester's last hope, hit a high, bouncing ball to the third baseman. By the time the ball came down, the batter was standing on first. McAlester's next hitter was their eighth hitter in the line-up, but Bobby recalled he had been on base all four times he had batted. And, he could also run and had two stolen bases in the game.

Shadduck decided to blow fast balls by him. He got two quick strikes, wasted a third pitch, and threw a fast ball down the middle. The McAlester hitter swung and hit a line drive into the right field corner. The ball rattled around and the right fielder didn't pick it up cleanly. By the time he caught up with the ball and threw it back into the infield, the McAlester speedster was sliding home with an inside the park home run, tying the game.

Shadduck looked dazed, but recovered enough to get the next batter on a grounder to first. Bobby noted that Shadduck had only thrown fastballs, nothing off-speed or breaking.

In the bottom of the ninth, Muskogee's first batter was Urf Bratkowski. The McAlester pitcher started him off with an off-speed breaking ball. Bratkowski swung and missed. Then the pitcher made the mistake that cost his team the game—he grooved a fastball right down the middle of the plate. Bratkowski didn't miss and put it over the center field wall for his second home run--the game winner.

Brookside and Muskogee would play for the championship of the Eastern Oklahoma Region and the chance to advance to the state finals.

TWENTY-ONE

When Bobby and Coach Albright returned to the Hampton Inn, the team had already come back from their dinner at Jamil's Steak House, and settled into their rooms, with strict instructions from Coach Brawley for lights out by ten. Bobby and Coach Albright found the Coach pacing in the lobby, waiting impatiently for them. "Let's go to my room and see what you got."

They sat down at the small table in Coach Brawley's room and the two scouts got out their notes. Coach Albright went first. "Muskogee has some big bats. They hit .295 as a team, which is about eight points higher than us. But, it didn't seem to me they were very effective hitting breaking or off-speed stuff. All their big hits came on fastballs. Also, they tried to bunt several times with some of their weaker hitters, but never could get them down. That guy Bratkowski can hit the ball, though. I think, when we can, we'll want to pitch around him. Walk him intentionally, maybe. What do you think, Bobby?"

"I tried to see what each of the hitters did with different pitches. None of them handled breaking balls very well; I don't think they got two of their nine hits on curve balls. A change-up, or slow breaking ball right after setting them up with a fastball out of the zone seemed to be effective. I never could figure out why McAlester didn't do that more often. I agree we need to be careful with Bratkowski, but he looked bad every time he got anything but a fastball. I think Al, with his junk, is the perfect match for their line-up. His fastball is just okay, but it's got movement and should be good enough to set them up for the other stuff."

"I know you didn't see their starting pitcher for tomorrow, but you did get to see their hot shot closer. Can our guys hit him?"

Coach Albright and Bobby exchanged glances. Coach Albright said "We can, if we can hit a fastball."

Bobby said, "I didn't see him throw anything but fastballs, so we should be able to dig in and be ready, without having to worry about anything else. Also, if I understood correctly, the pitcher Muskogee threw was their best starter. He looked like someone our guys could hit. In fact, we faced better pitchers several times during the season—harder throwers with better stuff. If he was their best, we should be able to get to the guy they throw tomorrow. If we do, maybe we won't even see Shadduck."

They talked a little more about the upcoming game and finally Coach Brawley said "Let's call it a night. I think we know as much as we can for now. But, be alert during the game. Some situation may come up that makes you think of something. Murphy, I want you in your usual spot on the end of the bench, by Tarkinton and Jones. Give Tarkinton all the intel you can before the game. Get Moore in the conversation, too. If we have to replace Tarkinton early, I plan to go right to Moore and let him finish the game.

"Be in the breakfast room no later than eight. I don't want us to have to rush around; we need to be at the ballpark by ten thirty. The game's at one."

Bobby and Coach Albright headed for their room. Bobby said, "Coach, I want to go outside for a few minutes before I settle in."

"Go ahead. I'll see you when you get back. Oh, and tell Laura Sue hello."

How did he know I was calling her?

"Hi," Bobby said, when Laura Sue answered. "It's me. Sorry to call so late, but I had to help Coach Booger scout the game after ours, and then we had a meeting with Coach Brawley."

"It's not too late, Bobby. Did the drive down go ok?"

Bobby assured her that it did. "I wish you were coming to the game tomorrow."

"Oh, I'll be there. Your Mom called me a little bit ago and invited me and Buddy to ride down with them. I thought that was really nice. I'm excited."

"It'll be tough," Bobby said. "Muskogee can really hit. But, Muskogee's not the only place Okies come from." *Lame joke.*

"Good one, Bobby." They chatted on for a few minutes, and hung up.

Well, I didn't say anything too stupid this time. I can't wait to see her. In his mind, he could see her perfect smile, blond ponytail, and those blue eyes twinkling like stars on a clear night.

TWENTY-TWO

Bobby woke early on Saturday morning. He was too excited to stay in bed, so he got himself up, finished in the bathroom, and was just about dressed when Coach Albright rolled over. He saw Bobby almost ready and jumped out of bed.

"What time is it? Did I oversleep?"

"No," Bobby said. "I just couldn't sleep any longer. Big day."

"Thank goodness. If I was late, Coach Brawley would never let me forget it. Let me get my shower and then I'll help you with your shoes and socks."

Coach Albright, wearing his Brookside Rangers white home baseball uniform with navy blue numbers and pin stripes, and Bobby left for the breakfast room with ten minutes to spare. Bobby was wearing new blue jeans and his Rangers baseball shirt and cap.

When they entered the breakfast area, most of the team was already there. The attendant looked a bit harried as the gang of strapping teenagers was eating everything in sight. Fortunately, the hotel had been alerted to the appetites of growing boys and had enough food.

After everyone had eaten their fill, the attendant brought out box lunches for the team to take with them. Coach Brawley didn't want them hungry, with the game starting at one. About nine, he cleared his throat loudly, a signal everyone recognized as, "Shut up. I have something to say."

"Okay, listen up. First, don't eat your lunches yet. We'll have plenty of time to eat them at the ballpark. Next, go back to your rooms and get ready to check out. We're leaving for home directly after the game. Finally, those of you who weren't smart enough to wear your uniforms put them on before you come out." His last comment drew a muffled laugh from the team. Bobby was thankful he had put on his shirt. "Bus leaves at ten sharp. Don't keep us waiting." With that, he turned and left the room.

There were no glitches and they arrived at the ORU stadium a few minutes after ten. As the team went through their warmups and batting practice, Bobby rolled himself out to the infield, where he set up near Red Freeman at second base and Charlie Levin at short. They both went through their infield drills flawlessly, and Bobby returned to the bench. First baseman Bennie Brown didn't need any special support, and there was no point in going down to third to offer Buster Talbot anything. When it was time for Al Tarkinton to begin his warm-up, Bobby joined him and Tommy Jones in the bullpen. When Al appeared ready, Bobby huddled with them.

"I watched these guys last night. They can hit, especially that guy Urf Bratkowski, their clean-up. So, Al, if they do get some hits, don't let it get to you. They look to me like they really like the fastball. So, don't groove any. Use it just off the plate to set up your off speed and breaking stuff. You might get away with a few fastballs the second or third time through their line-up, when they're not expecting them. But, whatever you do, don't throw Bratkowski anything fast or straight anywhere near the strike zone.

"Tommy, Coach is gonna call the pitches, like always. I've gone over this with him, so his calls should roughly follow what I just said. Good luck, guys. And, have fun." As nervous as Bobby was, he hoped his little pep talk would help relax Al and Tommy.

As they made their way back to the dugout, Bobby said quietly to Tommy, "Be real careful when Coach calls for a fastball. And, if he calls for one when Bratkowski's up, be sure Al doesn't throw it for a strike. I suspect there will be some times when Coach will call for an intentional walk."

"Thanks Bobby. We'll give it our best. Be sure you keep up the positive talk with Al between innings. He can let stuff get to him, and that won't help. What kind of a name is "Urf" anyway? Sounds like someone's throwing up."

"Maybe so, but, you and Al will be the ones throwin' up if he gets a fastball in the strike zone."

Before entering the dugout, Bobby looked up into the stands. He immediately spotted Laura Sue and his parents in the first row. They were sitting with Carl. Behind them were his buddies— Eddie and Riley. Buddy Medlin had hitched a ride with Bobby's parents and Andy Martin, who had been injured in the accident that crippled Bobby, was there, too. Bobby waved and they waved back. He gave a special sort of wave to Laura Sue, which earned him verbal 'raspberries' from his buddies. He didn't care and, for once, didn't even blush. *Did she just blow me a kiss?*

Then it was time for business. Al took the mound and looked confident. The only one Bobby thought looked nervous was Red Freeman, but that was normal for Red. Buster Talbot was his usual cocky self.

Muskogee's leadoff hitter dug in. Al started him off with a fastball just off the plate. Ball one. Then he threw a curve ball, off speed, and falling like it was off a cliff. The batter swung and missed. Two pitches later, it was two and two. Then, Al grooved a fastball and the right handed hitter hit a sharp line drive to left. Coach Brawley, Al and Tommy all turned as one and looked at Bobby, as if to say 'you were right!' Al threw a couple tosses to first to hold the runner a little closer, but on the first pitch to the plate, a fastball on the outside corner, he took off, sliding safely into second, just ahead of the throw.

Al got the next two hitters, one on a strikeout and the other on a weak ground ball back to the pitcher. Bratkowski strolled to the plate, looking like Babe Ruth. As Bobby had recommended, Coach

Brawley called for the intentional walk. Bratkowski frowned at the Brookside bench as he trotted to first. The next batter hit a pop-up to Freeman at second and they were out of the inning.

"I shouldn't have thrown that guy a fastball over the plate. Exactly what you said not to do," Al said.

"Shake it off, Al. You got away with it. And, it may help you with that guy next time. He'll be looking for another one. Give him one, but not for a strike. Be sure you hold their baserunners close. These guys can run. Don't show your best move on the first couple tosses over. Let 'em get confident and comfortable, then pick 'em off."

Brookside went down one-two-three in their half of the first. The game settled in and neither team mounted a significant threat to score until the seventh inning. Bennie Brown had two hits, both singles, Brick Nelson and Tommy Jones each had a single and Charley Levin had a double. Buster Talbot had gone hitless in his first two at-bats. Bobby noticed he was still swinging with an upward arc, trying to hit the long ball. Buster had also gone hitless against McAlester and Bobby knew Coach Brawley was very close to benching him.

In the top of the seventh, Muskogee's leadoff batter singled and again stole second. The next batter walked. Al looked a little shaken and walked the next batter, loading the bases with nobody out. Urf Bratkowski walked to the plate, with a bit of a strut, Bobby thought. He looked back at Tommy Jones and sneered. "You got to pitch to me now. Nowhere to put me."

Tommy called time and went to the mound. "We need to pitch around this guy. Bobby said he can't hit a breaking ball, or a change-up, so let's see if he's right." Al nodded his agreement, but looked unsure.

"We'll be ok," Tommy said. "You'll see. We'll start him with a fastball off the plate, then nothing but breaking and off speed stuff. Keep that guy at first close. Maybe you can set him up for a pick off."

The umpire came out and told them to get back to work.

Returning to the plate, Tommy looked over toward the Coach and gave him a nod, trying to indicate they had the situation under control and didn't need any more help right away. Then he glanced at Bobby with a grin, put on his mask and crouched down behind the plate. Coach Brawley made his way down the bench and sat down beside Bobby.

"I hope Jones and Tarkinton know what they're doing," he said.

"They do," Bobby said, desperately hoping he was right. He knew what they were going to do, and he knew who had suggested it. If it went awry, it would be his fault, he thought. He felt his skin crawl.

The runner at first took his lead and Al made a half-hearted toss over. Then, he unloaded a fastball, just outside to Bratkowski, who took it for a ball. Tommy thought he saw a smirk on his face. The runner took a little larger lead off first and Al made another toss over. The runner was back easily. Al went into his stretch. The runner led even farther off, knowing Al's move to first would too late to get him out. But, Al glanced over and fired a bullet to Bennie Brown. The runner was out by a foot. One down, but Bratkowski was still up and there were still runners on second and third.

Tommy decided to risk another fastball, this time low and on the inside corner. Bratkowski wound up and swung hard. But, he missed it. Strike one. Next Al threw a magnificent change up. Bratkowski swung from his heels, but was way out in front and managed only a weak foul ball that the third base coach fielded. One and two—pitcher's count. Al, who had gone into a windup, instead of the stretch he usually used with runners on base, threw what looked like a fastball, but at the last second broke down and away. Bratkowski almost screwed himself into the ground swinging, but missed the ball by a foot.

Coach Brawley looked over at Bobby, nodded and made his way back to the other end of the bench. Bobby, who had been holding his breath, exhaled. Al made short work of the next batter, getting the third out on another curve ball strikeout.

When Al and Tommy reached the bench and sat down, Tommy looked over at Bobby. "You da man."

"No," Bobby said, "Al's da man. He had to execute and boy did he ever."

Al just smiled. "Bobby, you called it. And, you called it right. I've never felt so confident out there. That pick off play was the coolest, even better than striking out the big boy."

As they were talking, Bobby saw Justin Moore coming down to sit with them. "I think you're gonna pitch one more inning, and then Justin will come in in the ninth to close it out. You're pitch count's getting up there, but you should easily have another inning in you.

"Come down here Justin and sit with Tommy and me." Bobby went over the same strategy points he had shared with Al before the game. "Just remember, they can hit fastballs, and they haven't yet proved they can hit anything else. Also, if you need it, use the same strategy Al did to pick someone off first. If all goes well, you shouldn't even have to face Bratkowski."

Brick Nelson led off the inning with a walk and promptly stole second. Bennie Brown, who already had two hits, nailed a long fly ball to right. It looked like it might leave the park, but the right fielder caught it just short of the wall. However, it was deep enough to move Brick to third. With Tommy Jones at the plate, the Muskogee pitcher threw a wild pitch in the dirt. It got by the catcher, allowing Brick to score. One to nothing, Brookside.

Tommy lined a double into the left-center gap and the Muskogee coach came to the mound to talk to his pitcher. Charley Levin hit the first pitch over the second baseman, scoring Tommy. Red Freeman dropped a bunt down the third base line and beat the throw by a step. With two runners on, and one out, Buster Talbot stepped to the plate. Bobby watched anxiously as Buster, swinging with his upward arc, hit a ground ball to the shortstop, who easily turned the double play to end the inning. But, Brookside had a two run lead going into the eighth.

In the top of the eighth, Al walked the first batter. Justin Moore was warming up in the bullpen, not quite ready. Tommy started out to the mound, but Al motioned him back behind the plate. Al had a look on his face Bobby had never seen, more focused and intent than normal. Having seen Al's good pick off motion, the runner didn't give Al a chance to get him. With a short lead, he took off for second on the first pitch, a fastball on the lower outside corner for a strike. Tommy came up throwing and nailed the runner at second. That was Muskogee's last base runner as Al struck out the next two hitters, all with breaking and off speed pitches.

Muskogee changed pitchers in the bottom of the eighth. Shadduck took the mound and immediately began throwing heat. All fastballs, no curves, no off speed stuff. The Brookside hitters were waiting for the fastballs, but, while they hit them hard, they all went right at a fielder. Now it was the top of the ninth, three outs away from playing in the championship game.

Justin Moore took the mound and his warm-up pitches were all fast balls. Bobby looked over at Al. "Didn't he get the message about fastballs?"

Al said, "Just watch. Those Muskogee hitters are watching him throw those fastballs and their mouths are watering."

"That's what worries me," Bobby said, as Justin threw a first pitch fastball, just missing the plate for ball one. Bobby closed his eyes. Justin then cranked off three breaking balls, striking out the first Muskogee batter. He followed exactly the same pattern for the second batter, who managed a ground ball to Charley Levin, who threw him out at first. One out away.

The third Muskogee batter stepped in, their season on the line. Justin threw a fastball, but this time it was not off the plate, but right down the center. The ball left the park twenty feet over the left field wall. Now things were serious. Muskogee was only one run down, but still had two outs. No need to worry. Justin returned to his formula and Muskogee watched their season end with a strike out—on a slow curve.

The two teams came out for the traditional post-game handshake. Bobby stayed at the bench. He didn't think it would be appropriate for him to go out in his wheel chair. As he sat there, to his great surprise, the Muskogee coach and Mark Shadduck came over to him. The coach said "Murphy, I remember you from the playoffs last year and I saw you and Coach Albright in the stands scouting us last night. You obviously did a good job because it seemed like your guys knew exactly what we were going to do, and you picked on our tendencies almost perfectly. Good job."

"Yeah," Shadduck said. "But, how did you know I was only going to throw fastballs?"

Bobby said, "I didn't for sure, but that was all you threw last night. You've got such a good one; I just hoped we could catch up with it."

"Good luck next week. I hope you guys win it. I don't like Lawton or Edmund either one." The two Muskogee men shook Bobby's hand and went back to their team, leaving Bobby stunned. *What a classy thing for them to do.*

The team all went out in front of the dugout to acknowledge their fans. The fifty, or so, fans whooped it up and waved back. Bobby rolled himself over to the railing where his Mom and Dad waited with his buddies. And, Laura Sue.

When they all finished congratulating Bobby and turned to leave, Laura Sue hung back. "Bobby, I'm so proud of you," she said. "I know you had a bigger part in this win than most people realize. I'd give you a big kiss if there weren't all these people around, and I could reach you."

Bobby didn't know what to say. "Maybe later," he said. After Laura Sue left, several of his teammates came by and they exchanged high fives. Al Tarkinton, Justin Moore and Tommy Jones all gathered at Bobby's chair. "Al, you and Justin pitched great. And, Tommy, you called a perfect game."

"We couldn't have done it without your help," Al said. "We all did our parts, but we were doing what you figured out would work. And, you nailed it. Can you believe we're goin' to State?"

"Let's go boys," Coach Brawley growled. "The bus is leaving." He looked his usual grouchy self, but Bobby could see a faint gleam in his eyes. "We haven't won anything yet. Next week is what counts."

TWENTY-THREE

The drive home with Coach Albright went by quickly. The coach was still riding the high from the victory. "We did a good job scouting Muskogee last night. I should say, you did a good job. You picked up stuff I missed, and got our pitchers to take advantage of it. I wish we could scout the Lawton-Edmund winner. It would give us a big advantage."

"If Lawton wins," Bobby replied, "I may have an idea. My cousin, Robin, plays for Edmund. If they win, he won't be any help. But, if they lose, he may be able to give us something."

Bobby dropped Coach Albright off at the school and drove home. When he pulled into the driveway, he saw his parents car, and knew they were already home. What he didn't know was that Laura Sue and Buddy were there also.

"Your Mom invited us to stay for dinner," Laura Sue told him, and gave him that smile that made him goofy. His Mom, Dad and Buddy were all in the kitchen; they were alone in the front hallway. She leaned over and said, "I told you I owed you a kiss, and here it is." She proceeded to kiss him right on the lips, just as Buddy came around the corner.

"Gross," he said and went back to the kitchen.

Bobby's Dad finished cooking the burgers on the grill and brought them to the table. "I forgot to ask everybody how they wanted their hamburgers. But, it didn't matter. I was going to cook 'em all the same anyway."

As they ate, they talked about the game. Mrs. Murphy said, "I noticed that Al didn't give that big guy anything but curve balls and off speed stuff. If I remember right, he has a pretty good fastball. But, it worked."

Buddy, who hadn't had much to say, piped up. "I heard some of the guys in the stands saying that Bobby had scouted their game on Friday night. Did that have anything to do with it?"

"It probably helped some," Bobby said, "but none of it would have worked if Al and Tommy hadn't done the real work. Al and Justin pitched great. That guy Bratkowski could really hit, but Al shut him down. Did anyone hear who won the Lawton-Edmund game?"

"Why don't you call Robin after dinner and ask him?" his Dad said. "Wouldn't it be neat if you played Edmund next week? One of you would have bragging rights for years."

"I'd rather play Lawton," Bobby said, but he didn't explain further.

After ice cream sundaes, complete with chocolate syrup, chopped nuts, whipped cream and a cherry on top, Mr. Murphy said, "Bobby, why don't you drive Laura Sue and Buddy home?"

Caught completely by surprise, Bobby said, "That would be great, but..."

Dad interrupted. "You did a good job driving you and Coach Albright down to Tulsa, and you've had enough practice that I think you're ready to have passengers. That is, if Laura Sue and Buddy aren't too scared to ride with you."

"I'd love to ride with Bobby. I think he'll be a good driver," Laura Sue said.

"I'm a little nervous, but I'll suck it up and hold my breath," Buddy said.

When they reached the Medlin house, Buddy, with a quick "Thanks for the ride," ran into the house. Laura Sue lagged, and when Buddy reached the house, she leaned over and kissed Bobby goodnight.

Why can't I ever think of something clever to say? So he said "Goodnight. See you in school, Monday."

"You could come over for dinner with us tomorrow, if you want," Laura Sue said.

Now's the time for a cool response, something smooth. He said, "OK, what time?"

"Come about two. We'll be home from church by then."

"I'll be here," he said.

TWENTY-FOUR

Monday morning, Bobby got to school early. He stopped by Miss Winn's office to say hello and was glad to find her at her desk. "Hey, Miss Winn," he said.

"Hi, Bobby. Congratulations on the big wins last weekend. Could you drop by for a few minutes during your study hall period?"

"Sure. Anything special?"

"Yes," she said. "We need to talk about college."

Bobby's study hall was the third period, just before lunch, so he made his way to Miss Winn's office. Bobby was always impressed with how professionally Miss Winn dressed and almost always reflected the school's colors.

"Come in," she said. Bobby took a seat. "Have you been thinking about what you're going to do next year after you graduate? If you plan to go to college, and I'm sure you do, it's getting very late to apply."

Bobby paused for a moment. "I do want to go to college next year, and I've been thinking about it. I guess I've put it off because it's a little scary thinking about how I can do it in a wheelchair. I can't even put on my own shoes and socks when I get dressed."

"Well," she said. "All of the colleges and universities in Oklahoma are set up to accommodate wheel chairs. So, it might take some adjustments on your part, but it's definitely doable. And, there are a lot of people who are wheelchair bound, not just you.

I bet you could find some help learning to put on your own socks and shoes. Have you talked to Carl about it? If I remember right, you were working with him."

"No, I haven't. But that's a good idea. Carl's really helped me a lot. I'll call him this evening. What do you think I should do about college?"

"First, what do you think you might want to study?"

"I don't really know. Maybe some kind of engineering," he said. "I'm pretty good in math and science, and I like the idea of working with those things. But, I also like history. Maybe I could work in the medical field. At this point, I really don't know what I want to do for sure."

"That's not unusual for an eighteen year old," Miss Winn said. "The big thing is to get started. You can always change your direction, and major, later. In fact, most people do. Very few people graduate from high school knowing exactly what they want to do with the rest of their life. Have you given any thought to where you want to go?"

"Yes, I actually have," he replied. "I've always wanted to go to OU, but I like Oklahoma State, too. And, it's a little closer to home. I know both schools have great programs. I also always thought I might be able to get a baseball scholarship somewhere, but that's out now. To be honest, I'm scared to go to a large school right off the bat. What do you think about starting at one of the community colleges?"

"I think that would make sense. Assuming you do well and keep your grades up, you should have no problem transferring into either OU or OSU after a year or two. And you could get a lot of your basic pre-requisites out of the way without the pressure of being in such a large place. You could probably keep living at home, since dorm space at the community colleges is either limited, or non-existent. Plus, the tuition at a community college would be less; and you'd save your parents a lot of money by living at home."

"I think that's what I want to do for at least the first year. I really need to get out on my own and learn to take care of myself, but I think I'd like to kind of ease into it, not all at once."

"Sounds smart to me," Miss Winn said. "There are two community colleges within a reasonable distance to consider. Rock Springs CC is about twenty miles east of here, and Will Rogers CC is about fifteen miles north. Both offer courses you'll need, whatever you decide to end up studying, and both are excellent "feeder" schools to either OU or OSU. Their courses will be fully transferrable to almost any four year college."

"That sounds like a good plan," Bobby said. "But, how should I go about deciding on which one."

"I have a brochure for each of them." She handed him the small brochures. "I suggest you take them home and talk it over with your parents. It'd be a good idea to apply to both of them, just in case. And, there are several scholarships you can apply for to cover your tuition. Some will even cover books and fees. There may even be scholarship money available based on your being in a wheelchair. Your grades are very good, so, unless it's too late and all of them have already been awarded, that will be a big help. Talk to your Mom and Dad tonight, and come see me again tomorrow. We'll get this worked out. Oh, here are a couple application forms. Since they're both state schools, the forms are the same."

"Thanks, Miss Winn. I really appreciate your advice. I've been putting off thinking about college, but I know I need to get started."

At lunch, he sat with his friends Andy, Eddie and Riley. He would like to be with Laura Sue, but her lunch period was the next one. When they got their food and sat down, Bobby asked, "What are you guys planning to do about college next year?" It struck him that this was something they normally would have been talking about for quite a while, but, with everything he'd been through this year, it wasn't a conversation he'd been in on.

Andy said, "I've been accepted at Wichita State. That's where my Dad went, and it's been my dream. Besides, they offered me a full scholarship."

Riley said, "I'm planning to go to Denver. We always used to take vacations in the mountains around there, and I plan to ski my way through." The others all looked at him and he laughed. "Seriously, I probably will ski, but they have a good accounting and business school. I want to go somewhere away from home. Not that I don't like it here, but I just need to get away and learn to be independent."

Eddie didn't immediately say anything. Bobby said, "Eddie, what are you doing to do next year?"

Eddie said, "I plan to go to Midwestern Tech in Oklahoma City. I want to be an electronics technician, and I'm not sure I'm really ready for college. Plus, from what I'm told, there's a big demand for people in the field, and the jobs pay pretty well. It's a two year program, and I can either go to work or go on to college when I finish."

"Sounds like you guys are way ahead of me," Bobby said. He told them about his meeting with Miss Winn.

"I think that's a great plan," Riley said. "It'll give you a chance to work some stuff out before you get in the pressure cooker atmosphere of a big school." The others chimed in their agreement.

When the school day ended, Bobby waited for Laura Sue before he went to baseball practice. She came out the door with a couple other girls, but broke away when she saw Bobby waiting.

"I wish we had some more time to talk," Bobby said. "I've been talking with Miss Winn about college. And, I realized I've never asked what you plan to do next year." He gave her a quick summary of his plan.

"I don't know what I want to do next year," she said. "I've been accepted at OSU, and they've offered me a partial scholarship. If I go to OSU, and you go to one of those two community colleges and live at home, we wouldn't be that far apart. Let's talk some more when we have more time."

Bobby agreed, and headed for baseball practice. As the team went through their warm-ups and drills, Bobby told Coach Brawley about his cousin, who played for Edmund. "Since Edmund lost to Lawton, Robin may be able to give me at least a little scouting report. He plans to be a coach when his playing days are over, so he pays attention to a lot of stuff most people don't notice."

Coach Brawley was skeptical, but said, "Give him a call, and see what you can learn. Never know what might help."

When Bobby got home, his Mom and Dad were ready for dinner. "You're running a little late today," his Mom said.

"Yeah, Coach Brawley did some extra batting practice, and we worked some on turning double plays."

Over dinner, they each talked about their day. When his turn came, Bobby told them about his conversation with Miss Winn. "What do you think," he asked.

"I think that all makes a lot of sense," his Mom said. "I'd be nervous about you going to one of the big schools right away. Much better to take it one step at a time. You'll have a lot less stress, and can really focus on making good grades."

His Dad nodded in agreement. "I've known several people whose kids took that route, and it was a really good experience for them. Didn't Carl go to one of those schools? You might talk with him and see what he thinks."

"Yeah, I need to call Carl this evening anyway."

They took a while longer, talking about college, looking at the brochures, and reviewing the application forms. After dinner, Bobby wheeled himself back to his room. Before he began his homework, he gave Carl a call.

"Hey Bobby. How're you doing?" Carl said. "How does the team look for next week? You guys were awesome against Miami and Muskogee. It almost looked like your guys knew exactly what their pitchers were gonna throw, and what their hitters couldn't hit. You really controlled that big boy Bratkowski. Did you know he has a full baseball scholarship to Texas?"

"No, I didn't know that. He's surly enough to go there," Bobby said. He told Carl about his scouting expedition with Coach Albright the night before they played Muskogee.

"Really good job," Carl said. "What's on your mind tonight?"

"Couple things," Bobby replied. "I'd like to pick your brain a little about college sometime. But, what I'm really thinking about is my shoes and socks. I can do a lot of things for myself, but I can't put on my own shoes and socks. Have you got any ideas on that?"

"I sure do," Carl said. "How about if I come by about this time tomorrow, and we'll see what we can do?"

"Sounds good to me," Bobby said. "Thanks."

The next call Bobby made was to his cousin Robin in Edmund.

"Hey cuz," he said when Robin answered the phone. "I need to get your take on Lawton's baseball team."

"Yeah, I heard you guys beat Muskogee last weekend. We should have won, but a couple errors at key times killed us. What can I help you with?"

"Let's start with their pitching. Tell me what you noticed. You know, tendencies, what kind of stuff they throw, like that."

"We only faced two of their pitchers. Their starter, a guy named Oren Hershman, or something like that, is a real tall guy. Must be about six five, but he's kind of skinny. When he comes off the mound at you, it looks like he's right on top of you. Throws mostly heat, but I didn't think his control was that good. We got a few walks, but had a lot of strikeouts on bad pitches. A little more patience and we'd have had a lot more guys on base. He had a curve ball but, when he threw it, you could pretty much tell it was coming by his motion. And, he didn't throw many curve balls over the plate."

"How about the second one? The one who came in in relief?"

"That guy was tougher. He wasn't quite as fast, but mixed in some off speed stuff and a nasty curve ball. He had a lot better control than Hershman, but still telegraphed it when he was throwing something other than the fastball. Marshall, or Marberry, or something like that. Still, he threw a lot more fastballs, and always threw a fastball when he really needed the strike. We should have hit both those guys, but we were too impatient at the plate."

"What about their other relievers?" Bobby asked.

"Those two guys were the only ones we saw. Mayberg, or whatever his name was, had pitched three innings in their game the night before, so I'm betting there's a pretty good drop off after those two."

"How about their bats? Are they mostly power hitters, or do they hit a bunch of singles? Do they run the bases; you know, steal and try to take extra bases?"

"It seemed to be a mix. Their leadoff hitter bunted for a single on the first pitch. I was playing third and was back in my normal place, so I had no chance. The second guy also bunted. I got him at first, but he moved the guy to second. But, the third, fourth and fifth hitters didn't look like bunters to me. They swing for the fences. They did seem to me to have trouble with off-speed and breaking stuff. But, they really peppered fastballs. The rest of the line-up didn't seem to have that much power, but they could hit, and they made contact most of the time. It was just the first two batters that looked like threats to steal. As far as trying to take extra bases, be ready. Their philosophy seemed to be 'try to throw me out' and force the defense to execute."

"This is really good stuff," Bobby said. "I hope we can use it. It's just one game, winner take all, so maybe we won't see any other pitchers."

The cousins continued to talk for a while. Robin was interested in how Bobby was doing and had a lot of questions. Before they hung up, they agreed they needed to get together over the summer.

When he got off the phone, Bobby made some notes from the conversation so he wouldn't forget anything.

TWENTY-FIVE

A fter school the next day, Bobby stopped by Coach Brawley's office on his way to practice. He told the Coach about his conversation with Robin. "Keep that stuff fresh in your mind for next Saturday," Coach Brawley told him. "Some of it may be helpful. I'm planning to bench Talbot. Hasn't had a hit in the last four games. He thinks he's a home run hitter, but all he does is strike out or hit weak ground balls. What do you think, Murphy?"

Bobby took a breath before replying. He had no love for Buster Talbot. The guy was a first class jerk. But, Bobby also knew how important to the team Talbot could be if he got his bat back. "Let me see what I can do before you make that call."

Coach said something that sounded like a bear growling. Coach Albright, who had been listening to Bobby's report, winked at Bobby and grinned.

During practice, Bobby spent most of his time observing infield practice. Red Freeman was looking more relaxed and consequently making better throws. Bobby helped Red with his turn on double play balls and, by the end of practice, Red and Riley were looking like major leaguers. He deliberately avoided Buster Talbot during infield practice. He wasn't looking forward to their discussion about hitting and thought, since Talbot seemed to resent any of his advice, he'd avoid antagonizing him as long as he could. He did want to watch him take batting practice, though.

As the team went through their batting practice, Bobby tried to watch each hitter carefully and offered occasional helpful comments. He noticed, for example, that Bennie Brown was not getting set before each pitch. When he pointed this out to him, Bennie's contact with the ball immediately improved. As Red Freeman prepared to take his turn, Bobby suggested he form a mental image of trying to hit the ball straight back at the pitcher.

Red said, "I've never thought about it like that, but I'll give it a try." Six consecutive line drives later, Red looked over at Bobby and grinned.

Buster Talbot stepped into the batter's box. "Watch this, Murphy. I don't need none of your bull crap advice." With that, he hit the first two pitches high and deep into center field. Bobby noticed he was still swinging up instead of level. Coach Albright, who was pitching batting practice, looked over at Bobby. They had discussed this situation before practice started. Bobby nodded and tipped his cap. Most of the team knew Coach Albright had been a pitcher at Oklahoma State, but few had ever seen him pitch seriously in a situation other than tossing batting practice.

Now, Coach Albright's approach changed. Instead of throwing at batting practice speed, he threw Buster some serious heat and a couple breaking balls that froze Buster in his stance. The balls Buster did hit with his "upswing" were weak ground balls that barely made it past the infield. When his turn ended, he walked back to the bench past Bobby without a word. *Tomorrow we'll have our chat.*

After practice, Bennie walked to the parking lot with Bobby. "Something's going on with you and Coach Booger, and Talbot. What's the deal? I haven't seen Coach Booger throw like that in batting practice before."

Bobby told him his plan to straighten out Buster's hitting. "I really don't like the guy, and I know he doesn't like me. But, if I can get him to hit, at least in one more game, it might mean the difference in winning State or not. And, I owe it to the team to try. If he won't listen to me, Coach Brawley's gonna bench him."

"I hope it works," Bennie said. "Good luck."

TWENTY-SIX

Bobby drove home slowly, his mind on the best way to approach the Talbot issue. As he turned in his driveway, his thoughts shifted to Carl's upcoming visit. He saw Carl's green Chevy parked on the street in front of the house. *He's really early.*

Bobby rolled up the ramp and into the house. Carl was sitting on the sofa in the living room talking with his Mom and Dad. "I invited Carl for dinner," Mrs. Murphy said. "I thought we could get Carl's thoughts about college while we eat. It's ready, so let's move to the table."

Mrs. Murphy had set the table ahead and served each of them a plate brimming with pot roast, a baked sweet potato, and fresh stewed okra. The salad, already on the table, had cherry tomatoes, sesame seeds and croutons. She pointed out the salad dressing, her homemade spicy Italian.

Carl said, "I can't remember when I've had a meal this good. My Mom used to spoil us kids with our meals, but I haven't been home for dinner in a long time, since my folks moved to Arkansas."

As they ate, they talked about Carl's life. He graduated from Brookside High and attended Rock Springs Community College before transferring to Oklahoma State to study physical and occupational therapy. After college, he moved back, secured a state license and started his business. Initially, he worked with his

127

clients, providing physical therapy, but realized there was a need for the kind of services he had been doing for Bobby. He still did a little physical therapy, but had formed a loose association with Karen, who was also a licensed physical therapist. Together, they started a small business that offered a full range of post-hospital rehabilitation services, including physical therapy and teaching life skills. It turned out they had identified a much-needed niche and the business had grown almost to the point of adding another therapist.

"I think your plan to start at a community college makes a lot of sense," Carl said. "Not only because it would ease you into a higher education environment, but also financially. OU and OSU are a lot more expensive -- and big. Not only that, but you'd be able to live at home while you adjust to a new situation."

Bobby asked, "Which one of the two community colleges do you think would be best?"

"Credits from either one will transfer to any of the state universities. I'm not sure about private colleges like Oklahoma City University or Tulsa. When I last visited Rock Springs for a reunion, I checked out the facilities for disabled students. They're coming along, but not quite as good as I saw when I visited Will Rogers. The curriculum at both is virtually identical, so from an academic standpoint, there's really no reason to choose one over the other."

"I just don't know what to do Bobby said. "It's a big decision."

"Why don't you do this," Carl said. "Go ahead and apply to both, so you can get your application in before the fall semester cut off. Then, go visit each of them with your Mom and Dad and see where you think you might be most comfortable. You really can't go wrong with either one."

"Good plan," Mr. Murphy said. "We can do that weekend after next. I know this weekend is busy."

They finished their dinner and Mrs. Murphy cleared the table. "Anyone for dessert," she asked.

Before anyone could say "no," Bobby said "Yes, please."

"Good," she said, "I'd hate for this cherry pie I made this

afternoon to get stale. It's still warm, so a dollop of ice cream on top might be good."

"If I ate this well every night, I'd be the size of a house," Carl said. Then, as though he were afraid the offer of dessert might be withdrawn, he added "But, I sure do enjoy it."

After they finished their cherry pie a la mode, Bobby and Carl went back to Bobby's room. "Let's figure out how you can put on your shoes and socks," Carl said. "I've been waiting for you to be ready for this. Remember how Karen worked with you to maintain flexibility and some muscle tone in your legs and torso, and also strengthen your arms and shoulders? Now we're ready to make use of that. Wheel your chair over beside the bed and lock the wheels with your brake." Carl pulled out a canvas strap from the small gym bag he had with him. "Notice this strap has a couple of loops at one end."

He handed Bobby the strap. "Try to put that bottom loop around your right foot." After a couple misses, Bobby succeeded. Carl took the strap and showed Bobby how to use it to raise his foot and cross his right leg over his left, putting his right heel on the edge of the bed. "Can you lean over and reach past your foot?"

Bobby leaned forward and found he could. Carl took off Bobby's socks and shoes and placed them on the bed. "Reach over and grab one of your socks. Put it over your toes and pull it up." A few tries and Bobby got the sock on his foot. "Now, put on your shoe. This is a little easier with your loafers since you don't have to tie them. But, after you get comfortable with this, you should probably learn to handle shoes with laces."

Bobby sat there with his sock and shoe on his right foot and grinned with pride. "I did it," he said.

Carl looked at him and said, "You did half of it. What about the other foot?"

Bobby's grin faded. "Yeah, that's a problem. I really need shoes and socks on both feet."

"But it's a solvable problem. Turn your chair around to face the other way." Bobby turned his chair. "Now, use the strap and pull up your left foot, just like you did the right one, and put on the other sock and shoe."

After a little more practice, Bobby found he could do it. "Wow," he said. "Now I can put on my own socks and shoes and I won't have to depend on Mom, or anyone to help me."

Carl said, "After a little practice, you should be able to get rid of the strap by pulling your feet up with your hands. But, don't rush it. Use the strap as long as you need to. And, remember, you'll need to put your socks and shoes on the bed where you can reach them before you get started."

Bobby sat there, basking in pleasure with his new skill. Carl said, "Time for me to go. Let me know after you visit the two schools what you think. We can talk some more about it, if you want."

Bobby rolled down the hall with Carl and said goodnight. "Carl, I don't know what I'd do without you."

Carl said, "You'd figure it out. It just would take you a little longer." He turned to Bobby's Mom and Dad, who had joined them at the door. "Thanks for the wonderful meal."

"We'll do it again," she promised. "And, thank you for all you've done for Bobby."

TWENTY-SEVEN

The next morning, Bobby woke early. Using the grab bar by his bed, he got into his wheelchair and went into the bathroom, where he made use of the grab bars to complete getting himself ready to get dressed. He rolled back into the bedroom, put on the clothes he had laid out the night before and prepared to put on his socks and shoes by himself for the first time since his accident. It was a struggle—not quite as easy as when Carl was there to help him. But, with persistence, and stubbornness, he got them on.

When he reached the kitchen, his Mom was fixing breakfast. His Dad was already at the table drinking a cup of black coffee. "Guess what you don't have to help me do today," Bobby said to his Mom.

"Bobby, look at you. You got completely dressed all by yourself."

"I really thought it would take a few days of practice to master that," his Dad said. "Way to go. Another milestone."

Bobby couldn't hide his satisfaction. "Mom, when I get home from practice, will you help me with the applications for college?"

"Sure I will. We should get those in the mail this week. Stop by Miss Winn's office today and ask her to send your transcript to both of them. That'll help get things moving."

Bobby got to school in plenty of time to see Miss Winn before his first class. He filled her in on his plan to apply both places, then visit the schools and make a choice.

"Good plan, Bobby. I'll get your transcripts off today. I don't think you'll have any problem getting accepted."

As he progressed through the school day, each of his teachers had pretty much the same message: "There are only three weeks left of school and, if you plan to get your grades up, now's the time to make an extra effort." Bobby thought his grades would all be at least "B's", with maybe an "A" in geometry and even chemistry.

He also had the matter of Buster Talbot on his mind. How to get through to Buster without a confrontation? He finally came up with a plan. *I hope it works for the team's sake.*

He got to the practice field before the team and waited for Buster to come out of the locker room. Since none of the others really liked him, Buster came out by himself. "Buster," Bobby called, "can I have a quick word with you?"

Buster came over to Bobby's wheelchair. "What is it now, Murphy?" he said. "You gonna bench me, or something?"

Bobby took a deep breath and said, "Maybe. We need to talk. Look Buster, I know you don't like me, and, to tell you the truth, you're not very likeable either. But, we're getting ready to play for the state championship on Saturday and I hope we can put the good of the team ahead of our differences."

When Buster didn't respond, Bobby continued. "You've got the potential to be one of our best hitters, and Saturday we'll need all the hitting we can get. We've talked before about your swing. If you level it out and try to hit line drives, you'll also hit more home runs. Right now, with trying to swing up, you're not hitting anything. Yesterday in batting practice, Coach Booger turned it loose when you came up. And you barely made contact."

Talbot looked at Bobby, a disgusted expression on his face. "Murphy, you think you know it all. If you weren't a weenie in a wheelchair, I'd pound the snot out of you."

Bobby didn't think he could have done that, but let it pass.

"Buster, you can try my suggestion, or ignore it. You might remember the time you did try it, and you ripped the ball. Since you've been back to the upward swing, you haven't had a hit. I'm trying my best to help you, but, if you don't get you're act together at the plate, Marty Ross is going to be playing third base on Saturday."

"You're full of it Murphy," Buster said, with a sneer. "Coach wouldn't bench me for a sophomore."

"Buster, you do what you want. But, I'm telling you, Coach is ready to sit your butt down. He was going to do it after the Muskogee game, but I asked him to give me a chance to talk with you first. If you don't pick it up, he's gonna bench you."

Buster Talbot turned and stalked off without another word. A few minutes later, Bobby saw him in what appeared to be a heated conversation with Coach Brawley. The discussion didn't last very long, and practice started. Bobby took his usual spot behind second base for infield practice, doing little but offering encouragement to Red and Charlie. When the team started batting practice, he moved to a spot behind home plate and made a few notes. He was anxious to watch Buster Talbot's swing. What would he do?

Buster came to the plate. Bobby knew Coach Albright would bear down a little extra. On the first pitch, a fastball, Buster lined it to left field. A right handed hitter, he had no problem pulling the ball. His swing was almost perfectly level. As he continued his turn at the plate, he drilled several more line drives and even put three over the left field wall. *Maybe his dislike of me won't keep him from taking my advice.*

Practice was finally over. Bennie, Charlie and Tommy all came over and greeted Bobby. Al and Ray Roberts stopped by. "Hope you've got a good line on Lawton," Al said.

"Yeah, after what you did for us against Muskogee, we're counting on you," Ray added.

Bobby gulped. "I hope what little I have will help," he said. The players headed for the locker room and Bobby rolled out to the parking lot. He looked for Buster Talbot after practice, but hadn't seen him. *He must really be mad.*

As he got closer to the van, he saw a figure standing by the sliding door. When he got there, he saw it was Talbot. *Maybe he's decided to beat the snot out of me even if I am in a wheelchair.* He remembered his conversation with Carl and put his hand on the can of tear gas.

"Murphy, you really did go to bat for me with Coach. I owe you."

"Buster," Bobby replied. "You don't owe me a thing. I just want what's best for the team, and I know you do, too. And, you hitting like I know you can, will be a great thing for us all."

"I'm gonna give it a try," he said. "Old habits are hard to break, but I'll do my best." Buster turned and headed for his car. "Thanks, Murphy."

Bobby got into his van, and settled himself in the driver's spot. He was relieved that his interaction with Buster Talbot had gone so well. At home, his Mom and Dad were waiting for him.

"Dinner's about ready," his Mom said. "Go wash up and we'll be ready to eat."

He returned from washing his hands and wheeled his chair up to the table. His Mom's meat loaf, mashed potatoes and Brussel sprouts, all favorites, filled his plate.

"Did you make this meal especially for me?" Bobby asked.

"As a matter of fact, I did," his Mom said. "You need to be well fed to complete those applications after we eat."

After dinner, they stayed at the table while Bobby told them about his day. "I have to admit, I was a little nervous about talking with Buster Talbot," he said. "Buster can be a first class jerk, and he doesn't like me at all. But, I was shocked when he met me after practice and said 'thanks.'"

His Dad said, "Bobby, you're a natural leader. That was a stressful thing you had to do, and you handled it very well. I'm not sure I would have done it that well. Oh, and I talked with your

Uncle Tom today in Edmund. He and Robin plan to come down to the City for the game Saturday. He said you and Robin had talked about what to expect from the Lawton boys."

"We did. But, you never know how much good it'll do. What if it turns out to be wrong? It's all based on what Robin said he saw, and he wasn't really scouting them. I guess we'll see. Anyway, it'll be nice to see them."

"Oh, and Laura Sue's riding down with us. I assume Coach Albright is riding down with you."

"Coach Brawley hasn't said anything about that yet, but it's a pretty good guess. I know he won't want me driving by myself."

He excused himself from the table. "Let me know when you're ready to work on those applications," he said to his Mom. "I need to make a quick phone call."

"Tell Laura Sue hello," she said.

When he reached his room, he dialed Laura Sue's number. "Hi, Bobby" she said, answering on the first ring. "I was hoping you'd call. How was practice?"

He told her all about the practice, likely more than she really wanted to know, and about his talks with Buster Talbot. "He really surprised me when he met me at my van after practice. He was almost. . . nice," he said, searching for the right word.

"Well, don't turn your back on him," Laura Sue said. "After all, it's in his own self-interest to take your advice. But, I'll be surprised if he gives you any credit for it. Did your Mom tell you I'm riding down to the City Saturday with them for the game?"

"She did. I'm really glad you'll be there." They chatted for a little while about school, their classes, and so forth when Bobby's Mom came to the door to tell him she was ready to help him with the applications. "I have to go," he said. "My Mom's helping me fill out my application forms for the colleges. I'll see you tomorrow at school. Good night, sleep tight, don't let the bed bugs bite." *That was so stupid. She'll think I'm an idiot.*

"That's cute, Bobby. You're the cleverest person I know. I'll see you tomorrow." *Unbelievable!*

Filling out the two applications turned out to be much easier than he had feared. "I just hope they accept me. Then, if they do, I'll have to make a choice. I have a little homework to do, and then I'm going to bed. I'm getting nervous about Saturday, and it just hit me that the prom is the next weekend, the same time we're planning to go look at the two schools. Lot's going on all at once."

"Indeed there is, but we'll get it done. We don't have to look at both schools on the same day." She left Bobby sitting at the dining room table, opening his geometry book.

TWENTY-EIGHT

The next two days were like a blur. The hot items at school were the upcoming state championship baseball game and the prom, which was set for the following weekend at the Brookside gym. Bobby reported to Miss Winn he had mailed his college applications and she told him she had sent his transcripts. She also gave him some information about applying for scholarships, although the deadline for several of them had expired.

Bobby spent most of his time at baseball practice offering encouragement to the younger players, urging them to be prepared when and if they were called on. Coach Brawley had not named his starting pitcher for Saturday's game, causing Al Tarkinton and Ray Roberts no little anxiety. He told Bobby he was waiting until Friday, at the end of practice, and that both would likely pitch in the game, along with closer Justin Moore.

Bobby didn't divulge Coach Brawley's intentions, but he devoted a good bit of time to reviewing what he knew of Lawton's hitters with them. "Sounds like a dangerous lineup," Al said.

"No question about that," Bobby said. "After all, they are playing in the state championship game."

"Right," Justin said, "but so are we."

Practice on Friday was short, just a quick run through of infield and outfield drills and a shortened batting practice. Before adjourning, Coach Brawley called the team together.

"All right team," he growled in his customary tone, "tomorrow we play for all the marbles. You know what to do, and how to do it. We've gone over it all. You're as ready as I know how to make you. What I want you to do now is have fun. None of you have ever played in a state championship baseball game, and there's a very good chance none of you will get there again, although we'll give it our best next year."

He went over the starting lineup—no change from the one they had used all season. Buster Talbot was in at third base, batting fifth behind Bennie Brown. He still hadn't mentioned the starting pitcher; Ray and Al were growing antsy.

Finally, he said, "Roberts, Tarkinton and Moore, stick around. You too, Murphy. Everyone else, be here dressed in decent clothes. Remember, you're representing your school, so no torn jeans or tee shirts. Bus leaves at 8:15, so be here no later than eight. We'll dress in the locker room at the stadium."

When everyone else had left, Coach Brawley continued. "Roberts, you're starting tomorrow. I plan for you to pitch four, maybe five, innings. You'll be on a pitch count, so you may come out earlier. Tarkinton, you're up next, probably throw three or four innings. Moore, you're the closer. We may need more innings than that from one or two of you, depending on how things go. As you know, we don't have anyone to throw after you, so there's some pressure for you to pitch as long as you can. Booger and I will make that call. Murphy, did you go over Lawton's lineup with them?"

"Sure did, Coach. These guys are ready." Tarkinton, a natural worrier, didn't look so sure, but kept his mouth shut. Coach Albright noticed his expression.

"Tarkinton, you're a good pitcher. And, with Murphy's scouting report, you'll know a little about what to expect. I've watched you all season, and you've pitched great against some better hitters than Lawton has. You'll be fine. Same goes for you, Roberts and Moore. Winners want the ball in their hand when it gets down to the wire, and you three are winners."

When the pitchers had left for the locker room, Coach Brawley looked Bobby in the eye. "What do you think, Murphy? Are they ready?"

"Coach, I really believe they are. All three of those guys will pitch in college next year, and, like Coach Albright said, they're winners. They'll be fine." *Sure hope I'm right. But, at this point, even if I'm wrong, it's too late to do anything about it.*

"I'm assuming you'll drive down to the City in your van. Coach Albright will ride with you. I'm sure you'd rather have some of your buddies riding with you, but insurance and county school policy won't let that happen because it's a school sanctioned function."

He turned to Coach Albright. "That ok with you, Coach?"

"Well, I'll be terrified the whole way, but I'll suck it up, maybe keep my eyes closed for the trip." He winked at Bobby.

"Then, you two can follow the bus down, so you won't get lost and end up in Ardmore or Dallas. If you can be here by eight, that would be good. Whole trip won't take more than a couple hours. We'll be there in plenty of time to get dressed, stretched out and get our infield warm-ups and batting practice in. Murphy, I hope you're right about Talbot. We're gonna need his bat."

So do I. So do I.

When he got home, dinner was waiting. The grilled pork chops looked so good, he momentarily forgot his anxiety. As the family ate, they each discussed their day. Bobby's Mom had resumed volunteering at the library and thought they would probably give her regular job back in the next couple months. His Dad tried to make his day at the office sound interesting, but approving some invoices and chairing a routine department meeting just wasn't very exciting.

"How was school, Bobby," his Dad finally asked, giving up on his entertaining workday report.

"Good. Miss Winn gave me some information on scholarships, so I need to look that over. And, practice went good, too. Ray Roberts is starting tomorrow, and Al will follow him, with Justin

Moore closing it out. I need to be at the school by eight in the morning. Coach Albright's riding with me again. I'm looking forward to that. He's a really nice guy."

"That'll work out good," his Dad said. "We'll leave here about eleven, pick up Laura Sue and Buddy, and head down. Probably stop off for lunch somewhere so we don't have to eat cardboard hamburgers at the ballpark. The game starts at two, doesn't it?"

"Right. Are you gonna see Robin and Uncle Joe?"

"We'll meet up with them at the ballpark," his Dad said.

"I hope I'll get to talk a little with Robin. Maybe we'll get a minute or two before the game."

Mom arrived with the remnants of last night's pecan pie, this time topped with whipped cream.

"I believe I may have died and gone to heaven," Bobby said, as he shoveled in the dessert.

TWENTY-NINE

The drive down to Oklahoma City was uneventful. Bobby and Coach Albright followed the team bus and chatted about the game. "I sure hope the info I got from my cousin was right," Bobby said.

"Me too," the coach replied. "By the way, that was some good work you did with Buster Talbot. I'm not sure he's smart enough to appreciate what you did for him, but Coach Brawley was impressed."

Bobby told him about how Talbot was waiting for him at his van after practice. "I was a little nervous at first. I can't do much to defend myself in this chair. But, it worked out. I think he meant it. Now, I just hope he sticks with the level swing."

"I guess we'll see soon enough. If he does, he can be a tremendous asset for the team, and I have a feeling we'll need all the help we can get."

Bobby followed the bus to the front of the stadium in Oklahoma City. The facility was only two or three years old and the home of the Oklahoma City Dodgers, minor league affiliate of the Los Angeles Dodgers. The team exited the bus and entered the stadium. Bobby and Coach Albright tailed the bus to a reserved parking space in a lot marked "Players Only." It was a short distance back to the stadium entrance. When they went in, they found the rest of the team waiting for them, most gawking at their surroundings.

Coach Brawley was talking to a man who looked official. They shook hands and the coach addressed the team. "OK guys, listen up. We're the home team, so we get the home locker room. Your uniforms are already there, so let's head on down and get suited up." He led the way to the locker room.

The team got on their home uniforms; white pants with a navy blue stripe down the leg and solid blue navy shirts with gold numbers and "Rangers" in gold script across the chest. The uniforms looked brand new, and slightly different from the home uniforms they wore all season. Those uniforms had white shirts with blue pin stripes.

"These new uniforms were donated by an anonymous supporter when we won our district. Had no doubt we would get this far, so wear them proudly. This team has a lot of pride, and I have a lot of confidence in you. Boys, I don't say this often, probably not often enough, but I'm really proud of all of you. We've overcome a lot, and even had some good luck along the way. Now, let's hit the field and get ready to play one more. When we get out on the field, take a minute to look around. This is a bigger and nicer place than you've ever played before. Get over it. Remember, it's just a ballpark, a nice one, but still essentially the same field you've played on all season."

They went down the tunnel that connected the locker room with the dugout. The tunnel was ramped with no steps. The dugout and the field were all on the same level, so Bobby was easily able to navigate his chair without any help. While the team was doing their stretching, Bobby looked around. *What a neat place for a game. I sure wish I were playing instead of watching. It would almost be like playing at Wrigley Field. Not quite, but almost.*

They transitioned into batting practice. Bobby suggested to Coach Albright that he have the outfielders go to their positions while the others were hitting so they would have a chance to see how the balls came off the outfield wall and also get used to the warning track. Overhearing the comment, Coach Brawley said, "Good idea, Murphy. You may earn your keep yet."

Bobby carefully watched each hitter as they took their swings.

He was particularly attentive when Buster Talbot stepped into the box. It looked to Bobby like Buster still had a little uphill angle to his swing. He didn't say anything, but made a mental note in case he needed to mention it later. After the Rangers finished their batting practice, the Lawton Cowboys took over for theirs. Bobby watched as they took their turn, but, with batting practice pitching, no particular tendencies were apparent. He noticed, however, several of them hit with a lot of power. Nothing he hadn't already anticipated.

When the Cowboys completed their batting, the Rangers began their infield and outfield warm-ups. Bobby took note of the infielders, and their performance in the drills. Red Freeman appeared to Bobby to be a little nervous, and a couple of his throws to first were over Bennie's head. *I'll have a little chat with him when he comes off the field.*

Turning back toward the dugout, Bobby noticed the fans beginning to file into their seats. He didn't see his Mom and Dad – or Laura Sue – yet, but leaning over the rail beside the Rangers' dugout was his cousin, Robin, and Uncle Joe. Bobby was struck by how much Robin looked like Uncle Joe, and how closely Uncle Joe resembled his brother, Bobby's Dad.

"Hey, Uncle Joe, Robin," Bobby called, and rolled over to the railing. "Thanks for coming. How are you doing?"

"Wouldn't miss this for the world," Uncle Joe replied. "We're doing fine. Lookin' forward to a good ball game. I sure hope you beat these guys. When we lost to them in the playoffs, I thought they were a bunch of jerks. They sort of looked down their noses at us, and just generally weren't very classy winners."

"Before I forget it," said Robin, "I remembered a little more. Their two big guns are Johnny Brewster at first base and Seth Rogers in left field. They hit three and four in their batting order. What I wanted to tell you is neither one can hit a curve ball. They're both easy to get off balance with a change-up right after a fast ball. Their fifth batter, Teddy Wilson, a real jerk by the way, loves curves, but can't hit a fast ball on the inside of the plate. But, groove one down the middle to any of them and you can probably watch it sail over the fence, even in this big ballpark."

"Thanks, Robin, this is good stuff. I'm just getting' ready to head out to the bullpen. Ray, our starter today, is warming up. I'll make sure he, and the other guys scheduled to pitch today, know all that. We probably won't have much chance to talk after the game, but let's try to get together when school's out."

"We will. Good luck today."

Bobby rolled himself out to the bullpen where Ray Roberts was just beginning his stretching routine. Al and Justin came over. Tommy Jones, already in his catcher's gear, joined them. Bobby reviewed what he had learned about the Lawton hitters. "Ray, make sure you don't give their leadoff guy a good pitch to bunt. Either on the knees or at the very top of the strike zone ought to make it harder for him. We'll have Buster and Bennie playing in, ready for the bunt, but not too obvious. Same thing with number two. Then, for three and four, a fastball out of the zone to set it up, then nothing but off speed and breaking stuff. Their fifth guy, Wilson, besides being a jerk, loves curve balls, so I suggest you bust him with heat on the inside first, then the outside. He's got a big ego and won't want to take a walk. The rest of their line-up are contact hitters. They'll probably put the ball in play, but you've got a good defense behind you, so that should work out okay.

"Oh," Bobby continued, "if you forget any of this, don't worry. Tommy has it all memorized. He'll let you know what to do." He looked over at Tommy, who took a big gulp.

"Right."

Bobby left the pitchers to their preparations and returned to the dugout. Coach Brawley asked about his pre-game "chat" with the pitchers. Bobby filled him in. "I like the idea of third and first being ready for the bunts, but not showing it. Perfect bunt will prob'ly work, but odds are against that, especially if Roberts is making it hard on them. Booger'll be calling the pitches and signaling

Jones, so while we're in the field, you need to stay close and help him. Then, get back to the end of the bench and sit with Jones and Roberts."

"Got it, Coach," Bobby said, hoping with all his might his scouting report was accurate.

The teams finished their pre-game warm-ups. The starters and coaches for both teams were introduced by the public address announcer. When the rest of the team joined them on the base lines, the announcer asked the crowd to stand and remove their hats. Then, he said, "Fresh from Nashville and back home to Oklahoma, let's give a warm Sooner welcome to one of our own, Reba McCall."

Wow. My favorite country singer of all time.

When Reba, who was wearing a western style skirt and shirt, with blue fancy stitched cowboy boots, finished singing the National Anthem, she flashed a smile that dazzled both teams, and especially the coaches. "She's got the prettiest red hair of anyone I've ever seen," Coach Albright said.

Bobby, who had joined the team on the first base line with the coaches, returned to the dugout, scanning the stands for a sight of his Mom and Dad, and Laura Sue. Just as he spotted them and waved, Coach Brawley growled, "Murphy, Brown, let's go. The umps are waiting."

THIRTY

Bobby turned and rolled back out to home plate for the pre-game meeting with the umpires and opposing coach, who had also brought his captains. The Lawton coach, Enos Schlacter, was a legend in Oklahoma baseball circles. After an all-American career at Oklahoma State, he played ten years in the majors with the St. Louis Cardinals. When he retired, he declined the opportunity to be a professional coach and returned to his hometown, where he coached for the last ten years. He won two state championships and was runner-up five times. Brookside hoped he would end the day with six runner-ups.

Coach Brawley and Coach Schlacter shook hands with each other and with the umpires. Then, each introduced their captains. To Bobby's surprise, Coach Schlacter said, "Murphy, I've heard a lot of good things about you. You've showed a lot of courage, and it's an honor to meet you."

Bobby was stunned. How would someone as famous as Coach Schlacter even know who he was? "The honor is mine, Coach," he stammered. "I've followed your career since I was a little kid."

Finally, it was game time—the game both teams had waited for and worked all season to get. The state championship was on the line, and only one would go home a winner. While it would be Lawton's third in the past ten years, it was Brookside's first time in the finals. The team's nerves were showing as Coach Brawley gathered them around.

"Boys," he began, "we've worked our butts off all season to get here. We can't let up now. But, remember this: it's only a baseball game. We all really want to win and go home state champs. If we do, it will be something you can be proud of all your lives. If we don't, you've got no reason to hang your heads. Let's go out and give it our best, but most of all, have fun." *Who is this guy? He looks like Coach Brawley, but he's not growling and he's telling us to have fun.* No matter, the team responded clapping each other on the back, jumping up and down and chanting "Rangers, Rangers."

The stadium was packed. It appeared to be about half full of fans from each team. The Brookside fans, clad in their navy blue shirts and caps were mostly on the first base side, behind the Rangers' dugout. Lawton's fans, in their green shirts and gold caps, anchored the third base line.

"Brookside. Rangers. Brookside. Rangers," the first base side yelled.

"Lawton. Cowboys," the third base side responded with equal fervor. The teams were ready.

As the home team, Brookside took the field first. Ray strode to the mound to begin his warmup tosses. Trying to look calm and composed, he launched his first throw five feet over Tommy's head. The ball hit the wall behind home plate and bounced straight back to the catcher. The situation was so ludicrous, with Ray trying to look so together and then throwing the ball like he did, he couldn't help but laugh at himself. It broke the tension, and he completed his warmups flawlessly.

Lawton's leadoff hitter, a lefty, came to the plate, took a couple mighty swings and settled into the batter's box. Buster and Bennie crept in, expecting the bunt. Ray went into his windup, and the hitter squared to bunt and, thinking he would catch them by surprise, he dropped the ball down the third base line. But, Buster was ready and fired a strike to Red Freeman covering first. Then, Buster and Bennie went back to their normal positions.

The second batter hit from the right side. Just like the leadoff, he took several mighty swings and stepped up to the plate. This time, the bunt went down the first base line, where Bennie was waiting. Bennie picked it up and underhanded it to Ray Roberts for the out. Lawton's trickery had not been successful. Coach Albright gave Bobby a 'thumbs up.'

Lawton's third baseman, Johnny Brewster, was next up. Remembering Bobby's scouting report, Ray cut loose with a fastball, high and inside, forcing Brewster to scramble to avoid being hit. Next, he threw an off speed breaking ball that started out for Brewster's head and broke languidly across the plate. Brewster bailed out, and the umpire said, "Strike one." Ray threw the next pitch fast and low, just off the plate knee high. Now, it was two balls and one strike. Tommy called for the slider, a hard fast pitch that broke sharply. Brewster took a hard cut at it, but missed. Two and two. Ray finished him off with another slider, this time low and breaking off the corner. Brewster swung hard again, and missed again.

Ray came to the bench and sat down between Bobby and Tommy Jones. "Did you see my first warmup pitch?"

"Yep," Bobby answered. "Best thing you could have done. In fact, I think it would be a good idea to throw one warmup wild every inning. It might keep them looser at the plate. You look good out there, Ray. Only seven pitches. Use the same strategy on the next two hitters. Then, you'll have to pitch to the rest of the line-up. Just remember, they don't strike out a lot and they'll make contact. So, if they get a hit here or there, don't worry about it."

In the bottom of the first, the Cowboy's ace, Orel Hershman, took the mound. With his slim six foot five inch frame, he was as intimidating as Robin had said. Brick Nelson led off, striking out on a curve ball at least a foot out of the strike zone. Charlie Levin hit a line drive on a fastball, but it was right at the second baseman.

Tommy Jones fouled off seven pitches before striking out, like Brick, on a curve ball way off the plate. One, two, three.

Neither team scored in the first four innings. Ray kept the Cowboys off balance, scattering three hits and following the strategy Bobby had suggested. But, Hershman matched him and had six strikeouts, mostly on pitches that would have been balls had the Brookside batters not swung. Through four, Brookside had no hits and had not hit a ball out of the infield. Bobby paid particular attention to the two players he thought of as his 'projects.' Buster Talbot had not made solid contact with the ball in two at-bats. It appeared to Bobby that the slight upswing was there in his second time at the plate. Red Freeman was also having problems, and had struck out twice swinging at balls out of the strike zone.

Bobby pondered how to approach the problems. He decided to wait to talk to Buster until he had one more plate appearance. But, Red needed some help now before he got even more down. Red already had some self-esteem issues on the diamond and didn't need to feed them further. "Red, can I see you a minute," Bobby called as Red returned to the bench after his second strikeout, his body language evidencing how discouraged he was.

"Bobby, look at me. I just can't hit this guy, or probably anyone else. I don't belong out there. I think I'm gonna ask Coach to take me out and put someone else in who can hit."

"Red, I know you're frustrated. But, look, no one else has a hit either. And, Charlie has looked every bit as bad as you have. You can do two things that I guarantee will help. First, stop swinging at bad pitches. Worst case, you walk. And then you're on base. Second thing; remember when we talked about picturing hitting a line drive right at the pitcher. Get the image in your head of the ball leaving your bat and hitting him right in the chest. If you visualize it, you can do it. You just have to be sure you're swinging at a strike and not a ball out of the zone."

"Okay, I'll try," Red said, not sounding convinced.

"Look Red. I know you're down, frustrated, discouraged— all

149

of that. But, think back to the talks we've had during the season. Whenever you took my advice, it worked, didn't it? I want you to do more than try. I want you to do it."

"I'll give it my best, Bobby. You're right. Your tips have all paid off. I'll do it."

In the top of the fifth, Ray missed his spot with a fastball to Brewster. Brewster hit it over the left field wall. As near as Bobby could tell, it was the only bad pitch Ray had thrown. "Hang in there Ray," Bobby shouted. "It was just one pitch." Ray gave him a thumbs up to indicate he was okay. He got the next two batters on weak ground balls. The Lawton "big three" still had only one hit. Unfortunately, that hit put them up 1-0.

Leading off the bottom of the fifth, Charlie Levin nailed a sharp single to right. While he was still in the on deck circle, Tommy looked over at Bobby. "Patient, patient, patient," he said softly. Bobby gave him a nod. Practicing his own preaching, Tommy took the bad pitches and walked. Brookside had two on, no one out and Bennie Brown, their clean-up hitter coming to the plate. Bobby called over to him, "Be patient, Bennie."

Bennie stepped in to face Hershman, a set look on his face. The first pitch was a fastball right down the middle. Bennie swung as hard as he could and whiffed. He stepped out, took a breath, looked over to where Bobby was sitting and set himself for the next pitch. This time the pitch, a breaking ball, was a foot outside. He took it. The third pitch was a fastball down the middle and Bennie made contact. Unfortunately, his contact was a sharp ground ball to the shortstop who flipped it to the second baseman, who threw to first to complete the double play. Now Brookside had a runner on third but two out.

While Bennie was on deck, Bobby approached Buster, unsure how he'd be received. "Buster, can I make a couple suggestions," he said. He and Buster had not exchanged any words, other than a cursory greeting, since that day in the parking lot.

"Whatcha got, Murphy?"

"I just wanted to remind you about the level swing, Buster. It looked to me like you let a little upswing slip in on your last at bat. Think about how well it worked when you did. Also, remember to be patient. This guy's wild and almost all his strikeouts have been on balls. We could really use a hit, but a walk would at least get us a base runner."

Buster didn't say any more. When Bennie went to the plate, he took his place in the on-deck circle. All Bobby could do at this point was hope for the best; and the best was what they got. Buster, with a perfectly level swing, drilled a double into the left-centerfield gap, scoring Charlie and tying the game. Even though Marty Ross, the designated hitter, grounded out to second, stranding Buster, the game was tied. New life!

But, that new life was short-lived. Al Tarkinton came in to pitch in the sixth. Before he settled down, Lawton scored two more runs on three hits. "Coach, you gotta go talk to him. Calm him down," Bobby said to Coach Albright.

"I think you're right," he said. Calling time, he headed for the mound. "Al, what's wrong with you? You aren't throwing the ball where Tommy's calling for it and you don't look sharp."

"Yeah, Coach. I don't have it today."

"Al, you better get it, and get it quick. Justin's all we got left, and it's too early to bring him in. Not only is the state championship on the line, you've got scouts from several colleges in the stands. If you want to win a championship, and pitch in college, it's time to suck it up. You've done it before."

"Break it up," the umpire said. Coach Albright returned to the bench. Al stepped off the mound, looked around the field and took a deep breath. Something in Al's posture or demeanor looked different to Bobby. He appeared to be more intense, more confident.

He looked over at the runner on first and chased him back to the base with a slow toss over to Bennie. As Al got set, the runner took a little larger lead. Al responded with a much quicker move to first and picked the runner off. One out and no base runners. The next batter was Lawton's leadoff hitter. He laid down an almost perfect bunt, but it was quickly scooped up by Al, who threw him out. He then proceeded to strike out the last hitter and they were out of the inning. But, Lawton now held a 3-1 lead.

Al held off the Lawton offense with precision pitching, following the formula that Bobby had suggested. Unfortunately, so did Hershman, and despite a couple hits and walks by each team, they entered the top of the ninth with Lawton still leading 3-1. As planned, Justin Moore came out of the bullpen to pitch the ninth for Brookside. The first Lawton batter was Ted Wilson. "You losers are going down," he said to Tommy. Following the plan, Justin struck Wilson out on three pitches.

"Not to you, though," Tommy told Wilson as the third strike buried itself in the catcher's mitt. The next batter was a pinch hitter. Bobby had no information that might be helpful. Justin threw him a fastball on the outside half of the plate, then turned and watched as the towering fly ball off the hitter's bat cleared the right field fence by two feet.

Coach Albright stood, gave Justin a palm down sign and called out "Don't worry Moore. We'll get it back." Although the stands, particularly the Lawton side, were as loud as they had been all game, Justin, who obviously couldn't hear the coach, shrugged. "Got it," he seemed to say.

Using a blazing fastball and a nasty off speed curve, Justin fanned the next two batters. But, it was crunch time for Brookside. They had worked their tails off all season to get here, and now in the state championship game, bottom of the ninth, they trailed 4-1. Things didn't look good for the Rangers, but they had the top of their line-up coming to the plate. When Brick Nelson stepped into the batter's box, the Brookside fans stood as one and cheered.

Lawton had changed pitchers for the ninth, putting in Cliff Marshall to close the game. While not as tall and rangy as Hershman, he had better control. He also had a better curve ball, but his fastball was not quite as quick. Bobby thought back to the scouting report Robin had given him. *This guy has a good curve ball, but he telegraphs it with a different motion.* Too late to get that information to Brick, but he got the next four batters together and let them know. "I'm not sure what the difference in his delivery is, so you'll have to watch him closely, but it should be there," said Bobby.

Brick hit a weak ground ball back to the pitcher on a nasty curve. The Lawton team was at the rail of their dugout, anticipating the win. Two outs away from a state championship. Charlie Levin took his place in the batter's box. Fans from both teams were urging on their favorites at the top of their lungs. Charlie calmly stepped out, calling time, just before Marshall went into his motion. Looking irritated, Marshall proceeded to walk Charlie, an uncharacteristic mistake for the Lawton closer. Tommy Jones also stepped out just before the pitch, and Marshall was clearly rattled. He tried to sneak a fastball by Tommy, but Tommy was ready for it and lined a single to left. The Brookside fans went wild.

The Lawton coach called time, and went out to try to calm down his pitcher. He appeared to have succeeded when Marshall immediately threw two curves to Bennie for strikes. Trying to lure Bennie into swinging at strike three, he threw him three curve balls in a row that just missed. Recalling that Bobby had told him Marshall always went to the fastball when he needed a strike, Bennie dug in. As Bobby had predicted, Marshall went to the fastball. Bennie was ready and hit a sharp line drive over Wilson's head into left field, scoring Charlie from second. Now, Brookside had runners on first and third with one out and Lawton's lead was down to two runs.

As Buster Talbot left the on-deck circle and strode to the plate, he glanced back at Bobby. *Anything but a double play ball, Buster.* Buster lowered his bat and, with his right arm, made a sweeping, level motion. "Now we'll see if you were right about Talbot," Coach Brawley said. Bobby felt the pressure. If Buster hit the double play ball, would it be his fault?

But, Buster didn't hit into a double play. He drilled the first pitch over the center fielder's head, and out of the ballpark for the game winning home run. It took a second or two for it to register, and then the team began jumping up and down and headed for home plate to mob Buster when he crossed. The Brookside fans went crazy. "Brookside. Rangers," went the chant, repeated over and over. The Lawton fans were totally silent.

After the expected 'dog pile', and more minutes of jumping up and down and patting each other on the back, the teams lined up to pass each other with a handshake. Most of the Lawton players had some brief congratulatory message for the Rangers, disappointed as they all were. But, third baseman, Ted Wilson, refused to shake hands, or even look at any of the Brookside players.

Bobby stayed in the dugout during the celebration and the handshake pass. But, when the team gathered to salute their fans, Buster Talbot broke off and came into the dugout. "Murphy, get out here with us. You had as much to do with our winning this game as anyone. Without you, I wouldn't have even been playing today. And, even if I was, I darn sure wouldn't have got that hit." With that, he pushed Bobby's chair out to join the team. As the fans in the stands saw Bobby clear the dugout, they cheered even louder. The team all gathered around his wheelchair, clapping him on the back, some even bending over and hugging him.

Bobby, already an inspiration for the team, had become a symbol of their success for the fans. He looked into the stands, searching for his parents and Laura Sue. He spotted his Dad first. Next to him were Uncle Joe and Robin, cheering madly. On his Dad's other side, he saw his Mom and Laura Sue hugging. *Are they crying? What's with that?*

Bobby's Dad made his way down to the rail and Bobby rolled over. "We're all going to Longhorn's for steaks to celebrate when we get home. My treat. Meet us there when you get back."

Bobby went back to the dugout where the team was gathering their gear. Coach Brawley was waiting for him. "Murphy, we absolutely would not have won this game without your scouting reports. You did more for Ranger baseball today than anyone. I'm proud to have you on our team." His words, and his manner, were so out of character for the normally gruff and aloof coach that Bobby was moved beyond words.

After a couple deep breaths, he managed a reply. "Thanks Coach. I just did what I could. Anyone could have done it."

"No, not just anyone could have reached Buster Talbot, or calmed our pitching staff, or given Freeman the confidence he needed. And, I still owe you and Booger a steak dinner for the one you missed in Tulsa last week." The Coach turned and walked away.

Bobby looked back at the stands, hoping to catch one more glimpse of Laura Sue. He need not have worried. She was down standing by the rail where his Dad had been. He rolled over to her. "We won," he said, still reeling with the thrill of victory.

"Bobby, I'm so proud of you," she said, tears still streaming down her face. "I've got to go. Your Mom and Dad are ready to leave, but I'll see you at dinner."

Waiting patiently behind Laura Sue were Uncle Joe and Robin. "Way to go," Uncle Joe said.

"Yeah," Robin chimed in. "You guys were great. Nothing like the drama of a walk off win to win State."

"Robin," Bobby said. "We wouldn't have done it without your help. I'm gonna ask Coach Brawley to make you an honorary Ranger."

"No, no, don't do that. If the word got out in Edmund, I'd be in trouble." They all had a good laugh.

"Well, thanks for coming," Bobby said to both of them. "Robin, we'll get together this summer and catch up. Now, I better go, Coach Booger, er Coach Albright, is waiting for me to chauffer him home."

THIRTY-ONE

obby dropped Coach Albright at the school. They passed the team bus just outside Oklahoma City and reached Brookside well ahead. Bobby headed for Longhorn. The word on their victory had obviously already gotten to the restaurant and, when Bobby rolled in through the front door, a lot of the diners began clapping and calling out congratulations.

Longhorn had a room in the back, where their group could eat all together. It was an intimate setting with western art displayed on the walls and even had a set of Texas longhorn horns over the door. There was a long table in the center with four place settings down each side. They had reserved a place at the head of the table for Bobby. On his right sat Laura Sue. Next to her was her brother, Buddy. The seat on Bobby's left was empty, and he noticed three other places down the side of the table were also vacant. Before he could ask about the empty seats, Carl entered the room. Bobby's Dad directed him to the seat on Bobby's left.

"We ran into Carl at the game and decided it wouldn't be a proper celebration without him," his Dad announced. Bobby started to ask about the other three seats, but his Dad said, "Eddie and Riley are on their way. We saw them at the game and, since they had a big part in getting you to the games early in the season, I decided they should be here, too."

Bobby was impressed with his Dad's generosity. *This is going to be an expensive dinner for Dad. I hope he can afford it.*

Eddie and Riley walked in a minute or two later. "Sorry we're late, Mr. M. We got a little lost leaving the City," said Eddie. "My navigator here," pointing at Riley, "got us into a parking lot and we had to ask directions to get out."

"It wasn't a parking lot," said Riley. "It was a parking garage. I thought we were on a level below ground, so we started winding our way upward and ended up on the roof. If Christopher Columbus here had just followed the sign that said 'Exit,' we'd have been out in no time."

"Well, "said Mr. Murphy amid the laughter, "if you two candidates for a National Geographic Explorer's internship can find your way to two of those empty seats, we'll get started."

Just before Bobby asked who the last seat was for, Coach Albright made his entrance. Bobby was surprised. He didn't even know his Dad knew Coach Albright. His Dad got up and greeted the coach. "In case there's anyone here who doesn't know Coach Albright, let me introduce him," he began. "Coach Albright was Bobby's companion and roommate for the playoff game in Tulsa and accompanied Bobby on his drive to the City today. After they won the first game in Tulsa, while the rest of the team went out and celebrated with a nice dinner, Coach Albright and Bobby stayed for the Muskogee - McAlester game to scout the winner. When I called Coach Brawley to congratulate him on beating Muskogee, he told me that it was largely because of the scouting report these two guys prepared. Coach Albright has worked closely with the team, and with Bobby, this season, and I wanted to include him in our little celebration tonight."

"Thanks for the kind words, Mr. Murphy," the coach said. "But, most of the credit goes to Bobby. I was there, but he's the one who picked up on the pitches we were likely to see, and what our pitchers needed to do to stop Muskogee, and Lawton today. And during the season, Bobby worked with some of the players on their mechanics and on their mindsets. We had the game winning home run today because Bobby had worked with Buster Talbot on his swing. Coach Brawley and I hadn't been able to get through to him, but Bobby got the job done." He sat down, looking a little embarrassed at the length of his speech. *That's the longest I've ever heard Coach Booger talk.*

Before anyone else could hold forth, the waitress came in and began taking their dinner orders. Since they were in a restaurant specializing in steaks, everyone ordered a steak. The two ladies, Mrs. Murphy and Laura Sue ordered small filets, while the men ordered sirloins, prime ribs and ribeyes. Bobby looked over at Laura Sue. "How did you like the game?"

"I thought it was the most exciting game I've ever seen. From what Coach Albright said, you were really important in getting the wins with Muskogee and today with Lawton. I'm so proud of you."

While they were eating their salads, Carl asked, loudly enough for all to hear, "Does everyone know the story about how I helped Brookside win its regional a few years ago?"

Almost as one, Eddie, Riley, Coach Albright and Bobby said, "Yes. A hundred times."

Carl looked kind of disappointed until Buddy piped up, "I haven't heard it."

"Neither have I," Laura Sue said, drawing a bemused look from Bobby.

"We haven't heard it either," Mr. Murphy said.

"Well then," Carl said, casting a look at the four who said they had heard it 'a hundred times.' He proceeded to tell them how he had been on the team that won the regional and had warmed up the relief pitcher in the bullpen. He also mentioned that he had major league scouts watching him, drawing a loud groan from Eddie. Carl just grinned.

When the steaks came, conversation stopped for the first few minutes while everyone prepared their baked potatoes and began eating. As the conversation began again, Laura Sue turned to

Bobby. "I know you've been busy and probably don't know about it, but the choral department's having its annual concert Tuesday night. I'm in the Senior Choir, and also a madrigal group. It would mean a lot to me if you could come." She gave him a shy smile.

Are you kidding me? I wouldn't miss it for anything. "Sure," he replied. "I can be there. What time is it?"

"It starts at eight," she said, "but you probably should try to get there a little early. There's usually a big crowd at these things."

After everyone finished dinner, and those who wanted desert finished that, Bobby's Dad stood up. "I want to thank everyone for coming. I know it was short notice, but who knew Brookside would win State today?"

Interrupting Mr. Murphy, Coach Albright interjected "Bobby and I did."

"You bet we did," Bobby said. "There was never a doubt."

"Now that we have that settled," Mr. Murphy said, "Bobby, do you want to say anything?"

Bobby, embarrassed, started to decline. But, out of the corner of his eye, he saw Laura Sue looking at him expectantly. He decided he better say something. "I also want to thank everyone for coming. It was a great day for Brookside, but I want to correct Coach Albright. He's the one that deserves the credit for the scouting report. I wouldn't have had any idea what to look for without him helping me. And, as far as Buster's hitting, Coach is the one who proved to him he needed to adjust his swing. Buster would never have bought into needing to make a change if Coach Albright hadn't been pitching batting practice that day. Remember that, Coach?"

"I remember, but I also remember whose idea it was to pitch him hard. And, I also know that you picked up stuff when we were scouting Muskogee that I didn't even notice. So Bobby, don't be so modest. You da man."

Bobby turned bright red, while everyone at the table clapped.

Not to be left out, Carl said, "I'd like to say something, too. I've been working with Bobby ever since he came home after the accident. In the years I've been doing this, I've never had a patient as determined as Bobby. He's accomplished an incredible, almost unbelievable, improvement. I'm proud of his contribution to the baseball team, but I'm most impressed with his character and determination." Carl sat down as they all applauded.

Dinner over, everyone began to leave, stopping by Bobby's chair to say goodnight and thanking Mr. Murphy on the way out. Eddie and Riley came over. "Don't know what the big deal is," Eddie said. "You're our friend, and friends stick together. I don't want to get all mushy, so I'll see you at school Monday." Turning to Mr. Murphy, he said," Thanks for including me and Riley, Mr. M. The dinner was great. I'm gonna tell my Dad about this place."

"Yeah, Mr. M. thanks," Riley said. "But, I bet Eddie's Dad already knows about it. He's just too smart to bring Eddie here." Realizing he had in effect implied Bobby's Dad was not too smart, since he had invited Eddie, Riley quickly added, "I didn't mean you aren't too smart." He looked embarrassed and said, "You know what I mean?"

Mr. Murphy chuckled. "I'm glad you guys could make it. And, I'm thankful Bobby has friends like the two of you."

Soon it was just Bobby, his parents, Laura Sue and Buddy, and Coach Albright. "Bobby, you're too modest, but thanks for the kind words. Mr. and Mrs. Murphy, thank you so much for inviting me. I have really enjoyed working with Bobby this season, and, I might add, I've learned a lot from him."

"Coach, I'm glad you could come. I invited Coach Brawley, but he already had another commitment. Just so you know," he said to Coach Albright and Bobby, "Coach Brawley kicked in a hundred dollars toward this meal. He said owed you two guys a steak dinner, and wanted to settle the score."

THIRTY-TWO

"I need to stop by the Minute Mart to pick up something on the way home," Bobby said to his Mom and Dad. He casually added, or at least tried to sound casual, "How about if I take Laura Sue and Buddy home?"

"I think that would be nice," Mrs. Murphy said, before her husband could object.

"Isn't anyone going to ask me if I want Bobby to take us home?" Laura Sue asked. Bobby, his Mom and Dad all looked at her.

"Well, don't you want me to take you home?"

"I do," she said. "I just wanted to be asked." Turning to Mr. and Mrs. Murphy, she said, "Thanks for taking Buddy and me to the game, and thanks also for the great dinner. This has been a wonderful day."

Laura Sue, Buddy and Bobby made their way out to Bobby's van and got in. Laura Sue took the front passenger seat, while Buddy sat in the rear. With the middle row of seats removed so Bobby's wheelchair could maneuver, Buddy was a long way back. "Don't forget about me," he called, holding his hands like a megaphone around his mouth. "It's a long way from way back here to way up there." Bobby and Laura Sue laughed.

"Don't worry, Buddy. You have rear seat duty. You're in charge of keeping order in the back. If anybody steps out of line, just let me know. I've got my pepper spray and my billy club right here."

"You've got pepper spray and a billy club?" Laura Sue asked. "Whatever for?"

"Carl talked me into carrying them as a 'just-in-case' thing. When he added these saddle bags to my chair so I'd have a place to carry stuff, he stuck in the spray and the club so, if I ever needed to, I'd be able to defend myself. You may have noticed my footwork is not too fancy these days. The only time I even thought about using them was that night after practice when Buster was waiting for me in the parking lot. But, luckily, I didn't have to. Still, it was kind of comforting to know I had them."

"I sure hope you don't need them when you're with me," she said. "I meant to say I hope you don't ever need them at all."

They arrived at the Minute Mart and pulled into a parking space right in front. There was only one other vehicle, a rusty fifteen year old Ford pick-up that looked like it had once been blue. Bobby noticed a Bixby High School Spartans decal in the rear window. *What are people from Bixby doing up here? They're a long way from home.*

"That old truck looks like it's from Bixby," Bobby told Laura Sue. "We beat Bixby during the season. Their fans and players were really nasty. They were the worst sports we played all year. One of their team parents got on Coach Brawley so bad that I thought Coach might go into the stands after him. When we got home, he dropped them from our schedule for next year and after."

"Maybe whoever has that truck will be nice," she replied. "Buddy and I'll wait here."

Bobby opened the door and rolled out of the van and up to the automatic door opener button at the store. As soon as he entered the store and the doors shut behind him, he knew something wasn't right. He looked to his left, toward the cashier. He recognized the young man behind the counter, but couldn't recall his name, maybe Ralph. The cashier was standing rigid and Bobby noticed a drop of blood coming from his nose. His face, upon a closer look, appeared bruised.

"Are you ok, Ralph isn't it?" Bobby asked.

Ralph didn't respond right away. Bobby heard a sound coming from behind the counter, but not from Ralph. He couldn't make most of it out, but someone apparently hiding behind the counter was talking to Ralph. "Turn around and get out. We're closed," Ralph said. But, the way he said it... his voice trembled.

Bobby assessed the situation. Someone was holding Ralph hostage, and probably robbing the place. *Was the perpetrator alone, or did he have accomplices?* He couldn't turn around and run away, leaving Ralph to the robbers. "I'm not leaving Ralph. The police are on their way." A bold bluff. *Hope they believe me.*

When he said that, the previously unseen figure behind the counter stood up. He was a tall, slim, rather unkempt character wearing a Bixby Spartans tee shirt. *Not too bright. Wearing his high school's shirt to a robbery.* But, what Bobby saw next sent a chill down his spine. The thug was waving what looked like a small pistol. It also turned out he was not alone. Another person, a little heavier and taller, with long hair that looked like it had not been washed in a couple months, came around the corner of the row of shelves in front of Bobby. *What if they see Laura Sue and Buddy in the van?* He rolled forward to try to put the front door out of their sight line, if possible.

"Well, look what we have here. You're that cripple from Brookside. You guys cheated to beat Bixby," the guy with the pistol said. "Let's teach him a lesson. Then we'll get the cash, a few beers and hit the road."

These lunatics are really stupid. They surely can't believe we wouldn't call the cops and tell them what happened. Unless they plan to kill us both. That would mean they'd see Laura Sue when they leave the store, and kill her too. They couldn't leave any witnesses.

The Bixby boy with the pistol came up to Bobby's chair and leaned into his face. "I'm gonna whip your butt," he said.

"I don't think so," Bobby said. "In fact, if you leave right now, you'll only have the police to worry about and I won't have to hurt you."

The guy with the gun straightened up. He and his buddy doubled over with laughter. "You're sitting there, helpless, in a wheel chair and you're threatening me?" He stepped back and looked at Bobby. He pulled his arm back. "You ever been pistol whipped?"

"Last chance," Bobby said. As the assailant started forward, Bobby completed his reach into his left saddle bag, pulled out the pepper spray and let him have it full in the face. Bobby was careful to turn his head so the spray would not hit him.

The gun fell as the pepper spray took effect. He screamed in agony, trying to wipe it from his eyes. The more he wiped it, the worse it hurt. His accomplice made a rush toward Bobby. "You're gonna get it now, you…" But, Bobby was ready. With a single motion, he slid the billy club out of its place in his left saddlebag and backhanded his attacker in the face. He heard the crunch of the fellow's nose breaking. While he seemed suspended in space right in front of Bobby, Bobby took the opportunity to strike another blow with the club and the guy went to the floor. Meanwhile, the first thug, still blinded and screaming, tried to salvage the situation by throwing himself toward Bobby. But, his perspective, as well as his sight, was off and he fell a little short. Bobby gave him a crack on the side of his head as he fell.

"Pick up the gun, Ralph," Bobby ordered, "and give it to me."

"It's Paul."

"What? One of these guys is named Paul?"

"No, my name is Paul."

"Sorry, Paul. I thought it was Ralph."

Just then, he heard sirens approaching. Within seconds, it seemed, two armed policemen, pistols drawn, burst through the door. "How did you know to come?" Bobby asked. They ignored him for the moment while they took in the carnage and removed the pistol from Bobby's hand. Then, satisfied that any threat was neutralized, the cop that seemed to be in charge said, "A woman called 9-1-1 from the pay phone next door and said there was an armed robbery in progress."

At the mention of a woman, Bobby suddenly remembered Laura Sue and his efforts to move out of the sight line from the van. He turned and she came running through the door. Ignoring the policemen and Ralph, or Paul, she leaned over and hugged Bobby hard around the neck.

Paul began telling the policemen what happened. The two robbers came in and immediately overpowered him, bloodying his nose in the process. Then, before they got any farther with their plan, Bobby arrived. Paul told the police he believed it was their plan to kill him so he wouldn't be able to identify them. He told them how Bobby had been so calm and single handedly took them both out.

Laura Sue had witnessed the action in the store from the van and called the police from the pay phone in the parking lot. But she didn't know what was said, or how Bobby had told the Bixby boys he would have to hurt them if they didn't leave right away.

After the police took everyone's statements and the two thugs were in custody, still unconscious, Bobby and Laura Sue went back to the van. Buddy, who Laura Sue had ordered to stay in the back of the van, had a million questions. Bobby did his best to answer them, leaving out the parts about how calm he had been, and the extra blows with the billy club.

When they pulled into Laura Sue's driveway, her Mom came out of the house. "Where have you been? Mrs. Murphy told me you left the restaurant three hours ago. I've been worried. Bobby, your mother is worried, too."

"Mom, I'll tell you all about it when we get inside. We need to let Bobby get home so his Mom can quit worrying."

"Bobby's a super hero," Buddy declared, leaving Mrs. Medlin even more confused. He ran inside without further explanation, his mother right behind.

Laura Sue looked Bobby in the eyes, "You scared me half to death, and that was before I knew the whole story. I'm sure glad you had that pepper spray and club. You're the bravest person I've ever known. You put your own life on the line to save me and Buddy. I thought I was proud of you after the baseball game today, but I didn't know what proud is until now. I think I love you, Bobby." She threw her arms around his neck and planted the biggest kiss he had ever imagined right on his lips. Then, she said "Goodnight," and went in the house.

When Bobby pulled into his driveway, his Mom and Dad came running out of the house. "Are you all right?" his Mom asked, with concern in her voice. "Laura Sue called to let us know you were on the way home and told us about what happened."

"I'm fine, Mom," Bobby replied. "Maybe a little shaky at the moment, but I'm ok. Honest."

"Bobby, thank goodness you're okay, and it sounds like you were pretty brave, at least from what Laura Sue told us." His Dad paused. "But, are you crazy? Two of them; with a gun? You could just as easily be dead right now, and . . ." He shook his head.

Bobby, moved by his Dad's show of emotion, said, "Dad, I didn't see a choice. If they had succeeded in beating me up, I was really afraid they would kill Ralph, or Paul, or whoever he is, so there'd be no witnesses to identify them. Then, they would have left the store and seen Laura Sue and Buddy were in my van. I just couldn't take a chance."

Bobby rolled out of the van and the three Murphys went into the house. Once inside, Bobby's Mom couldn't contain her emotions any longer and began to cry. Seeing his Mom so upset caused Bobby to finally show his internal strife. Mr. Murphy put his arms around the two most special people in his life and hugged them as hard as he was able.

THIRTY-THREE

By Monday, it appeared the whole town knew of the incident at the Minute Mart. All Bobby's classmates wanted to ask questions about it, or told him "way to go." He was a little embarrassed by all the attention, especially when Eddie told him, "Man, you're gonna have your own Marvel comic book." And, Laura Sue told all her friends how Bobby had saved her and Buddy from certain death.

Not to miss a chance to tease Bobby, Riley waited until he, Eddie and Bobby were in the cafeteria during their lunch period. Several classmates had come over to talk to Bobby about what he did. When the gathering around Bobby had grown to about ten, Riley announced Bobby would be at a table in the cafeteria after school to sign autographs for only fifteen cents each; twenty if they wanted them personalized. Laughing, Bobby denied it all. "Riley, you'll pay for that. Just wait until you're least expecting it," he said.

Although the buzz settled down that afternoon, Bobby had one more moment of notoriety when Mr. Akins, his taciturn geometry teacher, insisted on recognizing Bobby in class. "We don't often enough have examples of people being brave and standing up for what's right. Mr. Murphy's courage in the face of danger is an example for us all." The class applauded and Bobby wanted to hide somewhere.

Bobby didn't have much chance during the school day to talk

to Laura Sue. He called her that evening. "Sorry, I couldn't see you more today," she said. "We had a prom committee meeting right after school and it lasted almost two hours. You do remember the prom is next Saturday, and you're taking me, don't you?"

"Sure, I do," Bobby answered, although in light of everything else that had gone on in his life, he had momentarily forgotten the prom was coming up so soon. "And, I remember I'm coming to the choral program tomorrow night to hear you sing." They talked a little longer and said "goodnight." Bobby wanted to tell her he loved her, but . . . somehow he needed an ounce more courage.

He hung up the phone and rolled out to the living room, where his Mom and Dad were watching TV. "Mom, what am I gonna do," he said. "The prom's this Saturday and I don't have a clue. What do I wear? Do I need to buy flowers? How can I take her to dinner?" Bobby's parents looked at him with amusement. Not that long ago, this would have been the least of his concerns.

"One thing at a time," she said. "Tomorrow, you need to stop on your way home from school at Connelly's and arrange to rent a tuxedo. Then, you need to go by Margo's florist to order a corsage. I'd suggest white roses. After you get those things done, you need to talk with your friends and see if any of them want to take their dates to one of the nice restaurants in town. You'll probably need a reservation since it's prom night and you may not be the only ones who thought of taking your dates to dinner."

"But, I can't afford all that," Bobby said. "I don't even have enough money to buy my own gas for the van."

"Bobby," his Dad said, "we plan to give you some money in honor of your graduation. You can pay your prom expenses out of that. While we're talking about money, have you given any thought to getting a job this summer? You're going to need money for college. We plan to cover your tuition and room and board, at least for the first year. But, you'll need to earn your own money for other expenses. As far as the prom expenses go, we'll front you for those and deduct them from your graduation gift."

"Thanks, Mom and Dad. Even if sometimes I don't seem like it, I really appreciate everything you do for me. I'll figure something out about a summer job. By the way, the senior choir at school has their concert tomorrow night. Laura Sue's singing in it and asked me to come. Is that okay?"

"It's fine," his Mom said. "You and Laura Sue are getting pretty close, aren't you?"

Bobby, taken aback by his Mom's question, stammered "Yeah, I guess so. I'm getting tired, so I think I'll go to bed." He made his escape, displaying his bright red blush of embarrassment.

THIRTY-FOUR

Tuesday morning, Bobby woke up and got himself ready for school, his mind racing with all he had to do. When he rolled out to the kitchen, his Mom was already there. "Want some scrambled eggs and bacon?" she asked. "Your father had to leave earlier than normal to get to the airport. He's got a meeting in Lubbock, of all places, and won't be back until tomorrow."

"Yes, please, and when I stop at Connelly's, what should I tell them about paying for the rental?" Bobby asked.

"I'll call over today. Since your Dad buys all his dress clothes there, Mr. Connelly knows we're good for it. And, don't forget shoes. You'll have to rent a pair. Your loafers won't go with a tux."

Bobby ate his breakfast and headed for school, hoping yesterday's excitement over the Minute Mart incident had died down. At least Bobby hoped to go from class to class without being stopped every few feet for a pat on the back, or hear "way to go, Bobby." Try as he might, he was struggling to focus on his classes. He recognized this was an important week; the teachers were trying to get them ready for finals next week.

At lunch, he asked Eddie, "You taking Melissa out to dinner before the prom?"

"Hadn't thought about it," Eddie replied. "Guess I should. What are you doing?"

Tuesday before the prom and Eddie hasn't even thought about taking his date to dinner. Unbelievable! Then he remembered that he had not thought of it either until his Mom brought it up last night. "Eddie, I worry 'bout you. You need to be thinkin' ahead. I'm taking Laura Sue to Outback, if I can get a reservation. Why don't you and Melissa come along? In fact, we can double date."

"If you can get a reservation?" Eddie said. "Sounds like some real sharp advance planning. Yeah, let's do that, but you'll have to drive. Did you rent a tux, or are you wearing your own?"

"Yes, dufus, I'm renting one. I'm going by after school to order it. Where did you order your corsage for Melissa? I'm ordering mine at Margo's."

"You got me there, buddy. I forgot about that, too. At least I remembered the tux."

The remainder of the school day dragged slowly by. Finally, it was over. When he reached his van, Laura Sue was waiting for him. "Bobby, you didn't forget about the concert tonight, did you?"

"Are you kidding? That's all I've been thinking about all day," Bobby said, a little too eagerly, he thought.

"After it's over, they're having a little reception in the cafeteria. My Mom can't come to the concert, so would you come with me?"

"You bet I will. Listen, I've really got to run right now. I have to get over to Connelly's to order my tux for Saturday before they close."

"You haven't ordered your tux yet?" Laura Sue said. "I hope they still have some."

Bobby drove out of the parking lot as fast as he could, trying not to panic. *What am I gonna do if I can't get one? Please Mr. Connelly, don't be out.*

He got downtown and began searching for a handicap parking space. Luckily, he found one just a half block from the store. *Now I get to try out my parallel parking skills. Thank goodness for the back-up camera.* He carefully backed into the space, succeeding on the first try, rolled out of the van and up the street. *Oh, no. Connelly's doesn't have an automatic door, or a handicap button. And, the door opens out.*

This was the first time Bobby had run into this problem. He sat there for a minute, trying to come up with a solution, and growing more and more frustrated. *One more thing I can't do.* Mr. Connelly looked up and saw Bobby at the door. He walked out from behind the counter.

"Come in, Bobby," he said, as he held the door while Bobby rolled through. "Your Mom called and said you'd be by. Great job at the Minute Mart Saturday night. Probably saved Paul's life, from what I heard. I remember when Charlie, my youngest, was playing soccer. Bixby's fans were the worst sports I've ever seen. No wonder those two fools came from there.

"Bet you didn't know this: Paul's my grandson. And, you know what else? Your tux and shoe rental is on me. Least I can do to thank you."

"Mr. Connelly, you don't have to do that. I only did what anyone would have done."

"Have to or not, I'm doing it. Believe me, very few people would have done what you did. Now, let's get you measured."

As he was getting Bobby's measurements, Bobby said, "I was afraid you'd be out of tuxes this late."

"Oh, I don't have them here. There's a supplier in Tulsa all of us rent from. We place our orders and they deliver them right here. I have to get my order in today, though. Seems Brookside's not the only school in the state of Oklahoma holding a prom this weekend."

"I really appreciate it Mr. Connelly. When can I pick it up?"

"They'll deliver them here Friday morning. You can come by any time after about noon. But first, a couple decisions. I'd recommend the white dinner jacket instead of the more formal all black tuxedo. Is that ok?"

"Sure," Bobby said. "I like that."

"The other thing you need to decide is what color cummerbund you want."

"What's a cummerbund?"

"It's a thing you wear around your waist. I'll show you one."

Mr. Connelly went into the back room and came out with a bright red cummerbund. "This is what it looks like, but you should get one that goes with your date's dress. What color is it?"

"She told me it's blue, a light blue, I think," Bobby said.

"Perfect. If I'm not here when you come in, Ralph can help you."

"Who's Ralph?"

"My oldest grandson. Paul's older brother," Mr. Connelly replied. "He comes back from Stillwater on Fridays to help me out on the weekends."

"Do he and Paul look a lot alike?"

"Yes, they do. In fact, a lot of folks get them confused. Ralph is a sophomore at OSU studying marketing and, I hope, getting some real world experience here in my store."

No wonder I thought Paul's name was Ralph the other night. He didn't know Ralph, or Paul for that matter, but now he knew why he thought Paul's name was Ralph. Ralph would have been a senior at Brookside when Bobby was a wide-eyed sophomore and he must have seen Ralph around school. "I'll look forward to meeting him on Friday," he told Mr. Connelly.

Bobby left the store and drove the ten blocks to Margo's Florist Shoppe. He found a handicap parking space a block away and rolled over to Margo's. Luckily, Margo's had an automatic door opening button. A pretty young girl came out from behind the counter to welcome him. She had long black hair that came down over her shoulders and penetrating eyes the color of a stormy sea at sunset. Plus, she had a knock-out figure, and showed it off with a tight red tee shirt and short blue skirt. *She's beautiful. Almost as pretty as Laura Sue.* He found himself blushing, and feeling a little guilty about his thoughts.

Tearing his eyes away from her, he looked around the shop. There were several floral bouquets on display, a selection of greeting cards, and a cooler holding a large number of fresh flowers. The shop smelled sweet with the blended smell of all the flowers and plants. The aromas enhanced the girl's natural beauty.

"Hi. I'm Jennie," she said when he got inside the store. "How can I help you?"

"I need to order a corsage for my girlfriend for the prom. But, I don't know anything about flowers. I want something really nice."

"She must be a special lady," Jennie said. "I'd recommend either baby roses, or carnations. Do you know what color you want?"

"Um, how 'bout yellow or white?" He hadn't given the color any thought.

"What color is her dress?"

"I think she told me it's blue, a light blue."

"Then let's do one with both yellow and white. That would be really nice and a little unusual."

"OK," Bobby said. "Which kind of flowers should I get?"

"Roses send a special message, and yellow roses are perfect. Do you want a wrist corsage or one she'll pin on her dress?"

"I'll go with the roses, because she is really special," Bobby said. "What kind do most people get?"

Jennie thought a minute. "It's really a mixture. Some girls seem to like the wrist ones, but, if I were the lucky girl you're going with, I'd rather have one that pins on. If it's on your wrist, it's too easy to crush."

"I'll go with that, the one that pins on," Bobby said. "How much will it be?"

"We have a prom special," Jennie answered. "Only twenty-five dollars."

Bobby gulped. "Wow, that's a lot more than I thought it would be."

"Don't worry," Jennie said. "You won't have to pay until you pick it up. It'll be ready about midday on Saturday."

Jennie got Bobby's name and phone number, and escorted him to the door. "Thanks," he said.

"Thank you for shopping with us," she replied with a dazzling smile.

What a smile! Is she flirting with me? Naw. Couldn't be.

As Bobby drove home, he couldn't get the image of Jennie out of his mind. When he arrived at his house, his Mom was in the kitchen fixing dinner. "Did you get everything ordered?" she asked.

"I did," Bobby said, and he told her about the tux and the flowers. "I think Jennie will really like them."

"Who?" his Mom said, looking up in surprise. "Who in the world is Jennie?"

"Oops," Bobby replied. "Jennie's the girl at the florist who helped me pick out Laura Sue's corsage."

"You better be careful and not make that mistake when you're talking to Laura Sue. I'll stop by and pay for the corsage tomorrow, and check out this Jennie person. I'll stop by Connelly's, too."

"I almost forgot. You don't need to stop at Connelly's. Mr. Connelly isn't going to charge me for the tux rental. The clerk at the Minute Mart the other night, Paul, turns out to be his grandson. I told him he didn't need to do that, but he insisted."

"That's really nice of him," his Mom said. "Why don't you go ahead and get ready to go to the concert while I finish fixing dinner?"

THIRTY-FIVE

The concert started at eight, but Bobby left home at seven. He knew it would take him a little extra time to find a parking space that would allow him to easily get out of and back in his van. He pulled up to the entrance to the school's auditorium and parked at the end of the first row. The sidewalk on his right insured the access he needed. As he went up the ramp to the front door, he said hello to several of his classmates who were arriving to sing with the choir. He looked around, but didn't see Laura Sue.

The auditorium seated about three hundred people. At the rear were the wheel chair accessible places. He moved over to the center space and watched the members of the choir moving into their positions on the stage. He was so intent on the activity that he almost didn't notice the little tap on his shoulder. He turned and there was Laura Sue. She was wearing a western-style dress, complete with boots and a black cowboy hat. Her dress was white, trimmed in red. She looked spectacular. *How could I have been so taken with Jennie? Forget her.*

"Hi, Jennie," he said.

"Hi, Bobby. I'm so glad you came." Pause. "Who's Jennie?"

Thinking quickly, Bobby said, "Who?" *Boy, I've really screwed up now.*

"You said 'Hi, Jennie'. Who's Jennie? A new girlfriend?" she replied with an edge to her voice.

"What?" Bobby said. "I was sitting here thinking about ordering my tux and some flowers for you. The clerk at the florist was named Jennie. I was thinking about all this stuff and you walked up right as I was recalling ordering flowers. The clerk's name was Jennie. I wasn't actually thinking about Jennie. *Shut up, Bobby. Remember what you do when you find you're digging yourself into a hole?* Trying to change the subject, he said," I was hoping I'd see you before the show. I heard one time that people tell actors and performers to break a leg. I'm not sure exactly why they would say that, but 'break a leg.'"

"Oh, Bobby, you're a nut," Laura Sue said. *Good. She's already forgotten my slip.* Then, she added, "I'm gonna check out this Jennie person. I've got to go now and get ready. I'll see you after the show. Will you wait here for me?"

"I'll be right here," he answered. *She's going to check out Jennie. Not good. Maybe she'll forget.*

After Laura Sue left, Bobby was watching the people arrive. He spoke to several people, and a few came up to congratulate him on the baseball team's victory. A couple even said what a great job he'd done at the Minute Mart on Saturday, which embarrassed him. Then, Eddie came over.

"Can I sit here with you in the executive seating area?" Eddie asked. "Melissa's singing in the choir, and I told her I'd come listen."

"Sure," Bobby said, "but you'll have to find a chair. Check over there." He pointed to the side of the entrance way, where there were some folding chairs. As he looked, he gasped, "Oh, no." Jennie was coming through the door. Just then, she looked over and spotted Bobby.

Eddie arrived back with the chair just as Jennie came over . "Hi, Bobby. I didn't expect to see you here tonight. Is your girlfriend singing?" Eddie, looking at Jennie in her little black dress, gaped.

"Yes, she is. Jennie, meet my friend Eddie."

Eddie, melting into those killer eyes, managed a weak "Nice to meet you."

"My brother, Ray, is singing tonight. You may know him. Ray Roberts," Jennie said.

"You're Ray's sister?" Bobby exclaimed. "I sure do know him. He's a terrific pitcher. We wouldn't have won State without him."

"I'm going to sit down there with my Mom and Dad. They got here real early to get us good seats. I'll see you after the show."

Bobby glanced over at Eddie, who was still standing with his mouth open, watching Jennie leave. "Eddie, sit down. You're making a fool of yourself."

Eddie took his seat and said, "Bobby, I'm gettin' me a wheel chair. You attract the best looking girls I've ever seen. That Jennie is drop dead gorgeous. And, she's Ray Roberts' sister?"

"I guess so," Bobby said. "But, now I've got a problem. Laura Sue's coming by here after the show and, if Jennie comes by and Laura Sue sees her, I'm in trouble. I already slipped and called Laura Sue, Jennie."

"I can't wait to see how you get out of this one, Lover Boy," Eddie said.

The lights dimmed and Miss Marshall, the school's director of choral music, entered the stage from the left side. Miss Marshall also taught public speaking and was Bobby's teacher when he was a junior. He thought she was one of the nicest teachers he ever had.

"Welcome everyone to our annual year end concert. Tonight we will feature some of our seniors, both in small groups and in solos. Our theme this year is popular music from the 1950's, 60's and 70's, in honor of the parents and grandparents who have supported our students as they are growing up. I also want to thank Mr. Fuller, our director of instrumental music and our district champion marching band." A cheer went up from the audience.

"We have excellent back-up music to accompany our vocals and even a small country and western combo. Now sit back and enjoy 'A Look Back in Time.' You can follow along in your programs."

"Eddie, go get us a couple programs," Bobby whispered. "I didn't see them when I came in. Too early, I guess."

Eddie left and came back with two programs. While the choir marched onto their risers, Bobby quickly scanned the program. Then, the choir began to sing and he put it away before he got to the listing of the pieces being performed. From the first number, "God Bless America," sung by the whole choir, the audience was enthralled. When Anna Mae Marlow sang "Lara's Theme," from the movie, "Dr. Zhivago," she got a standing ovation. After an hour, the choir took a fifteen minute intermission.

During the intermission, Bobby opened his program. To his surprise, he saw Laura Sue would be singing a solo. *Dumb me. I've never even heard her sing. I didn't know she was good enough to sing a solo.*

Eddie leaned over. "Hey, Laura Sue's singing a solo. Good thing she's doing it before she meets Jennie," he added with a smirk.

"Thanks pal," Bobby replied.

The lights went down and the second half started with a rousing medley of songs from the Broadway play, "South Pacific." Then Maria Mengele took the stage and sang "I'm Gonna Wash that Man Right Out of My Hair." The audience applauded long and loud. After a couple more songs, the choir left the stage. A small combo, dressed in western attire and hats, came out. They had a guitar, a fiddle and a set of drums. As they began the musical introduction, Laura Sue, wearing her white and red-trimmed shirt, came onto the stage singing the Patsy Cline hit, "Sweet Dreams."

She's singing to me, Bobby thought. And sure enough, she did seem to be looking right at him.

When Laura Sue finished and took a bow, the audience rose as one and clapped until Bobby thought they would never stop. Miss Marshall finally came out to the microphone. "Would you like to hear Laura Sue do one more of Patsy Cline's songs?" The audience shouted "More, more."

Miss Marshall nodded at Laura Sue and the band, and left the stage. Laura Sue sang what Bobby thought was the best rendition of "Walking after Midnight" he had ever heard.

As she sang the final lyrics, the audience once again rose and clapped for a long time. Finally, Miss Marshall came back out and, laughingly, told the audience, "We have more music for you. Thank you, Laura Sue. Please give the band a hand. Weren't they terrific?" The audience clapped some more.

Finally, they settled down enough for the choir to do the next numbers. Before the finale, Miss Marshall came back out and thanked everyone for coming. "We think you'll like our last selection," she said. "You'll notice we didn't list it in the program, but I can guarantee you'll enjoy it." As the choir broke into the theme song from "Oklahoma," the entire crowd stood. Miss Marshall turned and invited them to sing along. It was a rousing ending.

The audience began to file out. Eddie moved away just a few feet. "I gotta see how this comes out," he said.

Bobby, watching the exodus, spotted Jennie heading his way. "Wasn't that great?" she said enthusiastically. "Did your girlfriend sing?"

"She sure did, she's the one who sang 'Sweet Dreams' and 'Walkin' after Midnight.'"

"Wow," Jennie said. "She was sensational. I can see why you like her so much."

At that point, Laura Sue walked up. Eddie took another step back. Bobby thought, *How am I gonna explain this? I guess just be honest.*

"Laura Sue, meet Jennie, Ray Roberts' sister."

"Hi, Laura Sue. You were sensational out there. Even if I could sing, I don't think I could do it in front of a big crowd. Bobby's told me all about you. Well, maybe not all," Jennie said with a smile. "He's a lucky guy to have such a talented girlfriend."

Laura Sue, who had been all ready to unload on Bobby, was not quite as sure of herself. "Thank you. It's nice to meet you," she said, a little coolly. Turning to Bobby, she asked, "Are you ready to go to the reception?"

"Sure am," Bobby replied. He looked at Eddie, "See you later, pal." Then, he turned to Jennie and said, "Goodnight, Jennie. I'll see you Saturday." *Oops. Probably shouldn't have added that.*

After a few steps, Laura Sue said, "You'll see her Saturday? Have you decided not to take me to the prom?" Without waiting for an answer, said, "Maybe I won't go with you anyway. Maybe you should just take Jennie." The she strode away, not even looking to see if Bobby was following her.

"Wait a minute, Laura Sue," Bobby called. "Let me explain." But, Laura Sue had gathered a head of steam and Bobby couldn't catch up. When he finally reached the cafeteria, where the reception was being held, he saw Laura Sue across the room, surrounded by a gaggle of well-wishers. He couldn't get anywhere near her. In fact, the only reason he knew she was there was because he could see the top of her black cowboy hat.

Bobby went over to the serving table and got a cup of some kind of red, fruity punch. There was a whole table of snacks and sweets, but Bobby had lost his appetite. *What's wrong with Laura Sue? Why won't she let me explain?*

As he sat there, growing increasingly miserable, Ray Roberts came over. "Hey, Bobby. Good to see you. How'd you like the concert? Wasn't Laura Sue great?"

"She sure was, but I think she's mad at me. I think she's jealous of your sister," Bobby said.

"My sister? Why would she be jealous of Margie? She's only a freshman, and I don't think you've even seen her."

"Isn't Jennie your sister?" Bobby asked, confused.

Ray began to laugh. "Yes, Jennie's my older sister. But, Laura Sue has nothing to be jealous about. I don't think you could compete with Jennie's fiancé. They're going to get married when he gets out of the Navy next fall."

"What? You've got to be kidding me."

"No," Ray said. "I'm serious as a judge. Laura Sue's got nothing to be jealous about. And, even if she did, you've got no chance with Jennie, anyway."

"I'm going back for more punch and some more of those chocolate chip cookies. Want me to bring you something?" Ray asked.

"No thanks," Bobby said. "I'm not really hungry or thirsty."

When Ray left, Bobby sat there alone. *How should I handle this? Shouldn't Laura Sue trust me? She said she loves me. And, I know I love her. But, we've got a problem if every time a pretty girl talks to me, she's gonna get all worked up.*

Time dragged on for Bobby. At last, he saw the crowd around Laura Sue thinning. Then, he saw Miss Marshall sitting across the room and rolled over to speak to her. "Miss Marshall, that was great tonight. I had no idea there was this much talent at Brookside."

"Thanks Bobby, I'm glad you enjoyed it," she replied. "Wasn't Laura Sue great?"

So even the teachers think of us as a couple. "She sure was," Bobby said, feeling himself beginning to redden.

Just then, Laura Sue came over to where Bobby and Miss Marshall were talking. "Thanks for all your work, Miss Marshall," she said.

"Thank you, Laura Sue. You were even better tonight than you were in rehearsals." Patsy Cline would be proud."

Turning to Bobby, Laura Sue said, less sweetly, "Take me home. I'm tired."

All the way to the van, Laura Sue did not say a word. When Bobby opened the door, she marched up the ramp and sat in the passenger seat. Bobby said, "Laura Sue, please let me explain."

"I don't want to hear it, Bobby. I'm tired and I've met Jennie. What did you think you were going to do? Spend Saturday with Jennie and then take me to the prom Saturday night? I don't think so."

Bobby locked his chair into place behind the steering wheel. He sat there, thinking for a minute. A long minute until the loudness of the quiet got to him. "Laura Sue," he began, "we're not moving until you hear what I have to say. The reason I'll see Jennie on

Saturday is because she works at the florist shop and I'll be picking up your corsage."

"Just take me home," she said. "Maybe I'll listen to you tomorrow. Maybe not."

"No," Bobby said, asserting himself in a way he'd not done before with Laura Sue. "You're going to listen to what I have to say. Then, you can do whatever you want.

"First, you know I love you, or at least you should know by now. And, only you. Sure, Jennie's pretty, even beautiful, but, if every time some other girl speaks to me, you're going to get into a snit, then you don't trust me. And, if you don't trust me, then we probably shouldn't be together. I've never loved you more than listening to you sing 'Sweet Dreams.' I felt like you were singing to me. But, if you don't trust me, and you think there's someone else, then there's nothing more I can do." Bobby started the van and drove out of the parking lot.

Neither of them spoke during the short drive to Laura Sue's house. When Bobby pulled into the driveway, he opened the door for her without a word. As she got out, Laura Sue turned and said, "Bobby, I've got to think this through. We'll talk about it tomorrow after school." He thought she might be crying as she walked quickly into the house.

THIRTY-SIX

After a restless night, Bobby didn't much want to go to school on Wednesday. The argument with Laura Sue was their first real disagreement, and it upset him. He didn't feel he had done anything wrong. She said they would talk about it after school. *What if she tells me it's over, whatever 'it' is?*

He got dressed and went to the kitchen to fix himself a bowl of Cheerios. His Mom was there. "Bobby, what's wrong? You seem a little down today. How was the concert last night?"

"The concert was great. Laura Sue sang a solo, and then had an encore. She sang "Sweet Dreams" and sounded just like Patsy Cline. Then, she sang "Walking after Midnight" and brought down the house." Bobby decided to ignore his Mom's' question about his mood. He wasn't ready to talk about the spat with Laura Sue yet.

When he drove into the parking lot at school, Eddie was waiting by his usual parking space. "How'd it go last night, buddy? Get everything all patched up on the way home?"

"Not really, but I hope to today."

"Good luck, then. She passed me a few minutes ago. Didn't give me much of a hello. She shouldn't be mad at me just because you've got another girlfriend," Eddie said with a grin.

Bobby bristled. "I don't have another girlfriend, Eddie. Quit saying that." He wheeled himself around and into the school building.

He didn't catch sight of Laura Sue when he was changing classes all morning. Usually, he saw her in the distance and they exchanged waves. But not today. *Is she trying to avoid me?* At lunch, Eddie tried again to pump him for what happened after the concert. Eddie must have told Riley about the meeting of Laura Sue and Jennie because Riley also started asking questions.

"Sounds to me like Laura Sue's jealous," Riley said.

"If you saw Jennie, you'd see why," Eddie said.

"Please guys, leave it alone. I don't want to talk about it."

"Okay," they said in unison. The two friends changed the subject and started talking about the prom. Bobby didn't join in, lost in his own thoughts.

"Riley, why don't you and Chelsi come with us to Outback for dinner before?" Eddie said. "That okay with you, Bobby?"

"If I go."

"You'll get this thing with Laura Sue patched up," Eddie said. "Did you make our reservations? We need to add Riley and Chelsi."

"No. I forgot. Would you mind doing it?"

"Will do," Eddie said. "Hope I'm not too late."

Bobby left Eddie and Riley at the table and began making his way to his next class. All he could think about was Laura Sue. Just before he went into his classroom, Ray Roberts passed him in the hall.

"How's it going, Bobby?" Ray asked.

"Not so good, Ray. I think Laura Sue's about to break up with me."

"Over my sister?"

"Yeah."

"No way," Ray said, and he continued down the hall.

The rest of the day dragged by. Bobby was apprehensive about what would happen next with Laura Sue. *What if I don't see her before I leave? Should I go by her house and try to talk with her?* He decided he would slowly make his way to his van. If she wanted to talk, she'd be able to easily catch him. If not, he guessed it was over. As he rolled out the front doorway, he saw Laura Sue out of the corner of his eye. She seemed to be listening to someone talking to her, but he couldn't see who it was. He kept going.

He was almost to his van when he heard, "Bobby, please wait for me." It was Laura Sue. He stopped and waited.

"I've made a mess of everything." Laura Sue had tears rolling down her cheeks. "I should have known to trust you. Ray Roberts just told me about his sister being engaged. But, that shouldn't have made any difference. Can you ever forgive me?"

"Laura Sue, you're the only girl I've ever wanted. I'm going to see Jennie on Saturday to pick up flowers for you. I can't help it that she's so pretty. And, I can't help but notice. But, even if she wasn't engaged, she's not you." Bobby took a deep breath. "Would you like a ride home?"

"I would," she said, and they proceeded to the van. When she had gotten into the passenger seat and Bobby had locked into position behind the wheel, she leaned over and gave him the sweetest kiss he had ever known.

THIRTY-SEVEN

After school on Friday, Eddie and Riley went with Bobby to pick up their tuxes at Connelly's. It turned out Riley had been the first of the three to order his. They all tried on their rented clothing. Mr. Connelly had installed a pair of bars in the dressing room so, between the bars and his chair, Bobby was able try his on without help.

"Have a good time, boys," Mr. Connelly said as they left the store. "And, be safe."

"Thanks, Mr. Connelly," they each replied.

"We'll see you on Monday," Eddie added.

"How come you didn't have to pay anything?" Riley asked Bobby when they got to the van.

Bobby was embarrassed to tell him the real reason, so he said, "My Mom already took care of it. They're loaning me the money for my prom expenses until I can get a summer job and start earning some of my own." *Sort of true.*

"Man, I've never had a tux before," Eddie said. "Fact is I've never even seen one except on TV or in the movies. Do you think I'll look like James Bond?"

"Yeah, right," Riley said. "With your red hair, you'll look more like that cartoon rooster."

"Look who's talking. People gonna be givin' you tips, thinkin' you're a butler."

"At least I'll have some income, instead of standing around looking like a red headed penguin," Riley replied.

As his two friends poked each other back and forth, Bobby thought, *No use making cracks about me. I'll just look like a dressed up lump in a wheelchair. I just hope I don't embarrass Laura Sue.* He found himself sinking into one of his depressed moods, feeling sorry for himself.

"Well," Eddie said. "What about our friend, Bobby, here? He's gonna actually look kind of cool. Like a piece of living room furniture in a museum." Bobby had to smile at the visual that came into his mind.

"Speaking of furniture, well sort of, did you and Laura Sue get things patched up?"

"Yeah," Bobby answered. "Ray Roberts helped bail me out." He didn't elaborate.

"McGee, you should have seen that girl, Jennie. If Romeo here convinced Laura Sue not to be jealous, he should be selling refrigerators to Eskimos," Eddie said, ever ready with a tired old cliché. "How'd Ray do that?"

Not wanting to share all the details, Bobby replied, "You already know Jennie is Ray's older sister. Ray just told Laura Sue that Jennie is all involved with someone else and was just being nice to me. She bought it."

"So, let me get this straight: you got Ray to con Laura Sue into believing that?" Eddie said, rolling his eyes.

"No, I didn't even know Ray was going to talk to her. Besides, it's true. She has a fiancé and she's getting married next fall when the guy gets out of the Navy."

Riley, looking perplexed, said, "Who is this Jennie? And, how'd you meet her?"

"She was working at Margo's when I went in to order Laura Sue's corsage. I met her there. Then, she came to the concert Tuesday because Ray was singing in the choir. After the concert, she came over to say hello to me just before Laura Sue walked up. Laura Sue went ballistic," Bobby explained.

"You think she might not have reacted quite as strongly if you hadn't slipped up and called her 'Jennie' before the show started?"

"Yeah, I really screwed up there," Bobby admitted.

"Let me come back to this corsage," Riley said. "That's flowers, right?"

Bobby and Eddie looked at Riley like he had just crawled out from under a rock. "Well, duh," Eddie said.

Riley continued, "And you guys got one for your dates Saturday night?"

"Riley, you're puttin' us on. Don't tell me you didn't get Chelsi a corsage. What's she gonna think when every other girl there's sporting flowers and she doesn't have any?" Eddie asked.

"What am I gonna do? She'll dump me faster than a load of mulch."

"Let's go by Margo's and see if they can still fix you one to give her," Bobby said. "What color is her dress? You need to know that so you know what color flowers to get."

No clue," Riley said. "I'm screwed."

They got back into Bobby's van and drove to Margo's. "When we go in there, if Jennie's working, don't make fools of yourselves, like slobbering on your shirt, or something," Bobby warned.

"What do you think we are, a pair of idiots?" Riley said.

"Close," Bobby replied.

They went in. Jennie came out from behind the counter. "Hi, guys," she said. "What can I do for you?" Jennie looked, if anything, more beautiful than she had when Bobby ordered his corsage, and when he saw her at the concert. Her outfit set off her black hair and stunning figure magnificently.

"Hi, Jennie," Bobby said. "You met my friend, Eddie, the other night at the concert. This is my friend, Riley." Since Riley was the one needing help, Bobby fell silent to let Riley tell her what he needed. When he heard nothing from Riley, he looked over at him.

Riley was standing there, as if in a trance, with his mouth open, staring at Jennie.

Eddie wasn't much better, but he poked Riley in the ribs with his elbow. "Tell her what you want."

"Flowers," Riley managed to mumble. Bobby was afraid he might actually slobber.

"He needs a corsage, but he doesn't know what color his date' dress will be. I know it's late, but can you help him out?" Bobby asked.

"Well, our deadline was yesterday, but since he's a friend of yours, I'll get him fixed up. How about some nice white roses?" she asked Riley. Riley nodded his head up and down.

"Okay," she said. "I'll have it ready by three tomorrow. Thanks for ordering from us."

The three boys left. When they got back to the van, Eddie said, "Riley, you're almost as smooth as Bobby. By the way, is that slobber on your shirt?"

THIRTY-EIGHT

Bobby didn't get up Saturday morning until a little after nine. He wanted to sleep late because he knew he would be out all night. He, Eddie and Riley had all signed up to go to the lock-in at the YMCA after the prom. They would have to be there by midnight and remain until six o'clock Sunday morning. To insure that all participants stayed the whole time, the sponsors had several door prize drawings planned to take place at five thirty. Bobby had his eyes set on a set of Yeti travel mugs. They also had a variety of games to be going on all night. A no alcohol rule would be strictly enforced and anyone who had been drinking before arriving would not be admitted. Laura Sue and Melissa had decided to come, but Riley's date, Chelsi, had to be home by midnight and would not be able to attend, so Riley decided to go home, too.

"What time are you picking up Laura Sue?" his Mom asked when he rolled out to the kitchen, still wearing his blue and yellow Superman pajamas. "Don't let Buddy know about those PJ's or he'll think you really are a super hero."

"Oh, Mom, he knows I'm not. We have dinner reservations at Outback for six, so I'll have to leave here by five to pick everyone up. Eddie's meeting me at Melissa's house, so I won't have an extra stop. Riley and Chelsi will meet us at Outback. I told Laura Sue I'd be there about five fifteen."

"You better get there earlier than that. Mrs. Medlin plans to take pictures of the two of you before you leave and that will add at least twenty or thirty minutes. She promised to send me copies."

"Good idea. I never thought about pictures, except for the ones they'll take at the prom. I better call Laura Sue and let her know."

After he called Laura Sue, he came back to the kitchen where his Mom had fixed scrambled eggs, bacon, grits and raisin toast. He picked up his fork as his Dad walked in and said, "Where's mine? Is Superman here the only one getting fed?" So Mrs. Murphy fixed another plate and his Dad sat down to eat with him.

"Bobby, I know you've been looking forward to the prom for a long time. And, I know I don't have to say this. But, I also know what it's like when a bunch of teenagers get together for a party. Remember you'll be driving, and you'll be responsible for all of your passengers. Whatever you do, don't drink any alcohol, of any kind." His Dad looked him in the eye.

"Dad, you're right. You don't have to say that. Even if I wanted to have a beer or two, I won't. Laura Sue would skin me alive if I had anything to drink. I told Mom, but I don't think I told you, we're going straight from the prom to the 'Y'. A group of the choir and band parents are having a lock-in, so we'll be there until about six Sunday morning. And, they won't allow any drinking, even before the lock-in starts."

"That's good," his Dad said. "Then I won't worry. You, of all people, know what can happen in an accident."

Bobby finished his breakfast and went back to his room to get dressed. When he came back to the kitchen, his Mom was still there putting the dishes in the dishwasher. His Dad had gone out to the garage to work on some project or other.

"Mom," Bobby said, "doesn't Dad trust me?"

"He trusts you. We both do. If we didn't, we wouldn't have bought you that van. But, a parent has to cover certain bases and set down some rules. We know you won't be drinking, but we still have to have that discussion. One day, when you have kids of your own, you'll know what I mean."

"Mom, like Dad said, I know what can happen in a car accident. If I caused one, especially if I'd been drinking, and something happened to Laura Sue, or Eddie, or Riley, or anyone, I don't think I could live with myself."

Bobby rolled into the living room and flipped on the TV. The Atlanta Braves were playing the Chicago Cubs. He was watching intently when his Dad came back in. They watched the game together, even having debates about whether the Braves should have tried to squeeze a run home in the seventh or if the Cubs should have brought in a reliever after the Braves scored two in the sixth.

The game ended and it was time for Bobby to get ready to leave. He went back to his bedroom, took a quick shower, and put on his tux pants. He thought the shirt that had come with the outfit was a little frilly for his taste, but he guessed that was what tuxedo people wore. He had a little trouble fitting the cummerbund. *Funny name for this thing.* Finally, he put on his coat and went back to the living room where his Mom and Dad were still watching TV.

Mrs. Murphy stood up. "Let me look you over. I know Mrs. Medlin is going to take some pictures, but, Jack, let's take a couple of just Bobby." As she approached his chair, she could not repress a laugh.

"What's so funny?" Bobby asked, with a bit of irritation. *What have I done now?*

"Oh, Bobby. I'm sorry. I don't mean to laugh at you, but your cummerbund is on backwards." And she broke out laughing even more.

His Dad came over to look, and began laughing, too. Finally, even Bobby had to join in. "Well, will you help me fix it right, so I can get on the road?"

THIRTY-NINE

With his parents waving goodbye, Bobby got in his van and drove to Laura Sue's house. He rolled up the ramp Buddy built and knocked on the front door. *Why didn't I ring the doorbell like a normal person would? Oh well, too late now.*

Mrs. Medlin was dressed in a pair of red jeans and a white blouse. *I see where Laura Sue gets her good looks.* She invited Bobby in. "Laura Sue will be out in just a minute. She's putting the last touches on her hair." Not understanding girls and their hair, Bobby felt that was nice, but had no clue why last touches would be required.

When Laura Sue entered the living room, she took Bobby's breath away. *How did I ever get lucky enough to have a girlfriend this pretty?* "You look great," he said. "I have this for you, but your Mom will have to help you put it on." He handed her the corsage box.

She took the corsage out and said, "Bobby, this is beautiful. And, it goes with my dress."

He started to say something smooth like, "And it matches your eyes." He had seen that line in an old movie, but realized just in time that yellow and white flowers matching her eyes might not be a compliment. Mrs. Medlin saved him by pinning on the corsage and telling Bobby he had good taste.

"Thanks, Mrs. Medlin, the girl at the flower shop, Jennie, helped me pick it out." *Bobby, shut up about Jennie, you idiot.* Laura Sue gave him a funny look.

"Let's get some pictures so you can get on your way. I don't want you to be late for your dinner reservation," Mrs. Medlin said. She had them pose in front of the fireplace and took several shots. "I promised to send copies to your mother," she said to Bobby. "You make a lovely couple."

Before they got to the door, Buddy came running out into the living room. "Gee Bobby," he said, "you clean up pretty good," earning a dirty look from both Laura Sue and her Mom. Bobby had to laugh.

"Thanks, Buddy," he said. "By the way, that's a nice ramp you built. Thanks."

"No problem," he said.

Bobby and Laura Sue got in the van and drove to Melissa's house. On the way Bobby asked, "Where was your Dad? I would have thought he'd want to see his beautiful daughter off to her senior prom."

Laura Sue didn't answer right away. Finally, she said, "Oh, Daddy had to work today and hasn't got off yet." She didn't add any more and Bobby let the subject drop. *There's something going on I don't know about. I guess she'll tell me when she's ready.*

They pulled up in front, but no one appeared. Eddie's car was parked in front of the house, so Bobby knew he was there. "Guess I better honk to let them know we're here," Bobby said.

"Don't you dare," Laura Sue said. "That would be rude. If they don't come out soon, I'll go to the door. And, when they do come out, be sure you tell Melissa how nice she looks."

After a couple more minutes, Melissa and Eddie came out the front door with Melissa's Mom waving goodbye from the porch. Bobby opened the door and let them into the van. "You really look nice, Melissa," he said. "And, I like your corsage."

"Did Jennie pick out hers, too?" Laura Sue asked.

Bobby had said all he had to say about Jennie, but Eddie blurted out, "Yeah. Boy is she a knock-out."

"Who's Jennie?" Melissa asked.

"She's the gorgeous girl that works at Margo's florist shop and has these dodo's all excited."

Bobby started to defend himself, but wisely kept his mouth shut. Eddie also seemed to realize he was about to enter a mine field and didn't respond either. Fortunately, they pulled up to Outback before the line of conversation could continue.

"Eddie, why don't you escort the girl's in and I'll park the van?" Bobby said.

"Will do," Eddie said. "At least we won't have to have any more conversation about Jennie."

"Don't be so sure," Melissa said. "We may come back to that later."

Riley and Chelsi were waiting by the hostess desk when Eddie, Melissa and Laura Sue came in. Riley was explaining to the hostess that they needed a wheelchair accessible table.

"No problem," the hostess said. "I already had that down. Follow me, please."

By the time they were seated, Bobby had joined them and they ordered a 'Bloomin' Onion' appetizer. Bobby, having been well trained, said "Chelsi, you look very nice tonight."

"Thanks," she said. "Isn't my corsage pretty? Riley picked it out 'specially for me." Riley beamed, but the other four just looked at each other; Laura Sue and Melissa looked like they wanted to say something, but, much to the relief of Bobby and Eddie, didn't. The waitress arrived to take their dinner orders, and the moment for risky conversation on the subject of Jennie passed.

"Can I take your order," the waitress asked. "Ladies first."

"I'll have the petit filet," Laura Sue said, "with a loaded baked potato."

"I'll have the same thing," Melissa said.

Chelsi added her order. "Me, too."

The three boys all ordered the twelve ounce sirloin.

Bobby looked around the restaurant. "Looks like a bunch of our classmates had the same idea to come here for dinner."

As she turned to look, Chelsi knocked over her water glass, spilling the cold liquid in Riley's lap. Riley let out a mild epithet. The others all laughed, but Riley didn't seem to find the incident all that amusing. Chelsi turned bright red with embarrassment and reached over toward Riley with her napkin. At the last second, realizing she might not want to pat the napkin in his lap, she pulled back, causing the others to laugh even harder.

When the laughter subsided, Laura Sue said, "Riley, don't worry. It's just water and, by the time we leave, it'll be completely dry and no one will think you wet your pants." Another round of laughter at Riley's expense broke out. This time it was Riley that turned red. For his part, Bobby was happy to see someone else turn a color.

The entrées arrived and the conversation slowed as they all dug into their steaks. Riley was the first to finish. "I'm still hungry," he said. "What's for dessert?"

"I'm stuffed," Laura Sue said. "I couldn't eat another thing." The other four nodded in agreement. "Besides, they'll have food at the prom. Might be just snack stuff, but it'll be enough to fill you up, Riley."

The waitress arrived and said, "How about dessert? We have a great fudge brownie with vanilla ice cream." All six declined dessert, but Riley did so grudgingly. "Shall I bring the check?" she asked.

Riley spoke up. "Might as well, if we're not eatin' dessert."

The waitress left and came back in a few minutes with the check, which she placed in front of Riley. He picked it up and gasped. Then, he began to hyperventilate. "Uuh, uuh," he said, gulping in anguish. No one had thought to ask the waitress to split the check.

Laura Sue, sitting on Riley's left, reached over for the check. "Give it to me, Riley." She took a small pencil out of her clutch. "Okay," she said, "we all had the same thing, each couple that is. So, we all owe a third, plus the tip." She quickly calculated an eighteen percent tip. She told each of the boys the amount they owed. Riley relaxed a little, but still showed residual signs of his initial shock.

Eddie said, "Laura Sue, you're assuming I'm going to pay for Melissa's dinner." Melissa gave him a look that would have turned him into a zombie, had he been looking at her.

"You're dumb as a rock, Eddie Smith, if you think you're not buying my dinner. Even Riley's buying Chelsi's."

"What do you mean, 'even Riley'?" Riley asked. Everyone ignored him.

"I'm just kidding," Eddie said. "I sold my pet hog to raise the money so I could feed you." That broke the tension, and they all laughed, even Melissa.

Changing the subject, Chelsi said to Riley, "Are you dry enough to walk out of here without embarrassing me?"

"Yes," Riley said, "but I suggest you don't get near me when I have a glass of water in my hand."

After they settled their tab, they all got up to leave. To Riley's further discomfort, they all looked at his pants to see if his lap really had dried out.

FORTY

Bobby, Eddie and their dates rode in the van, with Riley and Chelsi following. "Think Riley and Chelsi will still be speaking by the end of the evening?" Eddie asked.

Melissa looked at him and said, "If I were you, I'd worry about yourself, Mr. Smith. I wish we were having the prom somewhere else. Having it at the school gym just doesn't seem elegant enough for our senior prom." Eddie, unwilling to offer a contrary opinion, just nodded.

"I don't agree," Laura Sue said. "The prom committee put a lot of work into decorating the gym, and it should really be nice. Plus, we're all about to graduate and probably won't come back to the school very often. It's been an important part of our lives so far; lots of good memories. I'm glad it's here."

Bobby wisely agreed. He pulled the van up in front of the gym. "Eddie, if you'd escort the ladies in again, I'll go park."

Eddie, becoming smarter by the minute, said, "It'll be my pleasure." The girls smiled as Eddie took their arms and marched toward the door.

"Wow," Melissa said, as she went inside. "They really did do a nice job decorating. Except for the floor, you'd never know it's a gym." The dance floor was surrounded by round tables for six, and panels, normally used for separation of work spaces, were all around the edges. Light blue sateen cloth was draped over them, with gold specks sprayed on. The effect gave the room a cloudlike appearance. Spotlights focused on the ceiling were arranged to make it look like a starry night above. The overall effect was elegant. "I love it," Melissa said.

"Me too," Eddie said. He led them to a table on the front row, just off the dance floor and to the right center, across from the bandstand. Riley and Chelsi joined them and Riley moved the chair beside Laura Sue out of the way so Bobby would be able to roll up in his wheelchair.

Bobby came into the gym a few minutes later. Several of his baseball teammates greeted him as he went to the table. Bennie Brown came over with him and said hello to the others. "Laura Sue," he said, "you look fantastic. Sometime you're gonna' have to tell me what you see in this guy."

"Hey, dude, what about the rest of us," Riley said, feigning hurt feelings.

"Sorry, Riley," Bennie said. "You look lovely, too. A lot like a penguin that wet his pants."

As the others broke into laughter, Riley mumbled, "How...?"

Interrupting, Bennie said "Pretty much everyone's heard the story about Chelsi dumping water in your lap at the restaurant and then patting it dry."

Chelsi joined Riley's embarrassment. "Bennie Brown, you better quit while you're still dry yourself," she said. The rest of them laughed even harder.

The band arrived and distracted them from Riley and Chelsi. It was a group of five, a popular group from the Tulsa area, "Honus and the Hot Spurs." The group was well-known all over eastern Oklahoma. *We're really lucky to have these guys.* Then he noticed the fiddle player was a woman wearing tight black jeans and a yellow spandex shirt. *Good lookin',* he thought, feeling a little guilty.

Honus turned out to be the trumpet player. He was a big guy, over six feet and about two hundred and forty or fifty pounds. He had a full head of longish black hair, which almost looked a little too thick. Bobby looked across the table at Eddie. "Do you think Honus is wearing a rug?"

Eddie and Riley took a quick glance at Honus. "Absolutely," Eddie said.

"And not a very good one, either," Riley said. "The others look pretty normal, though. And, man, that fiddle player is hot," earning a poke in the ribs from Chelsi.

Honus stepped to the mike. "Welcome everybody. We're Honus and the Hot Spurs. As you may have guessed, I'm Honus. The pretty lady with the fiddle is my wife, Maybelle. If you're gonna play in Tulsa, you gotta have a fiddle in the band. Or was that Texas? We call our drummer Ringo. That's Waylon on the guitar, Pete on the sax, and Al on the trombone. We're gonna play a variety of music for you tonight. When Miss Marshall called me, she said we'd have to play everything from rock to country stuff. So, here we go." And they launched into their first number, a lively rock song from the Top Forty.

Riley and Eddie got up with Chelsi and Melissa and went out to dance, leaving Bobby and Laura Sue at the table. *Now what? I should have thought of this. I'm stuck in this wheelchair and it's not fair to Laura Sue. As much as I want to, I can't dance with her. She's gonna get bored and she'll see how boring it is to be with me. I bet she won't go out with me again after tonight.* He sat there getting depressed.

Laura Sue reached over and took Bobby's hand. "This is really nice, Bobby, just the two of us sitting here together with great music to listen to. I'm so lucky to be here with you. It's fun being with our friends, but it's more fun being here with just you." She smiled the smile he couldn't resist. He began to relax a little.

"But, don't you want to dance? I can't dance with you."

"Don't you worry about that. I have a feeling, I'll get in all the dancing I need. If you don't mind me dancing with some of the other guys every now and then, that is."

"I don't mind at all. I want you to have a good time," Bobby said, although he was hoping not on some of the slow ones. That might make him a little jealous.

The band started to play their second song, another rock piece, but an "oldie." Ray Roberts came over to the table. "Do you mind if I ask Laura Sue to dance this one with me?" he asked Bobby.

"Not unless she minds," Bobby said, smiling.

"Thank you, Ray. I don't mind at all," Laura Sue said. She looked at Bobby. "I'll be back in a minute. Don't get too worked up over that fiddle player while I'm gone."

Can she read my mind?

As the evening went on, one by one Bobby's baseball teammates came over and asked Laura Sue to dance. Eddie and Riley also each escorted her to the dance floor. By the time the band took an intermission, Laura Sue had danced several times. *Thank goodness she's gettin' to dance. Even if she won't want to go out with me anymore, she's having a good time tonight. I bet Bennie's behind all the baseball players asking her to dance.*

Meanwhile, Riley had eaten several plates of the finger food that was available. He even brought Bobby a plate and a cup of punch. Green stuff, but tasty.

The intermission was over. Honus went to the mike. "We're gonna start with a line dance, and then play a couple of two-step pieces for all you 'cowboy' dancers out there. Then, we've got a real surprise for you. You're gonna love it, if you love Patsy Cline's stuff like I do."

Bet they don't do it as good as Laura Sue.

About half the crowd, including Laura Sue took the floor to do the electric slide. Then, Brick Nelson came by to see if she would two-step with him. *Yep. Bennie has put them up to this. I need to remember to thank him later.*

After the second two-step, Honus returned to the mike. "I promised you a surprise, and here it comes. Would Miss Laura Sue Medlin please come up here?"

Bobby's mouth fell open. "Did you know about this?"

"Yes," she said. "But, I wanted to surprise you."

To loud applause, she walked to the mike. "As many of you know, I think Patsy Cline was the greatest female singer who ever lived. Miss Marshall asked me if I would sing a medley of her songs tonight, so here goes."

Honus cued the band and Laura Sue launched into "Sweet Dreams." As she sang, she pointedly looked Bobby straight in the eyes. She segued into several others of Patsy's hit songs, concluding with "I Fall to Pieces." The entire audience rose, cheering. Laura Sue took a bow, and returned to the table.

"Bobby," she whispered in his ear, "that was for you." He was afraid he might cry. That wouldn't do at all. He reached over and squeezed her hand.

The music and dancing continued until eleven-thirty when Honus and the Hot Spurs played "Turn out the Lights, the Party's Over." They decided to let most of the people leave so Bobby would not have to jostle with a crowded exit. As they sat there waiting, a large number of their classmates came by to tell Laura Sue how much they enjoyed her singing. Listening to all the kind words, Bobby felt so proud of her that he thought he'd burst. *I guess I didn't need to worry about her enjoying the prom. She's really wonderful. But, I still don't know what she sees in me.*

FORTY-ONE

They made their way outside, almost the last ones to leave. Riley and Chelsi went to Riley's car, while the others boarded Bobby's van and headed for the 'Y.' They entered and found themselves in another gym, but with no decorations. Tables and chairs were set up and, under one basketball backboard, a table with big speakers and a disc jockey. On one side of the room was a longer table with snacks and soft drinks. On the other side, the door prizes to be given out at the end of the lock-in.

Eddie led the way to a table for four, as far away from the speakers as they could get. "No need to be closer with the size of those speakers." The room seemed about three-quarters full. Several other members of the baseball team were there with their dates. Bennie Brown, at the next table, waved greetings. The DJ began playing a song. A lot of people got up and danced.

Laura Sue had a small gym bag. She said to Bobby, "I brought a change of clothes. I don't want to sit around in this dress all night, so I'm going to the rest room to change. I'll be right back. Oh, if you'll give me your keys, I can put my dress in the van."

Melissa picked up her own bag. "I'll go with you."

The two girls came back to the table. Laura Sue had changed into a pair of snug blue jeans and what appeared to be the same western style shirt she had worn at the choral concert. *Could she look any better?* He looked around the room. *None of these other girls are even close to her. I'm so lucky and proud that she's my girl.* He felt himself blushing at the thought.

Eddie and Melissa left to go dance. Laura Sue said, "I'm going to go get us something to eat. Do you want me to bring you a Coke?"

I could go get it myself. But he said, "Thanks. That would be great."

When she returned, Brick Nelson came over. "Mind if I dance with Laura Sue? She's looking pretty bored with your stimulating conversation."

Bobby laughed. "Sure, if she's willing to put up with you stepping all over her feet." Laura Sue gave them both a dirty look and got up. Over the next two hours, several others of his baseball buddies came by and asked her to dance, each time asking Bobby if he minded. He always gave his consent, but he couldn't help but feel a pang of jealousy, or maybe it was envy, as he watched Laura Sue having a good time dancing with his friends. But, deep down he knew: *These guys are really my friends. They're helping make sure Laura Sue has a good time.*

Finally, Laura Sue declared she needed to rest; she was "danced out for a while." Bobby had to admit he was glad he would have her to himself. Eddie and Melissa were moving around from table to table visiting with friends and Bobby and Laura Sue were alone for the first time since they'd been there.

"Laura Sue, did I tell you how pretty you look tonight?" Captain Cool blurted out.

"Ten times, so far," she said. "But, you can keep telling me that all you want. Am I as pretty as Jennie?" she added with a wink and a smile, to be sure he knew she was teasing.

Bobby said, "You're the prettiest girl I know, or ever imagined. Jennie's a knockout for sure, but she can't hold a candle to you."

"That's sweet, Bobby. You're exaggerating, but I still like to hear it."

They continued talking about the prom, the concert, school

and so on until Bobby said, "Laura Sue, can I ask you a question? If you don't want to answer, you don't have to."

"What do you want to know? Are you going to ask if I love you? Well, you don't need to ask that."

"No, I sort of hoped I already knew the answer to that. It's something different." He grew serious. "As many times as I've been over to your house, I've never met your father. You hardly ever mention him. Is there something I should know? Doesn't he want to meet me?"

Laura Sue took a deep breath and didn't say anything for a minute or two. She seemed to be trying to regain her composure. Finally, she said, "Bobby, I'm sorry I haven't told you this, but the truth is I'm embarrassed and ashamed." Not the answer Bobby expected!

"I guess you need to know. Please don't think less of me or my Mom. It's been really hard. My father is, or was, in prison for the last five years. He'd get drunk and stay out late, running around with floozies he'd picked up in bars. Mom and he would have awful fights, mostly yelling and screaming. He'd cuss at her and finally one time, he beat her badly. Buddy was just ten, but he came running out and tried to stop him. We were both awake; it was so loud we couldn't have slept through it. He punched Buddy and knocked him back against the wall. Then, he sat down in a chair in the living room and passed out. I think Mom might have let it go, but, when he punched Buddy, she'd had enough. While he was out, she called the police. They arrested him and, before he could post bail, she got a restraining order.

"He ended up going to prison for assault and battery. Mom got a divorce while he was there, and he's not allowed to come anywhere near us when he gets out."

Bobby swallowed hard. This was not what he thought he was going to hear. "When does he get out?" he asked.

"I think he got out on parole last week sometime," she said.

"But, I don't know for sure. The restraining order is still in effect, so he can't come around or he violates his parole and goes back to jail."

As she concluded the story, Bobby saw tears rolling down her cheeks. He took her hand and gently pulled her closer. Then, he put his arm around her. She turned her face into his shoulder and began to softly sob. Bobby didn't know what to say, but he instinctively knew she needed his support. "I'm so sorry. I can't imagine how hard it's been for you."

Neither had noticed Eddie and Melissa return to the table. Since Laura Sue had been talking softly, they hadn't heard what she was saying, but, when they saw she was crying, Eddie said, "Are you guys alright?"

"We're fine," Bobby said, and gave him a look that told Eddie to walk quietly away.

Before either could say any more, one of the chaperones, Mary Lou Reed's father, wearing a Texas A&M golf shirt, said into the mike, "Okay everyone. Can I have your attention? We promised we'd start drawing door prizes at five-thirty. It's five-thirty, so here we go." Bobby was amazed. *Where did the time go? Seems like we just got here.*

Laura Sue wiped her eyes with her napkin and said, "I'm okay now, Bobby. Thanks for understanding. I don't know what I'd do if you didn't." She still looked a little shaken, so Bobby took his arm from around her and just held her hand.

Mr. Reed continued. "You each got a ticket when you came in, so pull them out. Now, throw them away." The room gasped. What? "Reach under your chair. There's a piece of paper with a combination of letters and numbers. If you aren't in a chair," he said, looking Bobby's way, "I stuck one under the table in front of you when you weren't looking earlier."

Everyone reached under their chairs and Bobby under the table. Sure enough, they all came up with the promised paper. Bobby looked at his. It had "Baseball#1" written on it. *Wow! That's cool.* He looked across the room at Bennie. *Wonder what his says!*

"The first prize tonight goes to: 'StarWars78,' a Brookside official t-shirt."

Charlie Levin, sitting at the table with Bennie, let out a whoop. The whole crowd broke out laughing when Mr. Reed said, "You didn't win the lottery, Charlie. It's just a t-shirt."

"Doesn't matter," Charlie said. "I'm a winner." The crowd good naturedly booed.

Mr. Reed continued with several more drawings, giving away Brookside caps, key chains, and a soft side cooler. The prizes were increasing in value. No one at Bobby's table had won anything yet. Earlier, he and Eddie had noticed the last two prizes were a Yeti cooler and a set of four Yeti insulated cups. They had agreed that, if any of the four of them won the set of four cups, they would each get one.

Mr. Reed held up the Yeti cooler. "The next to last prize is this beautiful cooler. And the winner is "Baseball #..." He paused. Bobby said to himself, *Yes. I'm gonna win that cooler. I'm gonna give it to my Dad. Oh, boy!* "Two," Mr. Reed finished. Bobby couldn't help feeling disappointed. Who would have the paper that said "Baseball #2?"

"I've got it," Bennie Brown said. "But, I'm number two?"

As he drew the next, and last, prize winner, Mr. Reed looked at what he drew and said, "Well, Bennie. We'll see who's number one. 'Baseball #1' wins the set of four Yeti mugs." Eddie, Melissa, Laura Sue and Bobby all let out a cheer.

Bobby couldn't resist looking over at his friend and holding up his index finger. "Number One," Bennie." As Bobby rolled up to claim his prize, the other attendees cheered. "Way to go, Bobby. You da man," someone yelled.

When he got back to the table, he gave each of his friends their mug. "We should plan to get together every year for the rest of our lives and have a drink of something out of these mugs," Eddie said.

"Good idea," Laura Sue said. "At least we should do it once this

208

summer, before we all leave for college." Bobby didn't want to think about Laura Sue leaving for college.

Laura Sue and Melissa left to go to the restroom. When they were alone, Eddie said, "You and Laura Sue looked like you were having a pretty intense conversation. Is everything okay?"

"I think it'll be alright," Bobby said, and didn't elaborate.

FORTY-TWO

They left the 'Y' and made their way across the parking lot to Bobby's van. "I'm so tired, I think I'll sleep for a month," Eddie said.

Melissa looked at him. "Eddie, you sleep for months at a time even when you haven't been up all night." Eddie yawned.

Bobby drove to Melissa's house, where she and Eddie got out. "Thanks for driving us," Melissa said. "I had a great time."

"Yeah, buddy," Eddie said. "Good times."

Bobby pulled out of the driveway. "It's six-thirty in the morning. Do you want to stop at the Waffle House and get some breakfast." He wasn't sure he was really hungry, but he didn't want their time together to end.

"I think I should probably get home. My Mom's gonna be up waiting for me. I don't want our night to be over. It was everything I hoped for. You made me feel so special. And, I think you're the most special person who's ever come into my life."

Before Bobby could respond, they turned down Laura Sue's street. A police car was in front of the house, lights flashing. "Oh, no," Laura Sue cried. "What's happened?"

Bobby turned into the driveway and parked. Laura Sue threw open the passenger door and ran into the house. Not knowing what else to do, Bobby got out of the van and followed her inside. When he got there, he found Laura Sue hugging her mother in the kitchen. Buddy, still in his red pajamas, was sitting at the kitchen table. He mother was wearing her nightgown and a blue robe. All three were crying.

A policeman was standing by the door. "Don't worry, ma'am. He won't be back. We've already got him in jail, and I don't think he'll be out for a long while. Judges don't look kindly on parole violations. I'm gonna leave now. If you need anything at all, just call us, or call nine-one-one."

Bobby, still trying to understand, said, "What happened?"

Mrs. Medlin was too upset to reply. Laura Sue finally said, "Remember I told you my father was due to get out of jail on parole? Well, apparently he got out yesterday. He got drunk last night and, sometime this morning, he tried to break into the house. Mom heard him and called the police. He tried to put up a fight with the cops and they maced him."

Recognizing this was a family moment, and he didn't need to be there, he said, "It looks like everything's under control. I guess I better head home. Mrs. Medlin, if you need anything at all, please call me, or my Mom or Dad. I'm really sorry you've had to go through this."

"Thank you, Bobby," she said. "And thanks for being so good to my little girl."

Laura Sue blushed and said, "I'll walk out with you, Bobby."

She and Bobby went outside. Dawn was just breaking and the sun was only minutes from the horizon. When they reached the van, Bobby looked up at her. "Laura Sue, I really had a good time. I'm sorry it had to end this way. But, I meant what I said. If you or your Mom need anything, know my folks and I will be ready to help." He thought a moment. "And, maybe it would be a good idea for me to try to spend a little time with Buddy. This has got to be upsetting to him."

Laura Sue caught her breath. "Bobby, you're the most thoughtful person I've ever met. If I didn't know it before, I know now. I love you." She leaned down, put her arms around him and gave him the best kiss he had ever imagined.

"I love you, too," he said.

FORTY-THREE

Bobby drove home, dead tired. After giving his Mom and Dad a short summary of the prom, the lock-in and the events at the Medlin house, he went back to his room and crawled into bed. When he awoke about three that afternoon, he called Laura Sue.

"Are you and your Mom okay?" he asked.

"I think so," Laura Sue said. "Mom is still a little shaken, but I think she'll be all right. I'm kind of worried about Buddy, though. He's gone into a shell and I can't get him to talk to me. I hate to ask you, but would you try talking to him? He really looks up to you; maybe you can get him to open up."

"If you think I can help, I'll try. Tell him I'm coming over to take him out for some ice cream; just me and him. See what he says."

"Hang on." Laura Sue put the phone down. Bobby could hear bits of the conversation in the background.

"I don't want ice cream, and I don't want to go anywhere."

Laura Sue returned to the phone. "Did you hear that? He says he doesn't want to go."

"I'm too worried about Buddy to just accept that. Try this. Tell him I'll be there in twenty minutes and to be ready," Bobby said. "And tell him to come out when he sees me pull in the driveway. Tell him I'm gonna sit there until he comes out. When you tell him all this, don't make it sound like he has a choice. I don't know if it'll work, but we'll see."

Twenty-two minutes later, Bobby pulled into the driveway and opened the side door. Buddy slowly emerged from the front door and made his way to the van. He got in and sat in the front passenger seat with his arms folded.

"I don't want any ice cream," Buddy said.

"Well I do, so, if you don't want any, you can sit and watch me eat while you tell me what's on your mind." Bobby drove to the Village Creamery downtown. It was a small, intimate store with bright green walls. Small as it was, the booths had high backs, giving the customers a measure of privacy. Since it was a little after five on a Sunday afternoon, they were the only customers when they entered. Buddy followed Bobby up to the counter.

"What would you like, Buddy?" he said.

No answer.

"How about a dish of the Funky Monkey chocolate?" Bobby asked.

Buddy still had his arms folded and a defiant look on his face. "Whatever," he responded.

"Give me a dish of the chocolate peanut butter, please, and a dish of Funky Monkey chocolate for my friend," Bobby said to the clerk. "And put some sprinkles, nuts and whipped cream on both of them."

They got their ice creams and Bobby asked Buddy to carry them over to a table near the window. "Buddy, you and me are pals, right?"

"Yeah, I guess."

"Well, we are. You came over with Mr. Dowling to help widen my doors, and you built a ramp so I could get into your house. Those are the kind of things real friends do for each other. Well, now I want to pay you back. You had an awful thing happen to you this morning. How'd that make you feel?"

Buddy offered a one word reply: "Bad."

"What about it made it feel so bad?" Bobby decided he would have to draw Buddy out slowly and patiently. But, Buddy surprised him.

"My Dad tried to hurt me and my Mom. Dads are s'posed to love their kids, protect 'em, do stuff with 'em. Look at your Dad. Mine's been gone since I was a little kid, and first time he gets a chance, he tries to hurt us. Bobby, it's not fair." Buddy began to cry. "I wish I didn't even have a father. And, I hope he rots in prison. I don't have anybody but my Mom. And Laura Sue. Laura Sue has you, but Mom and I don't have anybody. None of my friends care. And, I can't talk to 'em anyway. Bobby, I just want to … I don't know what I want."

"Buddy, let's start at the top. First off, you're right. You do have your Mom and Laura Sue. They really care about you, and they'll always be there for you. And you have me. But, you're right, it's not fair. Life's not fair. Do you think it's fair for me to be in a wheelchair the rest of my life?" Bobby let that sink in for a minute.

"For whatever it's worth, I think your Dad has a drinking problem and, from what I know, when people get drunk, they say and do things they wouldn't otherwise. I don't really know what he thinks; maybe you're right. Or maybe he just can't help himself. But, Buddy, either way it's not your fault. I bet you feel like you did something wrong to make him do what he did, don't you?"

"Yeah, I do. But, I don't know what."

"Buddy, listen to me. You didn't do anything. It's not your fault," Bobby said again. "Now, you need to be strong for your Mom and sister. You're the man of the house, but the three of you need each other. You can lean on them, and they'll need to lean on you some. And, when you need someone else to talk to, call me. I'll be there for you."

They finished their ice cream, went back to the van. On the short drive home, neither said anything, but Bobby noticed Buddy seemed to be deep in thought. Gone was the sullen demeanor when he had picked him up. When Bobby pulled in the driveway, Buddy said, "Bobby, you really are my friend. Please don't break up with my sister."

"Buddy, you can bet the ranch that's the last thing I intend to do. There may come a time when she isn't interested in me anymore. But, that wouldn't mean you and me won't always be friends."

"Thanks, Bobby. Are you gonna come in and see her?"

"No, this visit was just for you. Tell her I'll give her a call later."

Buddy smiled for the first time since Bobby had picked him up. He got out and ran into the house, stopping at the door to wave goodbye.

When Bobby got home, his Mom and Dad were waiting for him in the living room. "Did you and Laura Sue get Buddy to go with you?"

"No, it was just me and Buddy," Bobby said. "I wanted him to feel special and, if Laura Sue had been with us, he wouldn't have felt that important."

"Very perceptive," his Dad said. "How did it go?"

Bobby gave them a capsule summary of the discussion they had at the ice cream parlor. "I'll call Laura Sue in a little while to get her take. I think it went pretty well. He seemed to feel a lot better by the time he got home."

"Maybe we can have the three of them over one night. We can do burgers on the grill. I can make some potato salad and baked beans," his Mom said.

The telephone rang, interrupting their conversation. "Hello. Hang on a minute. Bobby, it's Laura Sue," his Mom said. He rolled himself back to his room and picked up the extension.

"Okay. How're you doing? How's Buddy?"

"I'm all right," she said. "But, I think you've worked some kind of miracle with my brother. He's been talking almost non-stop since he got home; mostly about his good pal, Bobby. I think he's starting to look at you as the big brother he never had."

"That really makes me feel good," Bobby said. "I didn't do much more than listen, but I'm glad it helped. We need to keep an eye on him to be sure he doesn't start to get down again. And you need to let me know if he does so we can get right on it."

"Bobby Murphy, you're the best thing that's ever happened in my life. I don't know what I'd do without you."

FORTY-FOUR

With graduation approaching, the remaining school days took on a different feel. The seniors' days at Brookside were coming to an end. Friends they saw everyday would be leaving, some never to return. It was a time for excitement, anticipating the next chapters of their young lives. It was also a bit melancholy. But, the students couldn't let down yet. Finals were approaching.

The question of who would be the valedictorian seemed to be settled It had to be Mary Lou Reed. On the other end of the spectrum, a few people in the class needed to pass their finals to be part of the graduation. Buster Talbot was one of them. He had a baseball scholarship offer from Central State in Edmund, but it was contingent on his graduating.

Final exams for all of the classes were scheduled for Friday, adding one more element to the week's emotional toll. Teachers would grade them over the weekend and give the students their results on Monday. Yearbooks would also be distributed on Monday; it would be a frenzy of gathering signatures in the books from their friends, and in return writing best wishes for the future.

Monday morning, before classes began, Bobby stopped by Miss Winn's office. "Have you heard anything yet?" he asked. She knew he was asking about his acceptance at either of the community colleges. He had decided he wouldn't worry about his scholarship applications until he knew he was accepted.

"Not yet, but we should be hearing something soon."

After the final bell, Bobby waited for Laura Sue in front of the school. *What's taking her so long? She didn't forget did she?* Finally, he saw her heading his way.

"Sorry to keep you waiting," she said. "I needed to talk with Miss Winn. I've decided I want to go to Will Rogers Community College next year. She said it wasn't too late to apply. And the two scholarships I already have will be good there."

Bobby was shocked. "But, you've been dreaming about going to OSU. Why'd you change your mind?"

"A couple reasons," she said. "First, it'll save a lot of money if I do my first two years at a community college. And, we don't really have a lot of extra money right now. But, the biggest reason is Mom and Buddy need me. Mom's a little fragile, and I'm afraid for Buddy. I can live at home and keep an eye on both of them. It's time for me to step up and take some responsibility for my family." She paused. "And, maybe I can catch a ride with you now and then over to Will Rogers, if that's where you decide to go."

"Now and then? I'll be your dedicated chauffeur. Course, I have to get accepted first."

"You will."

They drove to Laura Sue's house. Bobby said he'd like to come in for a minute or two just to say hello to her Mom and to Buddy.

Mrs. Medlin looked up from her chair. "Hi, Bobby. I really want to thank you for talking to Buddy yesterday. He needs a big brother bad. Someone he can talk to, you know. There's stuff a boy just can't talk to his mother or his sister about."

"Buddy's a really good kid," he said. "You're right; he does need another guy he can talk about that kind of stuff with. And, I'm happy to be there for him. I told him that yesterday, and I think it took."

Buddy came through the front door. "Hey Bobby. Guess what?

I talked to Coach Brawley and he said I could go out for the baseball team next spring. I haven't played in a year, but I'm gonna sign up for the Babe Ruth league this summer. Tryouts are next Saturday at the rec center."

"How 'bout I pick you up and take you over Saturday? Just let me know what time. Have you got your shoes and glove? I've got an extra Brookside Rangers cap I'll bring you. I think it'll fit you. Gotta look like a ballplayer, too."

"That'd be great," Buddy said. "They'll really be impressed when I get there with you. I've got a glove and Coach Brawley said Mr. Bardahl will be there tomorrow selling shoes."

Laura Sue and Mrs. Medlin exchanged discrete smiles. Bobby prepared to leave. "I'll walk you out," Laura Sue said.

The driveway was on the right side of the Medlin house, so when Bobby and Laura Sue went to the right side of the van for Bobby to get in, they were shielded from view. Laura Sue gave Bobby a big hug and kissed him tenderly. "I better go," he said, "before we get out of hand right here in your driveway, and in the broad daylight, to boot."

She laughed and ran back into the house.

When Bobby got home, his Mom was pacing the floor. "You got two letters today in the mail. One's from Rock Springs and the other's from Will Rogers," she said. She gave them to Bobby. "Hurry up and open them."

Bobby took the letters, his hands shaking just a bit. He opened the letter from Rock Springs first. "I'm accepted," he said. He read on. "They're offering me a scholarship for full tuition, too. Wow!" He handed the letter to her and opened the letter from Will Rogers.

"This one says the same thing, but the scholarship includes fees, along with tuition. Wait a minute." He looked at the envelope and then back at the letter. This envelope was mailed to me, but the letter inside's addressed to someone I never heard of."

"Maybe Miss Winn can help you sort it out in the morning."

"I sure hope so. Laura Sue told me today she's changed her

mind about going to OSU next year and is going to Will Rogers instead. She said it'll save them a lot of money, and she feels like she needs to be around to support her mother and to keep an eye on Buddy."

"That's a very mature decision. She's a keeper. You better not let her get away. Oh, I almost forgot. Mr. Nelson, at the Ford dealer wants you to call him this evening. He didn't say what he wanted, but he said to call anytime."

"I guess I'll go ahead and call him now. Wonder what it's about?" She handed him a piece of paper and he dialed the number on it.

Hello. Mr. Nelson? It's Bobby Murphy. My Mom said you called."

"I did," Mr. Nelson said. "I want to offer you a job this summer. I just got promoted to General Sales Manager for our dealership. I have in my budget to hire two summer employees and I want you to be one of them. In case you're wondering about the other opening, I've offered it to Brick."

"Wow, Mr. Nelson! This is really a surprise. What would I be doing?"

"A variety of things. Nothing you can't do from your wheelchair, though. We need to have some market research done, some filling in for vacations in the parts department, doing some support for the finance manager, and helping salesmen with their paper work. There may be other things. Basically, you'll be like a general utility man, filling in wherever you're needed. Same with Brick. It'll be a terrific chance for you to learn about our business. You'll probably have to work a few Saturdays, but not every one."

"That sounds good, Mr. Nelson. I need a job this summer to save some money for college next year, so I'll take it."

"If it works like I think it will, we may be able to keep you on part time during the school year, if you're interested. Where are you planning to go?"

"I hope to go to Will Rogers, so that'd probably work. I'll be living at home. Course, I've got to get accepted first."

"Do you want to do this for free, or do you want me to tell you how much we plan to pay you?" Mr. Nelson said with a chuckle.

"I guess that would be good to know," Bobby said. He was hoping for eight or nine dollars an hour.

"We can pay you twelve dollars an hour. You'll get paid every two weeks. Does that sound okay?"

Bobby, trying not to sound overly excited, said, "Yes. That'll be great."

"Graduation is next Wednesday, so how about if we schedule you to start the following Monday. That'll give you a chance to enjoy a couple days off before you start."

"I appreciate this, Mr. Nelson. I'll try to make you glad you hired me. Thanks."

"If I had any doubts, I wouldn't have offered you the job," Mr. Nelson said, and hung up.

Bobby turned to his Mom and was just starting to tell her about Mr. Nelson's offer when his Dad arrived.

"Well," his Dad said, "that takes care of any summer job questions. That's really a good offer, and a good opportunity to learn a lot. If you sock your money away, you should have enough to cover most of your expenses next year."

Bobby told him about the letters from Rock Springs and Will Rogers.

"We'll get the confusion with Will Rogers cleared up tomorrow," his Mom said. "Bobby's going to talk with Miss Winn in the morning. I'm sure she can help."

"Altogether a good day," Mr. Murphy said. And, he didn't even know about Laura Sue's decision.

FORTY-FIVE

Bobby got to school early the next morning and went straight to Miss Winn's office. When she looked up, he said, "Hi, Miss Winn. I hope you can help me. I got this letter from Will Rogers yesterday. It's offering everything I'd hoped for, and then some. But, it's written to someone else. Could you check with them and find out what's the deal? Hopefully, it's just a mistake, but you never know."

"Sure, Bobby. I'll be glad to give them a call today. Why don't you check back with me at lunch time?"

"Thanks, Miss Winn. Don't know what I'd do without you."

Bobby had trouble concentrating on his classes that morning. He couldn't get the letter from Will Rogers off his mind. Finally, his lunch period arrived. Before going to the cafeteria, he stopped by Miss Winn's office.

"Come in Bobby. I called the admissions office at Will Rogers. The lady I spoke with assured me it was just a mix-up and they're gonna send you another letter. So, you can quit worrying about that."

"What a relief," Bobby said. "Thanks for doing that for me. I really appreciate it."

"No problem," she said. "I was glad to do it. Now go eat lunch and get your mind back on your classes."

After school let out, Bobby decided to stop by Coach Brawley's office to see if Buddy had any problem getting his shoes. He didn't think he would, but Buddy was pretty fragile and, for some reason, he decided to check. Mr. Bardahl was there visiting with the coach. Bobby had known Mr. Bardahl for several years, and had bought all his own athletic shoes from him. Mr. Bardahl also umpired summer league baseball games. He walked with a slight limp because one leg was shorter than the other. He was slim, and looked official in his navy blue slacks and matching polo shirt.

"Hi, Bobby," Mr. Bardahl said. "Coach Brawley was just telling me about Brookside's championship season. Sounds like you played a big part in that."

"Not all that much," Bobby said. "The guys playing were the ones that won it."

"Don't be so modest, Murphy," Coach Brawley said. "We wouldn't have won it without your scouting reports."

"Thanks Coach. I'm glad my reports helped, but the guys playing were the ones who won it. I really stopped by to see if Mr. Bardahl had sold Buddy Medlin a pair of shoes."

"He came by and picked out a pair that fit him," Mr. Bardahl said. "But, he was five bucks short and I couldn't let him have them. I'd like to have let him off the hook, but, if I did, I'd have to do it for everyone. And, I can't afford to do that. He paid me for all but the five and said he'd figure something out and get it back to me tomorrow."

Bobby reached into his wallet and pulled out a five. "Have you got the shoes? Here's the five."

Mr. Bardahl went out to his truck and got out a pair of shiny new black baseball shoes. "Here you go," he said, and handed them to Bobby. "I felt bad not giving them to him."

Bobby said his goodbyes and left. On the way home, he stopped by the Medlin's. When he pulled into the driveway, Buddy was in the front yard and came over to the van.

"I couldn't get my shoes. I paid the man fifty dollars, but he said

223

they were fifty-five. I told him I'd be back tomorrow with the rest, but Mom's running short. I guess I'll just have to wear my sneakers."

"No sweat," Bobby said, and reached down beside him. He pulled out the box with the new shoes and handed it to Buddy. "I went by Coach Brawley's office after classes and Mr. Bardahl was there. He told me he'd made a mistake on the price of your shoes. They were really fifty bucks. So I told him I'd bring them by for you."

Buddy let out a whoop. "Bobby, you're the best. Thanks. Oh, in case you were wondering, Laura Sue's not home yet. She had an interview for a summer job after school."

"Who's her interview with?" Bobby asked. "She didn't tell me she had one."

"I don't think she wanted anyone to know. In case it falls through, you know."

"Well, let's hope it works out," Bobby said.

He drove home, wondering where Laura Sue had an interview. When he rolled himself up the ramp and into the house, before he could tell his Mom what Miss Winn had learned, she said, "You need to call Laura Sue. She said she has some news for you."

"Okay, but first let me tell you this. Will Rogers got my letter and that other letter mixed up in the wrong envelopes. They're sending me another one. Same deal, though."

"That's great news," she said. "I'm sure your Dad will be happy."

Bobby went to his room and called Laura Sue. "Hi," he said when she answered. "What's up?"

"First, thanks for helping Buddy with his shoes. He's so excited."

"Happy to deliver them," Bobby said.

"Well, I know you paid the five dollars. That man didn't make a mistake on the price."

"Not saying I did," Bobby said. "But, don't tell Buddy that. I know that fifty bucks was a lot for your Mom, and he needs to thank her, not me."

"I won't," she said. "Let me tell you my news. I got offered a summer job today. I went by Margo's and had an interview with Mrs. Price, the owner. She's opening a new store in Pawhuska and needs someone to help out Jennie in this one. I'll work forty hours, and she's going to pay me ten dollars an hour. Plus, after I start at Will Rogers this fall, she said I can work some Saturdays. I'm so excited."

At the mention of Jennie, Bobby was not sure exactly how to respond. So he said, "That's great news. We both have summer jobs now."

"You didn't tell me about your job. When did that happen?" she said.

"I haven't had a chance. Things are happening so fast." He told her about his phone call with Mr. Nelson. "Besides being a great job, it sounds like a good opportunity, too. And, I hope if I do a good job, I'll be able to work some during the school year, and maybe next summer. Wanna celebrate our new employment with an ice cream after dinner tonight?"

"Let's. I haven't seen you all day, and I miss you."

Bobby's heart skipped a beat.

FORTY-SIX

On Friday, the Brookside students took their final exams. Amid all the excitement of the past couple weeks, Bobby had carved out time to study. He felt pretty good about most of his courses. History and geometry were easy for him. Chemistry was his only worry. He just didn't know what to expect. Earlier in the week, his lab partner, Billy Bachman, had told him the rumor was that a couple of students had somehow gained access to the final. How they did that, Billy didn't know. But, he said, "They offered to give me a copy for twenty-five dollars. What do you think I ought to do?"

Bobby thought for a minute about the best way to answer that. "Billy, you could do that, if you want. But, all your life, you'd know you're a cheater. I know, if I did that, I'd be ashamed of myself."

"Thanks, Bobby. I guess I knew that already, but hearing you confirm it, makes me feel better about myself. Are you gonna turn them in? Cause, if you do, they'll think it was me."

"No," Bobby said. "I'm not. They'll have to live with themselves. I don't even know who it is. And, if I don't end up with a very good grade, at least I'll be able to look at myself in the mirror."

The chemistry exam did not turn out to be as tough as Bobby had expected. He was easily able to complete the test in the hour allotted. He did notice, however, that two of the students he thought were the smartest in the class, Lester Pratt and Roy Biggs, both finished in a little over thirty minutes, turned in their papers and left. *That's odd. I didn't think it was that easy.*

Saturday morning, the seniors were all required to report to the auditorium at First Baptist Church to practice the graduation ceremony. It was the only facility in town with enough seating to hold two hundred and ten graduates, fifteen faculty members, the band and invited guests. Even so, each senior was limited to four tickets. The auditorium was much like a large theater, with room for over seven hundred people on the main floor and another fifty in the balcony. The walls were painted a pale blue with white trim, contrasting tastefully with the dark blue carpeting. The seating itself consisted of wooden pews with comfortable blue cushions. The stage in front went almost all the way across the room with five steps on either side. There was also room enough in front for a small orchestra pit, just large enough for the concert band from Brookside.

The band was made up of select undergraduates under the direction of Mr. Fuller. Mr. Doud, the interim assistant principal, was in charge. Mr. Doud was tall and slim, with a full head of light brown hair. He had the look of someone in charge, Bobby thought. Mr. Payne, the assistant principal Mr. Doud was replacing, was still on suspension awaiting his trial.

"Okay everybody, listen up," he said, using the battery operated megaphone. "I want you to line up single file in alphabetical order. Miss Winn and Miss Marshall are outside in the parking lot to help you if you can't spell." That drew a laugh.

Bobby looked up at the stage. *There's no way I can get up those steps or even sit with the class out front.* As he was contemplating his dilemma, Mr. Doud came over. "Bobby, we're going to have you sit up on the stage. When it's your time to receive your diploma, you can just roll yourself over to get it and then roll back. Sound okay?"

"That sounds fine, Mr. Doud," Bobby said. "I feel a little bit like I'm cheating, not walking in and out with everyone else. But, I know I can't climb those stairs."

227

"Don't think that. You're not getting anything you didn't earn fair and square."

The practice proceeded with the graduating seniors marching in to the strains of "Pomp and Circumstance" and taking their seats. After they were seated, Mr. Doud, this time using the microphone on stage, said, "It's very important that you remember who's in front of you and who's behind you. If you get out of order, someone else will get your diploma. Also, and this is even more important." The seated seniors got quiet, listening carefully. After all, none of them had ever graduated before.

"No, I repeat, no whoopee cushions. Anyone who brings one in will be immediately suspended, and will not receive a diploma." The prospective graduates began to laugh, just a few at first, and soon the whole class was in hysterics.

Mr. Doud looked at Miss Marshall. "I didn't think that was all that funny, did you?"

Miss Marshall was having trouble keeping a straight face and didn't reply.

The practice concluded with the band playing "Pomp and Circumstance" again as the class rose and marched out. Bobby met Laura Sue outside and they got in Bobby's van to ride home.

"I'll be sitting on the stage behind the speakers for the whole thing. I'd rather come in with the rest of the class, but then I'd have no way to get onto the stage," Bobby said. "I'd also rather sit with you. But, that wouldn't happen anyway since we're sitting alphabetically. Robert Mellon and Rachel Montgomery would be between us."

"It'll be okay," Laura Sue said. "This way you can look out over the crowd and smile at me."

"Good plan," he said.

FORTY-SEVEN

Saturday seemed strange to Bobby. He wasn't used to having a weekend when he didn't need to study. Looking out the window, it appeared to be another beautiful Oklahoma day—clear, sunny, not a cloud in the sky. Rather than get right up, he lay there reflecting on his life the last few months. He instinctively knew he'd have to put the past behind him and prepare for his future, which he also knew would be a dramatic change from his life in high school.

But, this morning he focused on how much progress he'd made since February. He remembered the day Bennie and the baseball team arrived while he was still in bed feeling sorry for himself. He thought about Eddie and Riley and how much their support and friendship had meant. *I'm gonna stay in touch with those guys the rest of my life.*

And, without the support of his Mom and Dad, he would never have achieved the level of independence he now enjoyed. Without Carl and Karen's help, he'd never have gotten this far either. With a bit of regret, he recalled the day he had lashed out at Carl and then been surly with Karen. That was a bad day all right. *But, if Carl hadn't said some of the things to me that he did, I might not be where I am today. Neither one of them gave up on me. I hope I can be as good in someone else's life as they were for me.*

That thought reminded him of how he was trying to be a big

brother to Buddy. *Buddy's gonna be okay.* Thinking about Buddy reminded Bobby he had promised to take him to the Babe Ruth League tryouts. *I told him I'd be by about nine-thirty. Tryouts don't start until ten, so that ought to be plenty of time. But, I better get up. I sure don't want to be late.*

He got out of bed and into his chair and his mind moved to Laura Sue, as it always seemed to do. As close as they had become, he still had a fear deep down that she'd get tired of him, tired of having a boyfriend who couldn't walk, or dance, or ... . But, he put that depressing prospect aside and went through his routine of getting himself ready for the day. Most Saturdays, Karen came by for his physical therapy, but he had postponed today's session until next week. *Buddy's my priority today. I sure hope I see Laura Sue when I pick him up. I wonder if she wants to go to a movie tonight?*

When he rolled into the kitchen, his Mom and Dad were sitting at the table. The aroma of the fresh coffee was invigorating and the morning sunlight coming through the window gave the room a welcoming, pleasant feeling.

"Good morning, Sunshine," his Mom said. "You're up early. Are you going somewhere?"

"I am. I promised Buddy I'd take him to Babe Ruth tryouts today and I've gotta pick him up at nine-thirty. And, if it's okay, I thought I'd see if Laura Sue wants to go to a movie tonight."

"Well now," his Dad said. He cleared his throat and continued, "You and Laura Sue are getting pretty thick. You need to be careful and watch out for women. They'll corrupt your life. Not to mention, interfere with various 'manly' activities you may want to pursue."

"You hush, Jack," his Mom said. "I like Laura Sue and I think she's good for him. Bobby, don't listen to this nonsense. Certainly, it's okay for you to take Laura Sue out tonight."

His Dad cleared his throat again and turned his head away so Bobby couldn't see the grin on his face.

"Would you like some bacon and eggs? I'll fix you some if you do. I'll also fix Mr. Grouchy over there some, if he wants. Maybe it'll make him more agreeable."

"Hrumph," his Dad said. He slid his chair to the side of the table so Bobby could get his wheelchair in place.

Bobby finished his breakfast and told his Mom and Dad goodbye.

"Remember what I told you," his Dad said. "They'll mess up your life."

"Jack, if you don't quit, you're gonna be sleeping on the couch," his Mom said.

I'll really miss my Mom and Dad when I finally do leave home. They have such an easy, loving connection. I sure hope Laura Sue and I will have as good a relationship as they do. With a shock, he realized he had just made a big jump in his thinking about Laura Sue Medlin.

He pulled into the Medlin's driveway right at nine-thirty. Buddy came running out of the house wearing the blue Brookside Rangers cap Bobby had given him. He had on a light blue baseball shirt, jeans and his new shoes. "You look like a ball player," Bobby said. "We'll find out if you are one, or just look like one."

Buddy looked a little hurt when Bobby said that. "Don't worry, Buddy. I'm just kiddin'. You're gonna do fine. What position do you want to play?"

Buddy brightened up. "Third base, just like you did."

"That'd be neat, Buddy," Bobby said. "But, don't limit yourself. You might find out you'd be a great outfielder, or second baseman. Just do your best and let your coach put you where he thinks you'd be best."

"Okay." Buddy paused a moment. "But, it'd sure be neat if I could play third base."

They reached the park where the tryouts were being held. After Bobby parked the van, they went over to the registration table and signed Buddy in. "You'll need to have these releases signed by your parents," the lady at the table said. She was a large lady wearing a red baseball cap and a blue tee shirt that said "KANSAS JAYHAWKS."

Her expression seemed to indicate she'd rather be somewhere else; not at a baseball tryout on a Saturday morning. While she didn't actually growl at them, she didn't look very friendly either.

"I'll hold those forms for him," Bobby said. "When does he need to get them back?"

"He can give them to his coach when he's selected to a team. Are you his brother?"

Before Bobby could reply, Buddy jumped in. "If I had a brother, it'd be Bobby. This is Bobby Murphy and he's my best friend. You've prob'ly heard of him."

Bobby felt his cheeks reddening. "We'll get the forms back," he said.

"You need to go over to home plate. Coach Nelson is there. He and his son, Brick, are running the tryouts. Brick was the star player at Brookside High School this year. He practically single-handedly led them to the state championship." The lady turned her attention to the next person in line and Bobby and Buddy walked away.

Buddy turned to Bobby. "What's she talking about? Brick Nelson didn't lead the team. He just played on it. We should tell her."

"No," Bobby said. "If she wants to think Brick was the star on the team, that's just fine. He was an important part and he played a really good center field. Let's get on over there. I'll introduce you to Brick and his Dad."

They got to home plate and Bobby said, "Hi, Brick. Hi, Mr. Nelson. This is my friend, Buddy Medlin. He's here to try out for a team today."

"Hey Bobby," Brick said.

"Bobby, how are you doing?" Mr. Nelson said. "I didn't expect to see you here today. We could use some help, if you want to."

"I'd be glad to help out where I can," Bobby said. "Where do you want Buddy?"

"We're gathering all the kids trying out over there by third base. Our plan is to have each one take five or six ground balls, and then we'll do the same thing with fly balls in the outfield. After that, we'll see what they can do at the plate. What you could do is go out there by third. If you see anything that might help a kid do better fielding or throwing, you could offer some pointers. The coaches will all be here in the stands watching. After all the kids work out, the coaches will get together and have a draft."

"Sounds good," Bobby said. "Buddy, you go over there by third with that crowd of guys. They'll tell you what to do from there." Bobby looked back at Mr. Nelson. "Let me know when you're ready for me to go out there."

"You can go on out now, if you want. We've just got a couple more to get registered and we'll be ready to go. Brick's gonna work with the outfielders when we get to that part. I'm gonna hit the grounders and fly balls. I'm also coaching a team, so I'll need to make notes on the players."

Bobby rolled out to the infield. He couldn't help but overhear three or four of the kids gathered there talking among themselves. "That's Bobby Murphy," one said. "He used to be a really good player."

"Yeah," another one said. "He can't play anymore, but my big brother said he's a really good coach."

A third player said, "Yeah, and he had a big part in the Rangers winning State."

As Bobby looked over at them, he saw Buddy walk up to the three kids. "Bobby's here with me. He's like my big brother," he said, his voice bursting with pride.

"Okay," Mr. Nelson said into his battery-operated megaphone. "Everyone listen up." He told them what was going to happen and cautioned them to be sure he had their names right before they began taking their turns.

"Edwin Butterfield," Mr. Nelson announced to the coaches. Edwin nodded and moved out onto the infield beside third base. Mr. Nelson hit him a grounder. It was not straight at him and

Edwin didn't move. He tried to reach it to the side, but it went off his glove.

"Mr. Nelson, can you hold up just a minute, please?" Bobby shouted. Turning to the group waiting their turn, Bobby said, "Everybody listen to what I tell Edwin." Then, turning to Edwin, he said, "Move in front of the ball. Don't try to field it to the side or backhand it. Okay, Mr. Nelson, let's try it again."

Mr. Nelson hit another grounder, this time straight at Edwin. Edwin fielded it cleanly and threw it to Brick, who was at first base. When he had fielded his allotted five balls, plus the two practice ones, Edwin had cleanly handled two. He went off the field and Mr. Nelson announced, "Bart Brown."

"You any relation to Bennie?" Bobby asked.

"He's my brother," Bart said. He fielded the first three balls hit to him without incident. But, his throws to Brick were erratic.

"Bart, when you throw, get set and then, as you release the ball, take a step straight toward your target. Don't try to aim it. Just let it go," Bobby said. Same advice he'd given Red Freeman not that long ago. Turning to the group waiting their turn, he said, "Everybody get that?"

Bart got the next two balls and threw to first without incident. "Thanks, Bobby. Bennie's right. You're a great coach."

The infield portion of the tryout continued. Some of the hopefuls did very well, obviously having listened to Bobby's tutorial; some not so hot. Buddy had a good turn, fielding the grounders and throwing to first.

The drills moved to the outfield. Brick went with the group out to center. Bobby watched intently. Several of the boys had looked good in the infield drills, but Bart Brown and Buddy had seemed to stand out a bit. He was anxious to see how Buddy did catching fly balls. It was one thing to field a ball hit on the ground, but quite another to judge a fly ball and catch it.

Bobby needn't have worried. When Buddy's turn came, he looked almost natural, instinctively running to the right spot to make the catch and then putting the ball away with two hands. Only four or five of the others did as well. Bart Brown did not appear to be an outfielder. When Brick came in after the outfield drills, he told Bobby, "Looks to me like Laura Sue's got a ballplayer for a brother; not just a useless old boyfriend."

A coach Bobby didn't know took the mound to throw the batting section of the tryouts. He was a short, young man, wearing white baseball pants and a blue baseball shirt with the number "15". He appeared to be in top physical shape and just looked like a ball player. He also proved to have superb control and threw at a speed that the young prospects could hit. The boys batted in the same order they had done in the fielding drills.

The first hitter, Edwin Butterfield, had a horrible time trying to hit the ball. He had no talent for swinging the bat and failed to hit one out of the infield. Of his five swings, he only made contact at all on two. *I don't see much baseball in his future.*

The second batter, Bart Brown, set the standard for hitting. *He's been working with Bennie. He looks just like his brother at the plate, but he may be even better in a year or two.*

When Buddy's turn came, Bobby was nervous. He knew, no matter how well someone played in the field, the coaches were looking for hitters. And, if someone could hit, they'd find a place in the lineup for him. Buddy stepped up to the plate and took his stance. *His stance looks just like mine used to look!*

Buddy swung and missed at the first pitch. Then, he drilled four straight line drives, two to center field and two to left. *His swing even looks like mine. Where did he learn that? I didn't even play this year.*

A few of the others hit well, also. Bobby noted that they were generally the same ones who had done better in the fielding drills. After the batting ended, Mr. Nelson asked them to gather around him. "Good job everyone. What we'll do now is have all our coaches get together and pick guys for their teams. Then the coach who picks you will give you a call. You should hear from someone by tomorrow. I need to warn you: everyone may not get picked. But, we're gonna form a special "developmental" team for those not on a regular team. We'll work on skills and get you ready to play on a regular team next year. Thanks for coming out."

Bobby and Buddy headed for the van. "How did I do," Buddy asked. Bobby could tell he was nervous.

"Buddy, you did better than even I hoped for. I'll be surprised if you aren't one of the first players taken. But, I have a question: Where did you pick up your batting stance and your swing?"

Buddy said, "I watched you last year, and tried to do it just like you did. Didn't I do it right?"

Bobby thought about his reply for a moment. Then, he said, "If you watched that closely, did you notice how much Bart Brown looked like Bennie at bat?"

"Yeah," Buddy said.

"Well, I thought I saw myself at bat, watching you. Only, I think you'll end up being a better hitter than I was." Buddy beamed.

FORTY-EIGHT

When they got to the Medlin house, Buddy said, "Thanks for going with me today. I know I did better 'cause you were there." He got out of the van and started for the house. Then, he turned back. "Are you gonna come in? I bet Laura Sue'll want to see you." He grinned and resumed his trip to the front door.

Bobby turned off the ignition and got out of the van. Before he could get halfway to the house, Laura Sue came out and met him. "Bobby," she said, "I'm so grateful you went with Buddy this morning. It meant so much to him. He really looks up to you. I'm sorry I couldn't come out when you picked him up this morning. I was helping Mom in the kitchen."

"That's okay," Bobby said. "I'm just glad I could go with him. He's copied my batting stance and swing? I didn't even know he'd ever seen me play."

"Bobby, you're either the densest person I know, or you're just being modest. Buddy's idolized you for a long time. He went to all of the Rangers' home games last year. When he came home, all Mom and I heard was about how Bobby Murphy had played. Why do you think he was so eager to go over to your house with Mr. Dowling and work on the doors? And, the ramp into our house? Nobody asked him to do those things. He did them because of you."

Bobby was stunned. He didn't know what to say. Finally, he

said, "I had no idea. I didn't even know who Buddy was last year." He stopped to take a breath. "That's a big responsibility. He's a great kid, and I really enjoy doing stuff with him." Then, he took another deep breath.

"I guess I can only hope his sister thinks as much of me." Bobby blushed.

"She does," Laura Sue said. She leaned over and gave him a kiss.

"Wow," Bobby said. "Right here in the middle of the front yard; in front of God and all the neighbors, too." Glancing at the house, he thought he saw Buddy looking out the window, but he wasn't sure.

"I don't care," she said. "I love you Bobby Murphy, and I don't care who knows it."

Bobby looked up at her. "Well, I love you, too, Laura Sue, and I'd just as soon everyone knew it." With that, he reached up, pulled her to him and kissed her long and hard.

"Bobby, do you realize that's the first time you've ever kissed me without my starting it?"

"I didn't," he said. "But, it won't be the last, I promise. How about a movie tonight? We could get a little dinner first. I haven't started to work yet, but I've got enough money saved to feed us. I can sell my hamster, if I'm a little short. That reminds me, when do you start working at Margo's?"

"I start the weekend after we graduate. They're only open until one on Saturday, so it'll be a short first day. I'm looking forward to working with Jennie. She's nice. I can't believe I got so jealous when I thought you were interested in her. And you don't even have a hamster."

"Would you be saying all those nice things about her if you didn't know she was engaged?"

"I don't know," Laura Sue replied, with a twinkle in her eye. "She's awful pretty."

"Not as pretty as you," Bobby said. "How about I pick you up about six? The movie starts at seven-thirty, so that should give us plenty of time."

"See you then." She leaned over, kissed him again and went into the house.

Bobby drove home, feeling better than he had in a long, long time.

FORTY-NINE

Sunday morning, Laura Sue went to church with the Murphys. Bobby's' Mom and Dad had not ridden in Bobby's van much, and Bobby was proud to chauffer them. When they picked up Laura Sue, his Dad moved to the rear seat, allowing her to ride up front. After church, Bobby's Dad announced that he was taking them to brunch at Maloney's Eggs and Such.

Bobby dropped them off in front of the restaurant. "I'll go find a place to park," he said.

"Why don't you park in their parking lot?" his Dad asked.

"I didn't know they had one," Bobby said. "Where is it?"

"See that big green sign with the big green shamrock on it?"

Looking up, Bobby saw the sign. It was about ten feet in front of him and featured an arrow pointing into the lot, with large lettering saying "Maloney's Parking Only."

Flustered, Bobby could only say, "Oh. Okay."

He parked in a handicap space with room for him to lower his ramp and roll out in his chair. When he approached the front door of the restaurant, he was glad to see a button that opened the door automatically. He entered the spacious restaurant and quickly located the others.

Maloney's was located in an older building downtown. Inside, the walls were painted a light shade of green, with shamrocks prominently displayed. The hardwood floors and oak stained chair rails on the walls gave it a welcoming atmosphere. Hanging from the high ceiling were several large fans and Irish ballads serenaded the diners. There were wooden booths around the perimeter, but Bobby's Dad had secured a table in the middle.

"Find the parking lot okay?" his Dad asked.

Bobby was ready for the kidding. "I went around the block a couple times. I finally asked a guy standing on the corner with a sign that said 'I'll work for food.' I told him to wait by the van and you'd hire him when we came out."

"Very funny," his Dad said. "If I've gotta put this guy on my payroll, you'll have to pay for our meals."

A young waitress in a green dress and white apron arrived at the table. "Hi. I'm Janette, and I'll be taking care of you today. Is everybody hungry?" When they all agreed that they were, she continued, "What can I bring you to drink?"

Laura Sue ordered orange juice. Bobby said he would just have a glass of ice water, while his Mom and Dad wanted black coffee. "We have a special family-style breakfast today—a platter of scrambled eggs, with bacon and sausage, French toast, cinnamon rolls, stone ground grits made with real cream and, if you like, regular toast, white, wheat or raisin."

"Sounds like more than I can eat, but I'll do my best," Laura Sue said.

"Yeah, me too," Bobby chimed in, drawing an amused glance from his Mom.

Mr. and Mrs. Murphy both agreed the special platter would be good.

"It'll be right out," Janette said, and retreated to the kitchen.

"Laura Sue," Mrs. Murphy said, "what do you plan to do this summer?"

"I have a summer job at Margo's florist shop. Margo is opening a new store out of town, so I'll be working with Jennie Roberts. This fall, I'm going to Will Rogers. I'm really looking forward to starting college."

"What do you plan to study," Mr. Murphy asked.

"I don't know yet. I'll start with basic courses that'll be prerequisites for most fields. Then, after two years at Will Rogers, I hope to transfer to Oklahoma State and declare a major."

"I went to OU," Mr. Murphy said. "But, I've known a lot of people that went to OSU, and most of them turned out all right. Long as you're not a big football fan, it should be okay."

"Don't listen to this nonsense," Mrs. Murphy said. "I graduated from OSU."

Bobby's Dad started to ask about the florist shop and Jennie, but to Bobby's great relief, Janette arrived with the food. His relief was short-lived, however. Just as she reached the table, the large bowl of scrambled eggs slipped off the tilted tray and landed upside down in Bobby's lap. Bobby stifled the expletive that jumped into his mind, and everyone else gaped open mouthed at the spectacle of Bobby wearing their breakfast.

Almost before Janette could react, two other waitresses arrived to take the tray from her so the rest of the food wouldn't spill. Janette was mortified. "I'm so sorry," she said. "I'll get a towel." She fled to the kitchen and returned with two towels, which she handed to Bobby. By this time, the manager had arrived. Janette was crying and saying over and over how sorry she was.

Finally, they got Bobby relatively food-free. The manager apologized profusely. "Please be patient and we'll get you a fresh platter of food, which I promise we won't dump on you. Your check will be our treat. And, young man, if you'll bring me the receipt from the dry cleaner, I'll also cover that. I'm going to get you a new waitress. Janette won't be employed here any longer."

"That is most kind of you, sir," Mr. Murphy said. "But, if you fire our waitress, we'll have to go somewhere else to eat. She made a mistake that anyone could make. Please give her a break. She certainly didn't do that on purpose."

"Well, perhaps I could give her another chance," the manager said.

"That speaks well of you, and your restaurant," Mr. Murphy said.

When the manager left, Laura Sue said, "Mr. Murphy that was a very nice thing you just did. It would have been a shame for that poor girl to lose her job. Bobby always seems to know what the right thing to say and do is. I see where he gets it."

"Thanks Laura Sue. I appreciate your saying that. But, there's also an upside to this. I thought Bobby looked pretty sharp wearing breakfast." They all laughed at the vision. Janette came out with their food. This time, she made three trips and it was served without further drama. "Thank you, so much, sir," she said to Mr. Murphy. "I really need this job, and I'm pretty sure Mr. Maloney would have fired me."

They dug into the breakfast, all the hungrier for the wait. Janette came over several times while they were eating to be sure everything was okay and that they didn't need anything. When they finished, she came over and told them, "Mr. Maloney said your meal's on the house. I'm so sorry for spilling the food and I hope you'll come back." She left and went to take care of another table.

"Everybody ready to leave?" Mr. Murphy asked. All agreed and headed for the door. Bobby noticed his Dad leaving a twenty dollar bill on the table. *That's a nice thing for Dad to do.*

When they reached the parking lot, Bobby's Dad said, "Why don't you take your Mom and me home first? Then you can take Laura Sue home." Bobby liked that idea.

When his parents were getting out of the van, Laura Sue said, "Thank you very much, again, for the wonderful meal, and also for including me. I really enjoyed myself. Bobby's lucky to have such a good family."

"We enjoyed having you, Laura Sue," Mrs. Murphy said. "Maybe when we get settled after graduation, you can bring your Mom and Buddy over. We'll grill some hamburgers."

"That would be fun. She and Buddy think Bobby is special, and I'd like for Mom to get to know you better."

FIFTY

After taking Laura Sue home, Bobby realized he needed gas. He stopped at a QuickTrip and began to fill the tank. He looked toward the store and noticed a young man in a wheel chair sitting at the table in front of the store eating an ice cream cone. He finished putting gas in the van and decided to roll over to say hello. He was half way there when two rough looking young men approached the man.

In a loud, belligerent voice, one said, "Hey, crip. You got any money on you?

The fellow in the wheel chair looked intimidated. "No, I don't have any money. I had just enough to buy this forty-nine cent ice cream cone."

"Don't give us that crap, cripple. You got some more money. You ever have an ice cream cone shoved up your nose?"

Bobby rolled closer. "Hey, you guys leave him alone."

"Well now. What's this? Another one? Place is crawling with wheel chairs," the larger of the two said.

By this time, Bobby had arrived at the table. He reached in the pouch on the left side of his chair and pulled out his can of tear gas. *Thanks Carl. Again.*

"It's time for you to leave. I'm asking you politely to move on."

"What you gonna do if we don't?" the smaller one said. He

made a menacing step toward Bobby. He didn't notice the can of tear gas until Bobby gave him a blast in his face.

"You interested in seeing what that feels like?" Bobby asked the larger one.

Moving away from Bobby and the can of tear gas, the fellow said, "You sprayed that in his face. I'm calling the cops. You can't do that to people."

Just then, a man approached from the gas pump next to Bobby's van. "You do that, son," he said. "I saw and heard the whole thing. I think the police would be very interested to hear how you tried to shake this guy down. Maybe these guys in the wheel chairs would be willing to let this go if you two get out of here—now."

"C'mon Snake. These jerks aren't worth our time." 'Snake' was rubbing his eyes in obvious pain, but his buddy took his arm and they moved swiftly away. They got in an old, rusty Ford pickup and squealed out of the parking lot.

The man turned to Bobby. "You're a pretty brave young fellow. That took a lot of guts to confront those two bullies."

"It just didn't seem right for them to try to push a guy in a wheel chair around," Bobby said.

A child about ten years old came walking across the lot from the man's car. "Wow, Dad. Really cool."

"I'm Jack Frogge," the man said. "And this is my son, Freddy. We're just passing through town on our way back to Arkansas."

"I'm Bobby Murphy," Bobby said. "Thanks for coming over. I wasn't sure how that was going to work out."

The other wheel chair occupant was looking at the ground, still shaken from the encounter. He finally raised his head. "I'm Frankie McDougal," he said. "I live in the VA shelter down the street. Coming down here for an ice cream cone is the highlight of my day."

"Good to meet you," Bobby said.

"Yes," Mr. Frogge said. "And thank you for your service to our country."

"Thank you, sir," Frankie replied, appearing a little embarrassed. "And thanks to both of you for coming to my rescue. That was kind of scary. Stuck in this chair, I can't do much to defend myself."

"Well, it looks like the excitement's over. Me and Freddy need to get on the road. Nice meeting you both," Mr. Frogge said. He and Freddy walked back to their car.

Bobby and Frankie continued their conversation. "I've been at the VA shelter here for the last couple weeks. Before that, I was in the VA hospital in Virginia for about three months after returning from Iraq. They taught me a lot about how to get around in a chair, but no one ever said anything about carrying a can of tear gas. How long have you been in one?"

Bobby gave him a quick version of how he had been injured and how he had worked to deal with life's new reality. "I've had some great support: Friends, family, at school. And, I've got a terrific guy who's helped me deal with stuff, plus a physical therapist who won't let me quit."

"I've got a great physical therapist here, too. Karen comes twice a week and works with me for an hour."

Bobby turned to Frankie. "Is your therapist, Karen, a pretty blond with short hair?"

"Yeah," Frankie said. "How'd you know that?"

"Cause she's my physical therapist, too. It's a small town for sure. Karen's really helped me a lot. I didn't know she worked at the VA shelter, too. I gotta go, Frankie. My Mom and Dad are probably wondering where I am. Do you need a hand getting back to the shelter?"

"No, I can get back okay. I don't think those two clowns will be back."

"Okay," Bobby said. "Let's stay in touch. Maybe I could drop by sometime and we could hang out."

"That would be great. I really get lonely. My family's up in Kansas, but it's hard for them to get down very often."

Driving home, Bobby realized this was the first time he

had encountered someone else in a wheel chair, other than the man who had owned his van. *I wonder what Frankie's injury is. I wonder if he'll be able to walk again. He's all alone here. I've made a new friend.*

FIFTY-ONE

G raduation day. Finally! There wasn't much for the seniors to do at school, but they were required to be there. The day started with an assembly in the auditorium.

"Okay, everybody listen up," Mr. Doud said. "You need to be at First Baptist no later than six-thirty tonight. We'll have tables set up where you can pick up your caps and gowns. You'll be required to leave a $20.00 deposit, which you'll get back when you return them. Also, don't forget, you need to attend all your classes today. Your teachers are taking roll and anyone who's absent may not graduate tonight. You've come this far. Don't screw it up. And, remember, absolutely no whoopee cushions."

The students erupted with laughter. Mr. Doud looked puzzled and glanced over at Miss Marshall. "I still don't see what's so funny," he said. Miss Marshall looked away, keeping a stiff upper lip.

Everyone filed out of the auditorium, still chuckling, and headed for their classes. The teachers, for the most part, gave them a little pep talk about the future and congratulated them on their accomplishment. Then, they visited among themselves until the bell rang and they went to their next class.

When Bobby entered his chemistry class, he rolled over to his lab partner. Billy looked a little shaken. "What's wrong, Billy?" Bobby asked.

"I heard a rumor that. . ." Before he could get it out, their chemistry instructor, Mr. Teschley, called the class to order. Mr. Teschley was wearing his usual yellow and black plaid sport coat and black slacks held up with red suspenders, and a red bow tie. He was a short, stocky man who walked with a limp. His students all agreed he was no fashion statement, but they would never say that to one of their favorite teachers.

Mr. Teschley had taught chemistry at Brookside for the past fifteen years. No one was sure how it started, but a tradition had developed of presenting him with a home-made chocolate cake on the last day of school. Mr. Teschley graciously accepted the cake each year, thanked the students and told them he would take it home and eat it over the next week or so. He did take the cakes home, but, after the first one ten years or so ago, he learned the tradition included lacing the icing with ex-lax. He never admitted to his students he was on to their stunt and each year they thought they had done it again.

Today, after the presentation of the cake, followed by sincere thanks, Mr. Teschley looked solemn. He was normally a jovial fellow, opening class with a joke or light remark, and the difference in his demeanor grabbed the class's attention.

"I have disturbing and sad news to give you today. I think it is important for you to be aware of what's taking place. It's a lesson for life you should already know, but some of us apparently don't. There are consequences for your actions. Two members of this class found a way to steal the final exam from my desk and copy it. I don't need to say their names—they're the two who aren't here. Neither will receive their diploma tonight. Whether they'll be allowed to graduate at all hasn't yet been determined. For those of you who were not involved, and I assume that is all of you here, I commend you for your integrity. This situation is very upsetting to me. In all my years of teaching, I've never experienced anything like it. I have nothing more to say about it. Mr. Riggleman, thank you for the cake. Since we've completed our material, and already had our final exam, you may socialize with each other for the remainder of the period. Please do so quietly." Mr. Teschley left the room.

Before Mr. Teschley was out the door, the class had identified the culprits as Roy Biggs and Lester Pratt.

"That explains why they finished the final and left so early," Bobby said. "Is that the rumor you were gonna tell me about?"

"Yeah," Billy replied. "Thank goodness I didn't get a copy of that test. And, thank goodness I've got a friend like you to help me tell right from wrong."

"You didn't need me to tell you that. You already knew the right thing to do."

By the time school let out, pretty much everyone knew about Biggs and Pratt being expelled. Bobby had arranged to take Laura Sue home, and met her as he went out the front door. "Do you suppose there's anyone else in our class who won't graduate tonight?" Laura Sue asked him.

"I sure hope not," Bobby said. "But, I think it might be close for a couple. Buster Talbot wasn't doing very well in English class or history. Poor guy was really trying, but it was hard for him. I guess we'll see tonight."

As they drove, they talked about what might happen with Pratt and Biggs. "I hope they end up letting them graduate, even though they can't be there tonight," Laura Sue said.

"I guess I do, too," Bobby said. "But, Mr. Teschley was right. Our actions do have consequences. Sad thing is those two were the smartest ones in the class. Neither one of them needed to cheat to get an 'A'. I just don't understand. I wonder how they got caught. Someone must have told on them."

When they reached Laura Sue's house, Bobby said, "I'd like us to go together to the church tonight. Is that okay?"

"Sure is. And, I almost forgot to tell you. Your folks are going to pick up my Mom and Buddy."

"I'll pick you up about six," Bobby said as he opened the door and prepared to back out of the driveway.

"Aren't you forgetting something?" Laura Sue said. She was smiling. "I'm not getting out until I have a kiss."

"Since you put it like that." He reached over, pulled her close and gave her a big kiss.

When Bobby reached home, his Mom was in the kitchen. Before he could give her the news, she said, "We're going to pick up Mrs. Medlin and Buddy for the graduation tonight. Your father's taking us all to Outback afterwards for dessert. That includes you and Laura Sue."

"That'll be great Mom, but wait 'til you hear this. Roy Biggs and Lester Pratt stole a copy of the chemistry final and got caught. They've both been expelled. I don't know if they'll be allowed to graduate at all, or maybe just not go through the ceremony tonight."

"That's awful," Mrs. Murphy exclaimed. "I know Roy's mother, Lucinda, through the library. She'll be devastated."

"I heard he has a full scholarship to Reed College in Oregon to study chemistry. I wonder how this will affect that."

"I don't know," she said, "but, if he's not allowed to graduate, I bet he'll lose it." She turned back to the stove. "We need to eat as soon as your father gets home. What time do you need to be there?"

"I'm picking up Laura Sue at six," Bobby said. "I'll go get my clothes changed so I'll be ready to go as soon as we finish dinner." He rolled out of the kitchen back to his bedroom and put on his best navy blue slacks and a white shirt. Looking in the mirror, he put a little water on his hair and combed it neatly. *Now the hard part. Got to pick out a tie. Well, that shouldn't be too hard, since I only have one to choose from. Think I'll wear the red one.*

"Hey Mom," Bobby called. "Can you come help me pick out a tie?"

"I'll be right there," she said.

When his Mom came into his room, Bobby held up his red tie. "Which one do you think I should wear?"

Without missing a beat, she said, "I'd suggest the red one. Do you need help tying it?"

"That's my choice, too," Bobby said. "And, yes, I could use some help tying it."

As she completed a perfect Windsor knot for Bobby's tie, they heard the front door open. "Good timing. Your Dad's home. Dinner's ready, so let's go eat."

FIFTY-TWO

Bobby finished his dinner, brushed his teeth and left to pick up Laura Sue. When he pulled into the Medlin's driveway, Buddy came running out of the house. He was wearing a sharply pressed pair of khaki slacks and what appeared to be a new red polo shirt.

"Hey Buddy. You look sharp. Expecting to meet some chicks at the graduation?"

"No," Buddy replied, turning almost as red as his shirt. "But, Mom said I had to look nice tonight, especially since we're going with your folks. I got a call from Mr. Nelson yesterday. He picked me for his team this summer and he told me he was going to see if you and Brick would help coach."

"You bet. I'd really like to do that," Bobby said. "I haven't heard from him yet, but I'll give him a call tomorrow if I don't."

"That'd be great Bobby. I'll see you later."

Laura Sue walked up to the van, got in and gave Bobby a peck on the cheek. "Did my baby brother tell you his baseball news?"

"Yeah. And he said his coach is going to ask me to help with the coaching this summer. I'm happy for Buddy and it'll be fun to do some coaching."

They arrived at the church and Bobby found a close in handicap parking spot. The graduating students were beginning to assemble in the church's gym to pick up their caps and gowns.

Bobby and Laura Sue went in and immediately ran into Eddie and Riley. "You bring the whoopee cushion?" Eddie asked Bobby. Bobby said, "No. I thought you were." They were all still laughing over the idea of the whoopee cushion when they arrived at the tables where the caps and gowns were being issued. There were four tables divided alphabetically so Riley, Bobby and Laura Sue all went to the table that included the "M" names.

The tables were staffed by students who would become next year's seniors. The "M" table was staffed by an attractive young lady named Marcia Matsadosius. "Name please," she said before looking up. As Laura Sue started to give her name, Marcia looked up. "Oh, Laura Sue Medlin." She got up, went to the rack behind the table and returned with a cap and gown with a tag showing Laura Sue's name. "I have to collect a twenty-dollar deposit," she said. "You'll get it back when you turn them in after the graduation."

"No problem," Laura Sue said, and gave her a crisp, new twenty-dollar bill. Marcia gave her a pre-printed receipt for the deposit.

Before Bobby could give her his name, Marcia got up and returned with his cap and gown. "I know you, too, Bobby. You're famous." Bobby was embarrassed, but fought it off and gave her twenty dollars.

Riley stepped up to the table. Once again, she immediately went to the rack and came back with Riley's cap and gown. "I didn't know you knew my name," he said.

"Oh, Riley, I know you," Marcia said. Her cheeks were turning pink as she took his twenty dollars and gave him his receipt. "Be sure to bring this back to me after the graduation," she added.

As the three left the table, Laura Sue said, "Riley, I believe that girl has a crush on you." Now it was Riley's turn to blush.

They went to an empty corner of the gym to put on their robes. Riley and Laura Sue helped Bobby get his on and they headed for the door. Miss Marshall and Mr. Doud were there, guiding the newly gowned students to their assembly area. "Come this way,

Bobby," Mr. Doud said. "There's a ramp on the side of the stage you can use to get up there."

They made their way to the ramp and Bobby easily rolled himself up on the stage. Mr. Doud showed him where he'd be sitting. "You can stay backstage until you hear the processional. Then, as the class begins to enter the auditorium, wheel yourself out to your place. Miss Marshall and I will be handing out the diplomas, and we'll be sitting on your right side. Mary Lou Reed, our valedictorian, is going to give a short talk, and she'll be on your left. George Johnson's also giving us some words of wisdom, and he'll be there, too. Your name falls between Marvin Mudd and Brick Nelson, so when you hear Marvin's name, you can wheel yourself to the side of the stage where everyone's entering and fall in line. Then, after I hand you your diploma, come back to your spot."

Mr. Doud handed Bobby a program and left him. Since everyone else would be marching in the procession, he was alone. The procession, which the students referred to as "The Parade," would not begin for another twenty minutes, or so, leaving him time to reflect. He thought back to the day of the accident. *One minute we were having a great time, laughing and enjoying life. Next minute, our world turned upside down. I really miss Rog. And Andy and I haven't been as close since. I guess it scared both of us.*

He thought back to his days in the hospital, to the days in bed feeling sorry for himself, mad at the hand life had dealt him; angry, frustrated, scared. *What would I have done without my Mom and Dad, without Carl and Karen, without the help from Mr. Dowling and his class? They were my rocks. And my friends and baseball teammates. They wouldn't let me wallow in self-pity. They made sure I didn't give up; gave me things to look forward to; kicked me in the butt when I needed it.* Tears ran down his cheeks. *Thank goodness I'm alone.*

He thought about the day Eddie, Riley and Laura Sue came by to tell him they were taking him to the baseball opener. *I'll never be able to thank Eddie and Riley enough. And, that's when I started falling in love with Laura Sue.* He couldn't help himself; his emotions were in control. *Where's that handkerchief? I can't go out there in front of everyone blubbering like a baby.*

He got control, at least for the moment. *Another guy I can't thank enough is Coach Brawley. I sure didn't deserve the chance he gave me to be part of the team. And Coach Booger. Those two guys made me actually feel useful. And Miss Winn. How could I have gotten through school without her help and support? All my teachers, in their own way, helped; giving Mom my school work before I could come back. I'd have never made it without them. And Buddy. He's like a side benefit that came with Laura Sue. He really is like a little brother. I have so much to be thankful for.*

He heard the strains of "Pomp and Circumstance" begin to fill the air. Through gaps in the curtains on the side, he could see his classmates begin to enter the auditorium. Bobby rolled out onto the stage to the spot Mr. Doud had showed him and watched the procession. He looked out into the audience, where parents, friends and well-wishers sat, and searched for his Mom and Dad. He finally spotted them and gave a little wave.

Mary Lou Reed came up the front stairs onto the stage and stood beside him. George Johnson, the senior class president, took his place on the other side of Mary Lou. They each took a moment to great Bobby with a handshake. After the senior class filed in and went to their seats, the faculty and staff marched in and took their places. Those with a role in the proceedings came up on the stage. Miss Marshall and Mr. Doud came to the opposite side of Bobby.

After everyone was in place, Mr. Fulmer, the principal, went to the podium. "Welcome parents, friends and our seniors to the graduation ceremony for Brookside High School. Before we hear from our guest speakers, I want to offer my sincere congratulations to the graduates. They have worked hard and, I must say, this has been the most dedicated and diligent class I can recall in my fifteen years as principal here. Would you please stand for out National Anthem?"

Everyone rose and the small orchestra played "The Star Spangled Banner."

"And now, I want to introduce Dr. Marvin Pfuphelnagel, the Superintendent of Education."

Dr. Pfuphelnagel came to the microphone and made a few comments about the state of education in the county, congratulated the senior class and sat back down. *I'm glad he didn't go on and on,* Bobby thought. By this time, he had located Laura Sue and gave her a big smile. *I hope she saw me.*

George Johnson was introduced by Mr. Fulmer. George's remarks were also fairly short. He talked about the accomplishments of the class during the past year and how they were prepared to go out in the world, taking the next steps in life's great adventure. George planned to attend the University of Oklahoma and ended his talk saying "Boomer Sooner." About half the audience applauded.

Next, Mary Lou Reed came forward. She spoke about the challenges they would face in the coming years. "We can do anything we set our minds to. We can be forces for the good of society, or we can be bad. We can do extraordinary things, or we can sit back and let others do them." She ended with a special appeal to the other female students. "We cannot let ourselves be irrelevant. Years ago, women were relegated only to mundane jobs, although even then, we were the foundation for many of the things that happened. But, our mothers and our grandmothers have worked hard, and taken risks to prove that we can do any job to which we aspire, even be astronauts and go into space." She looked the graduates straight in their eyes. Her last words were: "You go girl." Her classmates and the rest of the auditorium gave her a rousing round of applause.

When the clapping subsided, Mr. Fulmer announced that the keynote speaker, U.S. Senator Robert Wilkerson, had, at the last minute, suffered an apparent heart attack and was at this very minute being treated at the local hospital. "Our thoughts and prayers go out to Senator Wilkerson and his family. Since we have no more speakers, I'll turn the mike over to Miss Marshall for the next part of the program."

Miss Marshall stood and motioned for the mixed chorus to also stand. "The underclass singers have prepared a medley of special music to honor our graduates," she said. "Next year's student director, Mary Brunson, will lead. Mary."

The chorus led off with "Oklahoma," followed by "The Impossible Dream," and concluded with the Brookside Ranger fight song. More applause from the audience.

Mr. Doud, Miss Marshall and Miss Winn came forward to present the graduates and award the diplomas. As Mr. Doud stepped to the microphone, the unmistakable sound of a whoopee cushion broke the silence. He glared out at the class, trying to discern the instigator. But, it was impossible. The entire class had broken into laughter. Miss Marshall and Miss Winn looked vaguely uncomfortable, but couldn't totally contain their amusement.

Deciding the appropriate way to deal with the situation was to move forward as quickly as possible, Mr. Doud told the graduates: "Please follow the directions of the ushers and come forward to get your diplomas." The faculty volunteers began directing them to the stage.

Mr. Doud started off introducing each graduate by name. Miss Marshall handed them their diploma in a navy blue leatherette folder. Those who graduated with special distinctions and members of the Honor Society were recognized with Mr. Doud's introductions. For those who had received scholarships, Miss Winn broke in to recognize them.

The first member of the baseball team to be announced was Bennie Brown. After accepting his diploma from Miss Marshall, he went over to Bobby's wheelchair and gave him a "high five" and a quick hug. Every member of the team followed suit when it was their turn. Laura Sue came over and gave him a hug on her way off the stage. This was greeted by whistling and cat calls from the other students.

When Marvin Mudd's name was called, Bobby began to roll out to enter the que. By this time, Mr. Doud and Miss Marshall had traded jobs. As Miss Marshall announced Bobby's name, the entire senior class, even those who were still seated, stood and cheered. As he rolled back to his spot, he could not contain the tears. Mary Lou Reed reached over and put her hand on his. "You deserve this, Bobby. And Laura Sue's a lucky girl. If she screws it up, give me a call," she added with a grin.

As the parade continued, Bobby saw Buster Talbot in the line. Since their interaction after the championship game, they had had little contact. In fact, Bobby was not sure Buster would even graduate. His academic achievements were 'iffy' at best. He also wondered if Buster would follow Bennie's lead. Buster's name was called and he received his diploma. He looked over at Bobby, executed a left turn and came over to Bobby's chair. Giving Bobby a high five and a brief hug, he said, "Murphy, I owe you. You're the man."

The procession continued until the last graduate finally crossed the stage. Mr. Doud told the assembled crowd, "We have one more award to give out. I'm going to ask Coach Brawley to come forward and make the presentation."

Coach Brawley came to the mike. "Seniors, check that, graduates," he growled. "I have the honor of presenting the award for the outstanding senior athlete. This year that award goes to a fellow who starred on the football, basketball and baseball teams. Bennie Brown, please stand and be recognized. I'll bring you your trophy after the recessional." Raucous applause and cheering followed, joined enthusiastically by Bobby.

"This year, we have one more award to give. This one recognizes the outstanding contributions of a young man who has overcome more than most of us will have to deal with in our lifetimes. He played on the football team, more than just played. He was instrumental in our winning the conference championship. But, his most significant contributions came with the baseball team. He was a three year letterman coming into his senior year. He came out to our opener and every practice after. He served as a student assistant coach and helped make every one of us better. He scouted our opponents in the Final Four of the state tournament. I doubt we could have won the championship without him. By now, you all know I'm talking about Bobby Murphy." Coach Brawley reached under the podium, took out a large bronze trophy and walked over to present it to Bobby.

"Murphy," he said in his growly voice, "I've never made a presentation I'm prouder of."

Barely able to speak, Bobby said, "Thanks Coach. Thanks for everything."

Mr. Doud came back to the podium. "Would everyone please stand?" He looked at the graduates. "Ladies and gentlemen, you have made your teachers, our school staff and your parents proud." Looking out to where the parents and guests were seated, he said, "Before we adjourn, let's give our graduates a round of applause." Clapping and cheering filled the auditorium as the new graduates marched out.

When the faculty and others on the stage joined the exit march, Bobby rolled backstage and down the ramp into the hallway and out to the area in the front lobby where his classmates were gathered, greeting and congratulating each other and meeting their parents. He saw his Mom and Dad standing with Mrs. Medlin and Buddy. He made his way through the crowded lobby, stopping to shake hands with classmates along the way.

Before he reached his parents, Bobby felt a hand on his shoulder. He turned into a big hug from Laura Sue. They continued across the lobby and finally reached their waiting parents. Mrs. Medlin and his Dad both had their cameras ready. They took pictures with every conceivable combination—Bobby alone, Laura Sue alone, Bobby and Laura Sue together, Bobby with his parents, Laura Sue with her Mom and Buddy, Bobby and Laura Sue with his parents, then with her Mom and Buddy, and so on. As they were taking the photos, Miss Winn came by and posed with Bobby and then with Laura Sue.

"Let me take a group picture with all of you in it," Miss Winn said. When that was done, she said to Bobby's parents, "You should be very proud of this guy. He overcame more than anyone I've ever had in school. In fact, he's done more than just overcome. He's excelled. Why, I'm proud just to know him." Then, winking at Laura Sue, she added, "The girl that ends up with him will be a lucky lady." Bobby blushed and Laura Sue joined him. Before she moved on, she gave them each a hug, and said "Congratulations; stay in touch."

"Is everyone ready for dessert," Mr. Murphy asked. "We're heading for Outback."

After turning in their caps and gowns, and recouping their deposits, Bobby and Laura Sue drove to Outback in his van. He turned to her and said, "Laura Sue, you know how special you are to me. I don't know what's coming next for either of us. But, I'm excited. We really have a lot to look forward to, even if we don't know what it's gonna be yet."

They drove for a little while in comfortable silence. Then Laura Sue took a breath. "Bobby," she said. "You are the bravest and strongest person I've ever known. Could I ask you a question that I've wondered about since you and I began. . . whatever it is that we began?

"You know you can," he said. "You can ask me anything."

"Well, I've never understood how you kept from becoming discouraged and bitter about losing your legs?"

"Simple," Bobby replied. "My friends wouldn't let me."

Made in the USA
Monee, IL
27 December 2022

23819790R00156